Flying against time . . .

"Anchorage Center, I'm not sure what to call this emergency," she confessed. "At any rate, the critical problem is that I don't know how to land this aircraft. I'm going to need some help."

The untroubled tone in the air traffic controller's voice vanished immediately. So much for training. "You don't know how to fly an airplane? And you're in a Lear?" His disbelief was almost palpable.

That didn't reassure Taylor.

"Negative, Center," she answered. "I do know how to fly, just not a Lear. I'm a King Air captain," she added. "I'm not a complete neophyte. But I will need some help in getting down."

That was a dramatic understatement.

"Four-lima-lima, Anchorage copies." The controller was back to his calm, professional tone. "You're filed for Nome. Is that still your intended destination?"

"Well, I'd like to get vectors back to Anchorage." She glanced back at her gauges to confirm that she had enough fuel for that return trip. When she saw what it read, the blood drained from her cheeks. . . .

COFFIN CORNER

Megan Mallory Rust

BERKLEY PRIME CRIME, NEW YORK

COFFIN CORNER

A Berkley Prime Crime Book / published by arrangement with the author

PRINTING HISTORY
Berkley Prime Crime mass-market edition / June 2000

The Penguin Putnam Inc. World Wide Web site address is
http://www.penguinputnam.com

ISBN: 0-425-17508-1

Berkley Prime Crime Books are published
by The Berkley Publishing Group,
a division of Penguin Putnam Inc.,
375 Hudson Street, New York, New York 10014.
The name BERKLEY PRIME CRIME and the BERKLEY PRIME CRIME
design are trademarks belonging to Penguin Putnam Inc.

PRINTED IN THE UNITED STATES OF AMERICA

10 9 8 7 6 5 4 3 2 1

DEDICATION

*To David Hill, who taught the class
that opened the floodgates*

ACKNOWLEDGMENTS

I am indebted to my friends in the Alaskan aviation world who offered numerous technical details for *Coffin Corner*. Allan Jones, a Learjet and King Air captain for Lifeguard Alaska, was very generous with his time and knowledge throughout the building of the manuscript; Mike Thomas, air traffic controller at Anchorage Center, gave me useful information concerning his duties and taught me to talk the talk just like ARTCC does; Bill Kunkler, chief of flight operations for Rust's Flying Service, drew from his extensive experience to answer a myriad of questions; and John Thorsness, lawyer/pilot/friend, knew a good title when he heard it.

On the medical side of the equation, I relied on several people to confirm or correct my plot lines: Paul Craig, Ph.D., diplomate in clinical neuropsychology, American Board of Professional Psychologists, went out of his way to give me much of the information I needed to make my story credible; Chris Hunt, CRRN, graciously answered my questions related to a number of medical subjects; Margaret Auble, RN, director of Lifeguard Alaska, was only a phone call away to retouch my ideas about medevacs; and as always Don Rogers, MD, State of Alaska Medical Examiner (retired), let me pick his brain about poisons and other ways of killing people.

I am grateful for the assistance I received from all of them.

COFFIN CORNER

ONE

"Taylor! He's crashing! Get us down, get us down!"

Those shrill words of alarm ricocheted across the cabin of LifeLine Air Ambulance's Beechcraft King Air, triggering a flood of adrenaline that surged into Taylor Morgan's body. She jerked around in the pilot's seat of the twin-engine aircraft, and stared into the cabin with a saucer-eyed expression. The adrenaline rush provoked a dramatic rise in her temperature like a shot from a heat lamp, and started a hammering in her chest.

Gaping at the two flight nurses behind her, she called, "What happened? What's going on?"

Ignoring Taylor's question, Jude Macabee flicked a penlight across the eyes of a twenty-something Alaskan Native man lying on the cabin's bench seat. Shoving a hank of her dark-brown hair behind her ear, she swung the light back and forth over his face as she lifted his eyelids. A stainless steel hemostat protruded from a cargo pocket in her navy-blue Nomex flight suit—the suit a utility version of the same garb worn by the pilots—and a stethoscope dangled from her neck. The navy-blue wool blankets draped over her patient's body contrasted sharply with the neon-yellow restraints strapping him down. "Pupils dilated and nonreactive, Colleen," she stated rapidly, but matter-of-factly, to her partner. "Breathing very shallow, no response to stimulus. He's out of it. Intubate him while I inject the mannitol."

The younger nurse, a slim blond with a pageboy haircut, grabbed a short length of rubber tubing attached to a hand-held oxygen delivery bag. Tilting the patient's head back, she threaded the hose down his windpipe toward his lungs and began to squeeze the inflatable sack. "He's bagged, Jude," she reported succinctly.

Her coworker poked a syringe full of mannitol into the IV tube inserted in one of the Native man's arms. "We gotta get him to the hospital stat," she yelled into the cockpit. "Where are we now?"

Reacting to the anxiety heard in the first nurse's voice, Taylor swung to peer at the panel in front of her. "We're starting our approach right now, about five minutes out. Hang on, we're coming down as fast as we can." She shot a glare out the window.

The dark of the late evening hour—and the pea-soup fog surrounding the descending plane—troubled her. The conditions would make a desperate situation worse. Even though they were only five minutes from the airfield, those remaining five minutes were the trickiest ones of the whole flight.

And the weather wasn't helping.

When they had left Anchorage International two hours earlier, the weather had been marginal at best. Her glance out the window told her it hadn't improved, but deteriorated. That low cloud ceiling could compromise the upcoming touchdown: if the overcast dipped below a defined level, the pilots wouldn't even be permitted to attempt a landing.

Regardless of having a critical patient on board.

But how bad was it? she wondered. Fifteen minutes earlier she'd checked it, and it had been poor but flyable. What was the actual weather she had to deal with then? She triggered the push-to-talk button for her radio headset and contacted the air traffic control tower miles away in the gloom. "Anchorage tower, Lifeguard three-lima-lima needs the reported weather."

"Lifeguard three-lima-lima, Anchorage. We're reporting two hundred overcast, one-half mile visibility, winds calm, altimeter two-niner-zero-two. Right at minimums."

Taylor frowned at that report. Her heart skipped a beat. "Roger. Three-lima-lima copies."

She *had* copied the communication from the tower, but it didn't please her. Having the ceiling and visibility right at the minimum specifications for landing gave her absolutely no margin of error. If the conditions dropped even slightly during her approach, she would be unable to break out of the soup before the landing and would have to abort. She didn't know if the patient behind her could last for another try at landing, or a detour to another airport with better weather.

Out of the corner of her eye she saw a narrow, white bar slide to the middle of one of the multicolored instruments. "Localizer captured, glide slope coming in," announced a smooth male voice from the right-hand pilot's seat. That was Seth Roberson, her copilot.

A second later, a quiet *bleep-bleep . . . bleep-bleep . . . bleep-bleep* sounded in the cockpit as a dime-sized globe blinked on, staining the area around it an intense blue.

That display reassured Taylor. Once they were inside the outer marker on their flight path—as the blue light indicated—even if the weather continued to deteriorate they could try their landing. They wouldn't have to abort until *they* were convinced the weather was too marginal.

A small advantage, but an advantage nonetheless.

Taylor glanced over her shoulder into the cabin, where Colleen pumped the oxygen-delivery Ambubag while Jude checked the patient's vitals. The older nurse was shaking her head as she worked with the blood-pressure cuff—not a good sign. The continuing emergency increased the tension in the air, and it was almost palpable.

Returning her gaze forward, Taylor trained her eyes on the instrument panel and assessed it. "Okay, one dot on the glide slope, gear coming down," she announced to her copilot, and flipped a wheel-shaped lever down. A slight grinding noise filled the cockpit as an electrical motor slid doors open under the wings and lowered landing gear into the damp air. A mechanical *click* sounded and three small green lights illuminated above a minuscule sign that read DOWN AND LOCKED.

"Thousand over decision height," she told Seth. "I'll take it when I get anything." She prepared to take the controls of the twin-engine turboprop from Seth as soon as she caught sight of the ground. Squinting out the windshield of the King Air, she tensed, waiting for sight of the striped asphalt below to appear. But since the weather had deteriorated, she might not see the ground until she was little more than a hundred feet above it.

That could be trouble.

Regulations required her to have sight of the ground by the time she reached two hundred feet of altitude. If she didn't, she had to abort the landing.

But she had a dying man in the cabin behind her, and he *had* to get to a hospital. This landing could mean life or death for him.

What would she do? Continue past two hundred feet, break the rules but save a life?

She pondered the question. Those rules were there for a reason, a safety reason. Who would be served if she busted minimums, got disoriented in the thick fog, and drove the aircraft into the ground?

But what if the patient died because she acted like a Goody Two-shoes and refused to attempt the landing?

She stared at the panel. "Five hundred feet to DH, nothing yet," she said to Seth, frowning. Her copilot nodded mutely. She knew *he* knew she had to make a decision soon.

As the King Air streaked down its final approach path, the twin needles of the horizontal situation indicator held steady without wavering, forming a right-angle cross where they intersected. The display of precision comforted her somehow— at least Seth was holding up his end of the bargain with his unerring control over the aircraft.

But would the weather god play fair, too?

"Four hundred, nothing," she muttered to Seth. The runway was still not in sight; very little altitude remained before the landing must be aborted. The fate of the critically injured man behind her depended upon the whims of nature then. Her body tensed. "Two hundred to DH . . ."

Seth's eyes darted toward her. He seemed to be asking for a signal to abort the approach—what was she waiting for?

She said nothing, ignoring his pleading look. And she *saw* nothing, either—no lights, no trees, no other aircraft on the ground waiting for takeoff. She stared out the King Air's windshield, willing something to appear.

Then something did.

"Decision height . . . Starting to pick up the lights," Taylor affirmed, quietly exhaling her held breath.

Numerous strands of flashing white strobe lights, staggered like a ladder, glimmered through the dense cloud cover and pointed toward the runway. Two rows of high-intensity red beacons bordered the column of white lights, forming a giant capital *H*. The top of the *H* carried a slash of green strobes that marked the runway's threshold. Single lines of white bulbs framed the runway as it disappeared into the evening's gloom, and marked the centerline of the asphalt.

"One-fifty AGL . . . Runway in sight . . . I'm outside, I got it." Taylor Morgan lightly clasped the control yoke in front of her after Seth released it, and guided the King Air down toward the runway. Seconds later, a *squeak!* from tires connecting with asphalt signaled that the aircraft had landed.

As the plane eased off the runway onto a taxiway, Seth changed radio frequencies and contacted the control tower. His sandy blond hair stood on end like he had touched a light socket, and he wiped a hand across his sweaty forehead before he spoke. "Anchorage ground, Lifeguard four-three-three-lima-lima is clear of six right, taxi to north ramp."

"Lifeguard three-lima-lima," responded the tower, "taxi to north ramp . . . Good night."

When the silver-and-burgundy King Air reached its destination on the airport, it was met by an ambulance. The emergency vehicle's flashing lights glanced off the dreary layer of clouds hanging near the ground, and added a sense of urgency to the setting. Taylor and Seth jumped from their seats and rushed to open the cabin door and aid the paramedics as they extracted the stretcher from the narrow compartment. Gently but quickly they loaded it into the nearby ambulance. The two flight nurses darted from the aircraft and trotted to catch up with the men.

Taylor and Seth stood at the top of the airstair as they watched the ambulance speed off toward Cook Inlet Medical Center. Once it had disappeared from sight, both pilots seemed to relax. The younger copilot had shown the anxiety prompted by the tricky landing with his sweaty palms and rumpled hair, but the aircraft's captain had felt it just as strongly. She was as wired as an electric fence.

"Kinda exciting tonight, huh?" Seth's eyebrows danced to punctuate his comment.

"Yeah. I thought I was going to have to bust minimums." Taylor reached out and grabbed the aluminum clipboard from him that held their flight paperwork. Stepping through the hangar door as she scribbled her signature on it, she handed it back to him.

He followed her into the cavernous hangar with a questioning look on his face. His boots squeaked as he walked across the spotless white surface. "Well, you *did* bust minimums," he pointed out. "We didn't have the runway in sight at decision height." He grinned at her as though to let her know that he wasn't criticizing her—his mien indicated he realized what she had faced when deciding about the landing. He wasn't going to turn her in to the FAA for it.

"Hey, I *had* the lights in sight at DH. That's good enough."

"Okay, whatever you say. Must be a gray area in the regs." He winked at her. "Anyway, I'm going to get this flight suit off, then hit the road. My wife always worries about me when I'm on nighttime call. She says she wouldn't know what to do without me." He leered at her. "And she proves it as soon as I get home. That way she makes sure I don't dawdle. If you know what I mean."

"Yeah." Taylor sighed. Ah, to be twenty-five again, with an anxious—and young—spouse waiting for your successful return from hazard duty.

Then she shook her head. Thirty-seven wasn't so bad. And she may not have a young thing stowed away at home, but she had something better. Steve Derossett, a Learjet captain for LifeLine—a coworker and a coconspirator. He may not be a youth, with youthful hormones and youthful adulation, but with age comes knowledge. He knew how to do a *lot* of things that interested her.

"Hmmm," she mumbled. "I bet Steve could make me forget that landing."

"What?" asked Seth. "I didn't hear you."

And I'm thankful you didn't, she mused. It would have embarrassed her if he had. She liked keeping her personal life private.

Ambling across the cement floor of the hangar, she tried to calm herself. "Go ahead and take off, Seth. I think I'll hang around here for a bit. Cool down, get detuned. I got kinda wired on that landing."

He stared at her in disbelief. "I didn't think you ever got scared, Taylor."

"Scared?" She opened the door from the hangar into the pilot's locker room and the Lifeline office. "I didn't say *scared.* I was just a little tense." She laughed. "I never get scared."

He shook his head and began stripping off his flight suit. His posture seemed to say that he didn't believe it when she said she never got scared. He probably got scared; why wouldn't she?

Watching him, she thought she should level with him, then decided not to allow him into her head. Let him wonder.

She *did* get scared. All the time. But he'd never see it.

TWO

Taylor leaned back in Nate Mueller's big upholstered chair, which stood regally in LifeLine's front office. Finally back in her street clothes, she propped her Levi's-clad legs on the blotter covering the desktop. A white turtleneck poked out of her navy-blue crew neck sweater, and a brown leather flight jacket was slung over the arm of the chair. Beams of incandescence from the street lights outside swam through the wide plate glass window and mottled the carpeted floor.

Glancing out the window, she saw that the cloud ceiling had risen some in the past half hour. Even so, the midnight darkness hid most of the nearby structures—only the lights on the tall air traffic control tower a half-mile away added any color to the blackness. In a contemplative mood, she daydreamed as she twirled one of Nate's pencils between her fingers like a baton. He had nearly chewed the end off that particular pencil in the process of completing his office manager duties.

Perusing the gnawed-on pencil end, Taylor wondered which of his tasks produced enough stress to culminate in biting the eraser off a writing instrument. *Hmmm.*

As she sat in the dimly lit room—letting the late evening's gloom soothe nerves rattled by the marginal landing of an hour ago—she heard the halves of the large hangar door grind open. Several minutes later, the smaller locker room door creaked open, too. Two male voices faded in and out as they stepped from the cavernous hanger into the room.

Smiling in recognition of the voices, Taylor swung her feet off the top of the desk. The speech bouncing off the walls belonged to Carter Masterson and Kai Huskisson, two of her coworkers. Both of the men were assigned to fly LifeLine's Learjet: Carter as captain and Kai as copilot. She always liked talking to them, so she stood and marched over to the locker room.

"Hi, guys," she greeted them upon poking her head into the room. Carter glanced up from unzipping his flight suit, and Kai looked sideways from lifting a binder out of his leather flight case.

"Hi, Taylor." Kai set the binder aside and shoved the case into his locker. "What are you doing here this late?"

"You didn't just come in, did you?" asked Carter in his gruff but fatherly voice. "It's nasty out there. Keeps vacillating up and down around minimums. We had to take another shot at it the first time we locked onto the ILS. We hadn't hit the outer marker before the field went down, but after about five minutes holding it opened up again. Made it second try." The Lear captain was in his late fifties, with thick, gray-free brown curls that belied his age. His well-kept form—sans paunch, due to the exercise regime required of all LifeLine pilots—stood erect without stooping. His only concession to the approach of his golden years was the aviator-style eyeglasses framing his hazel eyes.

"I musta just caught the beginning of the deterioration," Taylor acknowledged. "The weather was slightly above minimums when we started our approach, but it held for us. No wavering. No problem." She turned away from Carter as she spoke, afraid her expression would betray her. Her landing had not been no problem, but she didn't want to tell him that. He was such a stickler for details—*he* would have gone around on that landing, but *she* was the one that had had a dying man on board.

"Anyway," she continued, "where'd you guys come from?"

"Seattle," offered Kai Huskisson. "Transfer from Cook to the UW hospital." He pronounced it *ewe-dub*. "The patient had relatives in Seattle, wanted to do his recovery near them."

Taylor smiled again. She always smiled at nearly everything Kai said—she had a major case of the hots for him. Six-foot-two, mid-thirties, hair a shade darker brown than Carter's, well-trimmed walrus moustache overlooking full lips . . .

She caught herself before her thoughts got more lascivious.

That wouldn't do. Even though she and Steve were not married—and the company policy concerning employee relationships kept their at-work feelings for each other toned down—she had no intention of cheating on him. Kai was strictly look-but-don't-touch.

But she definitely had fun looking.

Carter had removed his flight suit and hung it in his locker. He'd worn jeans and a white twill western shirt underneath the Nomex coveralls, and as he fingered a scuff mark on his cowboy boot he spoke to Kai over his shoulder. "I have to stop at the grocery store before I drop you off at your house. That okay?"

"Well, I'm not quite ready to go yet." Kai unzipped his flight suit and pulled it back over his shoulders, then turned toward Taylor. "Maybe Taylor can run me home. You got time?" he asked.

"Yeah, right. Do I look like I have a pressing engagement to go to? At what"—she glanced at her watch—"one-twenty in the morning? I can take you." Then she peered at Kai. "But why are you riding with Carter? You guys on the buddy system? Fly together, drive together?"

Kai snorted. "Are you kidding? It's all I can take flying with this guy. He eats too much garlic." A grin followed.

"Ohhh. You're scoring big points there. Wait until he evaluates your performance around upgrade time." She shook her head dejectedly.

"Hey, he knows I'm kidding. Don't you, Carter?"

Carter Masterson shot him a look over the frames of his glasses. "Good thing you've got another ride home." He slammed his locker closed and stomped off in mock anger. The front door of the office slammed behind him as he left.

"Now I've pissed him off," Kai sniggered. He didn't appear too alarmed by his captain's mood—Taylor figured he knew Carter was acting. She doubted the young copilot was that mean-spirited.

Lowering himself onto the locker room bench, Kai pulled the legs of his flight suit over his hiking boots. The fabric snagged on the lug soles and he grunted. "So, Taylor. Tell me what *really* happened on that landing. You said 'no problem,' but your face didn't agree."

"Yeah, well." She stubbed the toe of her boot on the locker room linoleum. "I didn't want to tell Carter that I shot an approach right at minimums. He knows that the weather can fluctuate on approach, and that's exactly what it did. I haven't ever had to decide how low I'd go before I aborted. It was kinda intense there for a few minutes."

"How low *did* you go?"

Her eyebrows lifted, and she shrugged. "Technically I don't think I busted minimums. I was picking up the lead-in lights at decision height, so I figured that was good enough to continue."

Kai shook his head. "Technically, I think you *did* bust minimums. The regs say you need at least the threshold lights, not the lead-ins. But that doesn't really matter." He shrugged in turn. "There was nobody there watching you. What the FAA doesn't see, they can't give you a violation for. Why were you keyed up about getting in, anyway? Couldn't have been that bad."

"Shit, Kai! The guy was dying right behind me!" She bristled, then tried to calm herself. He had no idea of what had been going on with the patient. She should cut him some slack. "When we left to pick him up, he was just in pain from internal injuries. Flipped his four-wheeler. Typical village injury, happens all the time, like you know. Anyway, by the time we were picking up the ILS glide path, he was crashing."

"Crashing? What happened? Something burst in his gut, some lacerations from the wreck?"

"Yeah, you'd think. But that wasn't it. The guy had a *head injury*. Nobody picked up on it at the village health clinic. He was lucid, no signs of brain trauma. So the nurses gave him fluids during the trip back to Anchorage—you know, to combat the internal bleeding—and that must've triggered the brain swelling." She shuddered in remembrance of the anxious call up front from nurse Jude Macabee in the cabin. "He'd stopped breathing. Pupils dilated, all that. The nurses got him bagged right away, but the brain swelling had to be stopped. That meant get him to the hospital, stat. All they could do for him in the plane was give him mannitol, and that may not do enough."

"Ah." Kai hung his flight suit in his locker and grabbed his jacket from another hook. "I can see why you're still here, then. Trying to cool down from the excitement, huh?"

She nodded somberly, then brightened. "Want to go get something to drink? That might ease my return to the real world." She nudged him with a shoulder, urging him to take up her offer. "I'll treat."

Laughing, he reached to close his locker door. "I'm still on duty, so nothing alcoholic."

"Hey, I'm on duty, too. How about a Coke and some popcorn at the watering hole?" A local bar—in a hotel near LifeLine—put baskets of popcorn on the tables. It was a common tavern trick to make customers thirsty, but one that delighted Taylor—she loved popcorn.

"Okay, deal." He started to swing the locker door shut, then caught a glimpse of the aluminum clipboard on the bottom shelf. "Oh, shit. I forgot to get Carter to sign tonight's log entry." He grabbed the clipboard and shook his head. "We'll have to drive over to his house before we get our drink. I got to get him to sign this. Damn. That'll be a pain in the butt. I hope he gets back from the grocery store before we get there."

Puzzled, she dragged her car keys out of her pocket. "Hey, can't that wait until the morning? I'm thirsty."

"No, gotta do it tonight. I got my butt kicked for forgetting to get a log signed before. The FAA did a spot paperwork check—looking for duty time violations—and they found a couple of log entries that weren't signed by the captain. I was the copilot on those flights, so Nate gave me a spanking. He said it'd be my ass if I forgot again. And I don't want to get caught again—who knows when the FAA'll come calling again. Could be tomorrow."

"Aw, shit. He lives way over in Spenard." She pouted, doing her best to look irked. It was hard to look irked where Kai was concerned, though. "Okay. I can make a detour. Just for you."

"Thanks. You're a sweetie." He ruffled her hair and gave her a quick peck, which was exactly what she wanted from the encounter. It was okay for Kai to touch her as long as he was being playful and she didn't initiate it. Those were her unwritten rules.

They locked the office door behind them and headed for Taylor's Suzuki Sidekick. The compact four-wheel-drive vehicle got her into and out of the virtual wilderness where she lived—the winter's snow and the spring break-up's mud made it nearly impassable during two of the four seasons. True, the Sidekick had a reputation for tipping over, but that was only when driven recklessly. She was careful not to turn corners at high speeds—or do anything at high speeds—and figured that would save her from trouble.

"He lives on Twenty-seventh, doesn't he?" she asked as they clambered into her car. Kai nodded, so she started the engine and pulled out of the LifeLine parking lot onto Old International Airport Road.

Ten minutes later, after stopping for some gas and a stale doughnut at a convenience store/service station, they were tooling down Minnesota Boulevard. Driving past a grocery store parking lot, she noticed several vehicles. "Any of those cars Carter's?" She pointed at the well-lit asphalt square.

Kai peered over her shoulder and shook his head. "Naw. He drives an old Volvo station wagon, kinda hard to miss. Real beater." As they passed the lot, he leaned over his seatback and scanned the rest of cars. "He's not still at the store, as far as I can tell. Unless he shops at Safeway." Swiveling around, he looked out his side window to survey the parking lot in front of the rival grocery store across the street. "Nope, he's not there, either. Hope he's not asleep already."

She snickered. "Hey, if he wasn't really pissed at you for the garlic crack, he'll definitely be irate if you wake him up to sign a log book." She'd be a bit surly if one of *her* copilots did that. But in her case, she lived so far from town that nobody would drive to her house. They'd take their chances.

"Well, we'll just go to his apartment door. If we don't hear any sounds from inside, we'll leave. Maybe I'll luck out and the FAA won't pick tomorrow morning to do a spot check."

"Okay." She turned off Minnesota onto Twenty-seventh. Her alma mater, Romig Junior High School, sat directly across the street, a floodlight illuminating the purple-and-white Trojan painted on the building's side. *The Romig Trojans. Go, team, go.* She smiled. "This complex here?" she asked, gesturing at a two-story stucco structure.

"Yeah. He's in apartment one eleven. Ground floor, east entrance." Taylor guided the Sidekick into the lot, heading for the opposite side. No slots were empty near the stairwell, so she pulled up behind a parked car, blocking its egress. She shrugged. Nobody would be leaving at two in the morning, most likely.

Kai opened his door. "You coming in?" He nodded at the building.

"Of course. He might answer the door without any clothes on." She laughed.

Kai glared at her. "Isn't he a little old for you?"

She grinned at him. "I'm just looking. That's all I can do." She jumped out of the driver's seat and met him on the sidewalk with a question in her eyes. "What if this is a security building? We won't know if he's awake from out here unless he's got a light on. We'll have to ring his buzzer. That'll wake him for sure, if he's asleep."

Glancing down the building wall, he noticed a light on in one of the apartments. "I think that's his unit there. He's probably up, but the lock on the front door doesn't work anyway. People prop it open all the time, let their friends in. Come on."

Shoving the door open—and someone *had* taped the latch in the open position—they trotted down the stairs and took a right at the ground-floor landing. The sounds of a late-night party ricocheted down the hall as they walked down it, and Taylor wrinkled her nose. She was glad she didn't live there—she would hate being disturbed by inconsiderate neighbors.

"That's odd," Kai commented once he rounded the corner.

"What's odd? It's just a party."

"No, why did Carter leave his door open? Do you think he just went down to shut those guys up?" A flood of light seeped into the hall, obviously from inside an apartment.

He frowned and began to run.

"Wait up!" yelled Taylor, pounding down the hallway after him. Her heartbeat lurched into overdrive in response to his obvious concern. She tried to quiet it, telling herself that it was nothing. Carter was probably just down the hall at the party on his way to taking the trash out and hadn't bothered closing his door because his arms were full.

Kai skidded to a stop at the open apartment door, an incredulous expression on his face. His eyes had locked on something on the floor. "Carter?" he murmured, squatting to extend his hand.

"What is it? What is it?" Taylor cried out as she slid up behind him. Her gut seized as she scanned the object in front of her. Carter Masterson lay on the apartment's linoleum foyer, a crimson stain spread across his white western shirt. The fingers of one hand were curled as though he'd been grasping something.

"Oh, God," she wailed. "Is he dead?"

THREE

By three-thirty that morning, Taylor was slipping a key into the lock at Steve Derosset's condo. Kai Huskisson, Steve's best friend, stood behind her, anxiously stubbing the toe of his boot on the utility-grade carpet covering the hall floor. His action caught her eye, and she started. The carpet was similar to that used in Carter's building, and the likeness made her shudder—she didn't want to be reminded of the scene they'd just witnessed there. Waiting for the police at the scene of the Learjet captain's murder had been chilling, and that wasn't something she wanted to do on a regular basis.

Staring at a bloody, dead body—the body of a friend who had met a brutal end—had given her the heebie-jeebies. Even so, when the police had arrived and shooed her and Kai off after asking them some questions, she wasn't sure how she felt about that. On the one hand, getting away from the gory evidence of murder relieved her; on the other hand, she felt miffed. She wanted to know the circumstances that had led to the shooting. What did the police think? Did they have any likely suspects?

Other than her and Kai.

She knew that the person or people that report a dead body are often chief suspects. That made her shudder, too.

Pausing as she applied the key to the door's deadbolt, she turned to Kai. "I don't know if Steve's awake," she whispered to him. "I hope he doesn't hear me and think I'm a burglar."

Her face blanched. "That's *all* we need tonight. Have him shoot me with that loaded thirty-eight next to the bed. I better say something, just in case."

"Why does he have a loaded gun next to his bed?" Kai squawked under his breath.

"I don't know. Must be because of the break-ins they've had in the neighborhood recently. I wouldn't have one, though." She undid the lock and called to him. "Steve, it's me. Don't panic." After waiting a few seconds, she swung the door open and walked into the foyer.

Her voice had cracked with emotion when she'd announced her presence. If her words had woken him, she figured, he'd hear the strain in them and know something was wrong. Her late-late-night arrival at his condo itself wouldn't be enough to alarm him—midnight flights called both of them to the airport frequently, and their returns home were often in the wee hours. On the nights they stayed together, that meant interrupting *somebody's* dream time.

Easing the door closed, she beckoned to Kai and stepped into Steve's bedroom. A light in the parking lot outside illuminated the room, its beams seeping through the curtainless window of the fifth-story unit. The bed table blocked its sparse rays, mottling the wall with vague shadows. A lump on the bed was her sleeping beau.

His chest rose and fell, and the sound of his breathing was steady and deep. She took comfort in that—she hadn't woken him with her entrance, and he hadn't had a gun trained on her when she entered the room. That was a relief.

The bed's down-filled comforter hung haphazardly over one edge of the mattress, barely covering his body. That was typical—he was a restless sleeper, tossing and turning all night. Taylor couldn't count the number of times he'd woken her with an unconscious fling of his arm.

His thick blond hair was as tousled as the bedclothes. On a normal night, the sight of his well-developed form—only half-hidden by the comforter, and topped by a bad case of bed head—would have made her smile.

But it wasn't a normal night, and she didn't feel like smiling.

Hating to drag him away from his peaceful sleep, Taylor touched his shoulder lightly. "Steve, it's me," she gulped. "Kai's here, too. I've got bad news." When he didn't react, she shook him gently. "Steve, wake up."

Finally, one blue eye opened cautiously and focused on Taylor's face. When he noticed she wasn't alone, both eyes snapped open and he bolted up in bed. "Taylor! Kai! What's going on here? Has something happened?"

"Yeah," Taylor muttered. Settling down on the edge of the bed, she took a deep breath. Kai remained standing by the night table, his face grim. "It's Carter," she added. "He's been shot." She paused to catch a breath, feeling herself choke. "He's dead."

"Dead?" Steve glanced at Kai as though he wanted confirmation from him that her words were true. Surely she had gotten it wrong. When the Lear copilot nodded assent, the blond man pushed the comforter to the side and rolled over to sit next to Taylor. His eyes shot from his girlfriend's face to his coworker's. "What the hell happened?"

"I'm not really sure," Taylor replied. "Me and Kai had to run over to his house to get a log signature around two-something. We found him just inside his apartment, lying on the floor. He'd been shot in the chest. Blood everywhere." She shuddered as she recalled the picture. It hadn't been a pretty sight.

"My God." Steve stared at the comforter draped over his naked knees and digested the information. Looking back at Taylor again, he asked, "Do you know what happened? Did you call the cops?"

"Duh. Of course we called the cops," she snapped, before she caught herself. Undoubtedly he was still processing what she'd said—no wonder he was asking stupid questions. Give him some time. She'd asked a stupid question, too, when she and Kai had discovered the obviously dead body.

Kai broke into the conversational lull. "The cops ran us off as soon as they got some information from us, so we don't know much about what they found. But we did hear a couple of them talking. They were saying something about 'surprising an intruder, probably a burglar.'"

With one eyebrow raised, Steve pondered Kai's statement. "Does that make sense to you?" he quizzed them. "What did you see?" He wrapped an arm around Taylor's shoulders, and peered up at his coworker.

Taylor shook her head and shrugged. "As soon as I saw Carter lying there in a puddle of blood," she confessed, "my brain shut down. I wasn't assimilating anything. I couldn't even

have told you the color of the *car* I'd driven to his *apartment*."
That embarrassed her—she thought she had complete control
over herself at all times. Even in *extremely* difficult situations.

But not so. She'd turned into a blathering idiot when faced
with violent death. It was bad enough to admit that to Steve—
who'd seen her emotional side and would understand—but col-
lapsing in front of Kai at Carter's apartment really bruised her
ego. She had a reputation to uphold, especially with coworkers.
Shit.

"Okay." Steve stood up, grabbed a pair of Levi's off the
chair, and stepped into them. The room's cool air had created
goose bumps on his skin, and his nipples stood erect. Looking
down at his chest, he reached for a sweater and pulled it down
over his head. Partially dressed, he turned to Taylor and Kai.

He seemed to have control over *him*self, Taylor acknowledged, ashamed. But then again, she thought, he hadn't seen
Carter Masterson's bloody body and staring, lifeless eyes.

"Did you guys call Nate?" he asked them. When both she
and Kai shook their heads, he nodded. "Okay. That's the next
thing to do. Nate'd want to know. He'd *need* to know." He
reached for the phone and dialed.

Half an hour later, Taylor pulled her Suzuki into the nearly
empty parking lot in front of the LifeLine hangar-office complex. Steve sat to her right, Kai on the bench seat behind her.
Peering out the windshield, she noted that the slate-gray overcast still lingered, though it had risen to about a thousand feet.
The sodium-vapor street lights on International Airport Road
cast an eerie yellow string of illumination that looked like a
monstrous glowworm huddled next to the asphalt. Nate
Mueller's beater Datsun B–210 sat near the glass door to the
office, and a single lamp burned inside.

Steve gestured for her to swing in beside him, then jumped
from the still-idling vehicle. She silenced the engine and waited
for Kai to clamber out of the rear seat before she ran to catch
her beau.

The sight that greeted them when they approached the office
made her wince. Nathan Mueller slumped over the top of his
desk, one thumb mindlessly flipping through the Rolodex next
to the Touch-Tone phone to his right. Wrinkling his brow, he
pushed his aviator-style eyeglasses up onto the bridge of his
nose and leaned back in his chair.

His dark-brown hair looked like he hadn't bothered to comb it before he'd dashed from his house, and his sweatshirt and rumpled jeans matched accordingly. Glancing at his watch and comparing it to the clock on the wall, he fumbled to reset it to match the larger timepiece's reading of 4:16 A.M.

The swishing noise of Steve pushing the heavy door open brought Nate's head around. When he recognized his coworker, Kai and Taylor in tow, he looked at them desperately.

"What happened?" Nate croaked at Steve. "You got any more details? More than you told me on the phone?"

"Nothing but guesses so far," Steve replied. He and Taylor had been brainstorming the shooting on the way over to LifeLine, with Kai jumping in with points on occasion. "We figured Carter surprised a robber as the guy was rifling through his stuff, and the robber shot first and thought about it second."

"Did the burglar take anything?" Nate asked. "I haven't been to Carter's house. Did he have any expensive gadgets?"

Kai broke in, his eyebrows knotted. "You know, now that you bring it up . . ." He paused, thinking, then spoke again. "He told me he'd just bought that new WebTV. You know, that thing that attaches to your TV. It lets you get on the Internet even if you don't have a computer. I know those gadgets are pretty popular, might be easy to fence. A burglar would go after one of them for sure. Maybe that's what he was after." He paused. "Just a thought."

Nate nodded, then checked himself. The skin on his cheeks drew back as a thought surfaced. "What's really going on here, Steve?" He glanced up from the pencil clamped in his hands. "First we lost Robert Berndt, now Carter. Is this some kind of a bad joke? Are you Lear captains jinxed?"

Steve approached the desk, frowning. "Naw, that couldn't be, Nate. Things are just getting really violent everywhere. When we've got schoolkids shooting their classmates, you'd expect other crimes to happen."

Drawing her eyes away from Steve, Taylor trained them on Nate with a puzzled look. "Has this happened before? Someone got shot?" She turned back to her boyfriend. "Must've been before me and Kai got hired, huh?"

"Yeah." Steve grimaced. "We lost another Learjet captain, Robert Berndt, a few years ago. Right before you guys arrived. He didn't get shot, though." The blond man shook his head, contorting his face. "He was on his way home after a flight and some jerk hit his car with a big Suburban. Pretty bad wreck, too. I guess that's why the guy took off." Pausing, the pilot stroked his moustache in remembrance. "Anyway, Berndt couldn't go after the guy. He couldn't go anywhere. Got a pretty severe head injury from the accident, was unconscious when the cops arrived. Went into a coma. When he came out of the coma, he had enough brain damage so that he'd never fly a Learjet again. Probably not any kind of airplane again." He pushed his hands into his jeans' pockets and looked down at the floor. After a few seconds he raised his eyes, a question in them. "So, Nate, what do we do now? We're one captain short, and we can't handle enough of the medevacs if we're shorthanded. Summer's right around the corner and you know how that goes."

Nate's chair squeaked as he swiveled, and he tapped the eraser end of his pencil on the blotter. "Yeah, I know. We need somebody right away." He glanced at Kai, narrowing his eyes, then shook his head. "You don't have enough time, Kai. The insurance won't cover you. I'll have to look at some resumes." With a sigh, he opened a drawer in his desk and thumbed through a hanging file labeled PILOT APPS-LEAR.

He had several letters halfway out of the file before Steve interrupted him. "While you're looking for replacements, don't forget to get somebody lined up to stand in for me and Taylor. We've got refresher training scheduled for the day after tomorrow. We'll have to leave for Seattle pretty quick."

"Oh, shit. I forgot." He glared at the schedule board, tossed the paperwork on the desk, and shoved his chair back. Distractedly, he frowned at the pilot roster in front of him. "Now I'm going to have to rearrange everything to account for you guys being gone. There's going to be some pissed-off pilots when I'm done."

FOUR

After leaving Nate to his schedule rearrangement duties, Taylor walked out to her Suzuki with Steve and Kai in tow. "You guys want to go get some breakfast?" she asked, glancing at her watch. "It's only five, but I'm sure there's something open in town. One of those twenty-four-hour joints. A pancake house or something."

Steve perked up at the talk of food, but Kai shook his head. "I've been up all night, and I've got to get some rest. I'm on duty again at six tonight." Then he hesitated, seeming to remember that the man assigned to duty with him lay on a gurney at the medical examiner's lab. "At least, I *think* I'm on duty tonight. If Nate gets another captain for nighttime call." Seconds later he grimaced. "Shit. Nate'll probably reassign Ed Guralnik to nights with me. I hate that guy, he's such a macho jerk. Thinks he's God's gift to the world because he's a Lear captain."

Kai shuddered, though probably not because of the chill in the clammy, predawn air. The waterlogged clouds above the three pilots had risen another five hundred feet, but still hung low. The almost-spring-in-Alaska sunrise was imminent— even at five o'clock in the morning—but the dismal gray layer would only permit a vague glow to appear over the mountains. The apexes of those mountains—the sixty five-hundred foot-high Chugach Range, twenty-five miles to the east of the city—were hidden by the thick stratus, like the heads of so many ostriches stuck in the sand.

The bleak sunrise waxed further as Taylor drove to Kai's midtown apartment to drop him off. Virtually no traffic impeded her progress as she turned off International Airport Road onto Arctic Boulevard. Not even early birds were looking to catch the first worm of the day at five o'clock.

Within five minutes, she had her vehicle parked on a side street next to the complex where Kai rented a studio unit. "Here you go," she said, leaning forward so he could crawl out of the rear seat and squeeze past her. "Sweet dreams."

"Yeah, right. After what we've seen tonight?" He rolled his eyes and plodded toward the building, mental *and* physical fatigue obvious in his slow gait.

"So," Steve said eagerly once Kai had disappeared into the complex, "still interested in getting some breakfast? There's a Burger King right down Northern Lights. I know *they'd* be open."

"Well, maybe later. First I want to go take another look at Carter's apartment."

"Why would you want to do that?" His puzzled expression showed doubt. "Haven't you had enough of murders for one night? You said that the whole scene was too much for you."

Taylor put the Suzuki in gear and prepared to pull away from the curb. "Yeah, but me and Kai got shoved out of there pretty quick by the cops. We never got a chance to see what they saw. I'm curious about what happened, and I doubt I'd get any answers from the police if I called them. Why don't we go over there and do a little checking ourselves?" When Steve shrugged in noncommittal acquiescence, she accelerated down the asphalt.

Five seconds later, at the intersection of a side street and Arctic Boulevard, she halted and glanced at the blond man. "But if we do go to Carter's place, how do we get in? The cops aren't going to leave the door open when they're done examining the crime scene. For that matter, they might still be there when we arrive. They won't let us rummage around while they're working—"

"Yeah." He nodded, then something dawned on him. He looked at her encouragingly. "Wait a second, I just remembered. I still have a key to Carter's place. We *can* get in, even if it's locked."

"You have a key? For what? You had to water his plants when he went on vacation or something?" She laughed. She didn't give *her* house keys to coworkers. Except Steve.

"No, that wasn't it. When I was still a copilot, and we were flying together, he gave me his spare when we had flights scheduled back to back. I wanted to get a few minutes of sleep in between the flights, but there wasn't enough time for me to drive back to my house for a nap. I was living in Rabbit Creek then, you know the long drive. Anyway, he gave me a key for his place so I could crash there for an hour. He never asked for it back, and I never remembered it, either."

"Ahhh. Okay, that's how we get in, then. We'll just have to take our chances with the place not being cordoned off when we get there."

Pulling into the parking lot at Carter's, Taylor glanced around the neighborhood. A Chevron service station graced the corner they had just swung past, and the neon sign for a coin-op Laundromat glowed in the dull, early morning sunlight.

She scanned the street in front of the building. "Oh, shit. There's still somebody here." She pointed at the single white-on-white Anchorage Police Department cruiser, subtle shots of blue artistically scattered over the body. New paint scheme, one she didn't care for. "What do we do now?" she asked.

"I've got a novel idea. Why don't we go home? Quit putzing around where we don't belong?"

"No way, Steve. I have to know what happened. I would think you would want that, too." She glared at him. "So how do we get past the cop?"

Steve hiked his shoulders helplessly. "Don't ask me. I'm not used to sneaking past the police."

"You wimp," she sneered. Then she added a smile to show him she didn't really mean any insult.

Seconds later she snapped her fingers. "I got it, Steve. When I was here with Kai, I heard a loud party going on down the hall. If it's still going on—or even if it's not—we can talk to the cop guarding the scene and pretend to be neighbors that want him to shut them up. Maybe we can say the partygoers are getting kinda rowdy, starting to fight. Sound okay?"

Without waiting for a reply from him, she clambered out of the Suzuki. She was on a mission. After sliding out of the other seat, Steve followed her to the front door of the building.

When they walked into the foyer the odor of new carpet tickled her nostrils. She hadn't noticed that earlier, when she'd dashed after Kai toward Carter's open door. In contrast to the new carpet, the beige paint on the walls showed some wear and tear and the wooden baseboard molding sported nicks and scratches. The trim around the doors had its share of those furniture-moving marks, too. The whole building looked pretty typical for an apartment complex, if you didn't know what had happened in one of the units just hours ago.

When they rounded the corner, they saw an APD officer standing in front of the door to Carter Masterson's apartment. He glanced in their direction, obviously surprised to see anyone up that early. Taylor jogged his way, a damsel-in-distress expression on her face.

"Oh, officer, officer," she chirped in a vulnerable voice. "We need help. There's a party going on upstairs." She pointed above her head. A muffled bass beat sounded nearby. "They've quieted down some—they kept us up all night—but now it sounds like they've started to fight. We heard it when we got ready to leave for work, and when we saw your car in the parking lot we tried to find you. We didn't want to drive off and ignore what was going on. Can you check on it?"

The officer's eyes narrowed. "Where's the trouble?"

"I'm not sure. Sounds like it's farther down the hall on the second floor. Can you help?"

He looked over his shoulder at the door he was guarding, then back at Taylor, trying to make a decision. Finally he tested the doorknob to confirm it was locked, and turned back to her. "Lead the way."

"No, we're on our way to work at the bakery at Carr's. We're going to be late; we just wanted to notify you."

"Okay. You said second floor, west end?" He set off down the hall. Taylor and Steve headed in the other direction toward the building's front entrance, but as soon as they climbed a few stairs they stopped. She peeked around the corner to see the APD officer disappear into the stairwell on the opposite end of the hall.

She grabbed Steve's elbow. "We've only got a few minutes before he comes back. Let's go." She tugged him along down the hallway to Carter's apartment.

When they reached it, he fumbled with his key ring, then

applied one of the keys to the knob and shoved the door open. The solid wood door swung aside to reveal a blood-stained carpet just inside, and the big blond man made a funny strained noise as he looked down at it.

Oh, he *is* affected by the scene, she thought. And the body wasn't even lying there, like it had been when she'd arrived. His reaction made her feel better about *her* initial reaction to the scene.

Shivering in remembrance of the gory image, she shut the door and glanced around. The corpse of her coworker had immediately drawn her attention on her first trip to the apartment, and kept it, so this was her first real look at Carter's home. A sparsely furnished living room greeted her, with a lone sofa filling one wall. Several magazines and books lay on the floor near its far end. A card table and a single folding chair rested in what appeared to be the dining room. No decoration or ornamentation covered the ivory-colored walls. Nothing homey or personal sat on an end table, no knickknacks cluttered shelves. There wasn't even a calendar tacked on the bulletin board near a window.

"We gotta get out of here fast," she acknowledged. "You check this area, I'll check the bedroom." She didn't know what she was searching for, but she'd look anyway.

Trotting over to the bedroom, Taylor peered inside and scooted through the bedroom door. Her first look puzzled her. She saw a small box—like a cable receiver—placed on top of the twenty-one-inch TV. "What is that?" she wondered out loud, then just took mental note of it and scanned the rest of the room. She didn't have time for making guesses.

Finishing her survey, she turned toward the living room. She scanned the decor—or lack of decor—with interest. Carter was either a minimalist or he hated shopping, though neither of those points of view made any sense to *her*.

A few seconds into her scrutiny, her gaze fell on an open sliding window near the corner. "This is how the burglar got in, Steve," she called toward the kitchen, pointing at the window. "He came through here."

Over the countertop separating the kitchen from the living room, she could see him look over his shoulder and frown at the window. Then he gestured for her to come over. "Come look at this, Taylor."

"No, we're out of time. That cop'll be back pretty quick. If he finds us in here we'll get charged with fucking up the evidence. I don't want that." She took another glance around the living room, and trotted toward the front door. "Come on. You can tell me what you found when we get back to the car."

Seemingly unsatisfied with something, he swung around and scanned the kitchen a second time. Taylor saw him peer into each of the open drawers, one by one. When he passed the sink again, he halted and crouched down, disappearing from her view beneath the counter.

She trotted back to the kitchen and peeked over the counter. "Come on! What the hell are you doing down there? We gotta go!"

"Okay, I'm going. But there's a lot of odd stuff in here. It looks like Carter—"

Taylor interrupted him. "Tell me later. Now we gotta get out of here." She beckoned for him to join her at the front door. Finally, he walked out of the kitchen and headed for the door. Both he and Taylor grimaced as they maneuvered around the blood-stained carpet in the foyer. "Good thing we're leaving. This place was creeping me out," she confessed.

After exiting the apartment and locking the door behind them, they started down the hallway. When they were only ten feet from Carter's apartment, a sight startled them. Several men in APD crime-scene technician coveralls were rounding the corner. "Oh, shit," Taylor breathed. "That was close."

The trio of men marched past Taylor and Steve, briefly taking their measure, and stopped at Apartment .111. They tried the knob, found it locked, and glanced around. "Hey," yelled the tallest of the group to the fleeing trespassers, "you seen the cop that was supposed to be here waiting for us?"

Taylor swung around and looked at them, innocent as a wolf in sheep's clothing. "I think he just went upstairs to check on a disturbance. Should be back pretty quick."

FIVE

Back in the Suzuki, Taylor keyed the ignition and whipped out of the parking lot. "We better get out of here," she announced, "before the cop figures this one out." In her haste, she nearly sideswiped the APD crime lab van, an enormous Winnebago-style motorhome hugging the street near the exit from the lot. "Yikes!" she squeaked as she wrenched the steering wheel to the left. "That's all we need, getting a ticket for hitting the APD van on our way out."

After getting her bearings back, she sped down Twenty-seventh Avenue toward Spenard Road. The full parking lot at Steve's place could conceal her Suzuki, and they could disappear into the building in case the police decided to track them down for leading an officer on a wild goose chase.

She felt kind of guilty for doing that. She and Steve had acted like burglars themselves, scampering away from the murder scene just like the earlier criminal visitor had done. But *they* hadn't left any dead bodies in their wake. All they had done is look around.

She halted at the stop sign where Twenty-seventh crossed Spenard. The intersection stood a quarter-mile from Carter's—out of the range of imminent discovery—and she felt she could relax some. Her heart still pounded in her chest but not as rapidly as before, and her fight-or-flight response had reached a cooling-down point. Now it was time to talk.

With one foot resting on the clutch and the other on the

brake, she turned to face Steve. "So, what did you think of Carter's? You've seen his place before, but to me it looked like it *had* been burglarized. I mean, Carter didn't have anything. He must've lived like a monk. Was he always like that?"

Steve arched an eyebrow, obviously unable to understand how anybody could live so sparingly. "Yeah, his place has always looked like that. Apparently his wife got everything in the divorce—including the house—and he never got around to replacing any of the stuff he had when he used to live in Ocean View. He had moved into his smaller digs by the time I first met him, so I never saw the other house, but his apartment looked about the same this morning as it did last time I was there. Pretty bare." Steve frowned and tapped his fingers on the dash, thinking. "But I thought Kai said he had an expensive TV-something. He'd just gotten it."

Taylor nodded. "Yeah. Kai called it WebTV, and I think I saw it in the bedroom when I looked in there. Some box was set up on the TV console next to his bed. I didn't know what it was then—I figured it was cable—but now you mention it, I bet that was the WebTV Kai was talking about." Then her eyes squinted at Steve in confusion. "But why was it still there? Kai said it was kinda expensive, and that would make it the only expensive thing in the whole damn place. Why didn't the burglar nab it? It was small enough, he wouldn't have had any trouble carting it out of there."

As soon as she finished her sentence, she felt the urge to get moving again, and hung a right onto Spenard. They were away from ground zero, but she knew she wouldn't feel entirely safe until the Suzuki was off the street. Steve's condo was just a half-mile away, so she accelerated to the south. Two blocks later, she slowed to turn at Twenty-ninth.

Taylor shot glances at Steve as she drove, and picked up on his analytical expression. He was thinking hard about something. "What's bothering you?" she asked. "I can practically hear the wheels turning in your head."

Lifting a finger, as though to say, "Give me a second here," he remained quiet for a few moments. She continued down Twenty-ninth as she waited for him to finish ruminating, then he finally spoke.

"I think the reason why the burglar didn't lift the expensive TV gadget is because there was no burglar." He angled his head and stared at her as though daring her to play devil's advocate with him.

Halfway down Twenty-ninth, she jammed on the brakes and turned to gape at him. "What do you mean, no burglar? Did you find something that said there wasn't?"

"Yeah, I did. In the kitchen." Responding to the confused expression on Taylor's face, he continued. "Somebody'd pawed through all of the drawers, and most of the cupboards."

She squinted at him in bewilderment. "I don't know about you, Steve, but that spells burglar to me. What does it spell to you, maid service?"

Laughing at her, he shook his head. "There's more, Taylor. There's his garbage. I was looking at his garbage, and—"

She interrupted him instantly. "You were going through his garbage? You think we work for some tabloid newspaper or something?"

"Taylor, shut up and give me a chance to finish." He stared her down when she opened her mouth and got ready to speak again, but his demeanor convinced her to stifle her words. She ran a finger across her mouth in the universal sign of "my lips are sealed."

Assured of her silence, he spoke again. "I found one of those microwave-safe melamine plates in the trash, with half of a Salisbury steak dinner still on it. It didn't mean anything to me at the time, but now that I've had a chance to think about it, it's obvious." He didn't say any more, seemingly convinced that she would see the meaning in his words.

Instead, she pursed her lips. She wasn't going to talk anymore, even if she didn't get the message he thought he was sending. He had just handed her a pretty oddball clue—could he see messages in dirty dishes like they were tea leaves?

Shaking his head because his explanation obviously wasn't good enough for her to see the connection, he sighed. "Here, let me explain it to you. Carter wouldn't have tossed half of his meal like this, Taylor. Not the Carter *I* know. Plus, there's no way he would've thrown that plastic plate away in the garbage."

Her forehead wrinkling, she squinted at Steve. The skeptic in her had to object, regardless of the gag rule. "Oh, come on, Steve. How can you say an obvious burglary was something else on the basis of finding a half-eaten meal in the trash?" She shook her head. Steve had lost it, seeing demons around every corner.

He sniffed in irritation. "Hey, that dinner was on a *plastic* microwave plate. There's no way Carter would've discarded plastic like that. I know him better than you do, and he was the greenest guy I know. He recycled everything. His newspapers, anything plastic or glass, any metal cans. He had three different bins under his sink to separate the recyclables from everything else. He wouldn't have thrown that plate in the garbage. Someone else did that, that's clear to me.

"Plus, there was something else in there. A fork and a knife." He stared at her evenly. "Do you throw your utensils away when they get dirty? Or do you wash them?" When she lifted her eyebrows in response, he continued. "I admit it wasn't expensive stuff, but come on. Another person—the one that shot him—threw that stuff away after the murder to make it appear he had just walked in. Carter didn't surprise a burglar and get shot for his trouble; he was already home and eating when someone else surprised *him*. Then, *ka-blam!*"

Taylor frowned and her eyebrows snapped back down almost audibly. What Steve had revealed changed things radically. "Well, damn. You might be right," she conceded. "The rearranged drawers and the open window were just made to look like the work of a burglar. And that loud party upstairs hid the sound of the shot." She started when she realized they'd entered the scene of a much more serious, and puzzling, crime. "You didn't touch anything when you were looking at his trash, did you? You didn't paw around in the bag?"

He snorted, clearly offended. "I have more sense than that, Taylor. Sneaking into Carter's apartment was bad enough. I wouldn't rearrange the crime scene. I've watched *Law and Order* on TV enough times to know that's a no-no. I didn't even leave fingerprints on the cupboards. I used my keys to open them."

"Okay, then we didn't goof anything up." With her expression glum, she released the Suzuki's clutch and allowed it to continue toward Steve's condo building at a slower pace. "You know, your take on the crime scene really makes sense when you look at what the *alleged* burglar left behind. No experienced thief would've neglected to check the bedroom for valuables, and take off without the only expensive toy in the place. I don't care how worried he got when he shot Carter, he wouldn't have wasted his time by running empty-handed." She pulled into the building's parking lot with a quizzical expression twisting her features. "So, if this is the way it *really* happened, who was behind it? Carter seemed like such a nice guy. Did he have enemies I didn't know about? Ones that would *shoot* him?"

As Steve thought about her question, he guided her into a visitor slot on the striped asphalt. A red Mazda Miata and a black Toyota Celica flanked the space.

Looking at the cars, she decided most of his neighbors must be young singles to whom a car was a status and virility symbol. A sporty car said a lot about its owner; she wondered what her utilitarian Sidekick said about her.

Once she'd silenced the Suzuki, Steve turned to her. His eyes were unfocused as he thought about Carter's connection to a murderer, a fact clearly unpleasant to him. Nobody wanted to ponder a death, especially when the victim was a friend.

A minute later, he nodded when a possibility occurred to him. "I don't know if this means anything," he commented, "but Carter was talking to me the other day. He said he caught some training record discrepancies. I didn't think much of it then, but . . ." Ten seconds passed and his eyes refocused. "But now he's dead. I can't believe that's nothing but a coincidence."

Taylor's face registered puzzlement. "How could there be a connection between training record mistakes and murder? That's kind of a stretch."

"Hear me out before you decide, Taylor. He was looking at another Lear captain's recurrency paperwork and it was wrong. Unfortunately he didn't tell me who he was talking about at the time, probably because he didn't want me to know until he was sure of what he'd found—"

She interrupted. "But you can find out who the other captain is, can't you?"

"Well, yeah. It'll take a little poking, but I can do it if I can get into the records. Give me a couple hours by myself with the files, and *voila*!" He made a fist and drew an imaginary silk scarf out from between his curled fingers. When Taylor didn't appear properly amused by his magician imitation, he hiked his shoulders and dropped his hands back into his lap. "Anyway, back to the story. There were obvious discrepancies in the guy's records. The date of a class he had *supposedly* attended was during the two weeks he took for his vacation. LifeLine hadn't sent him down for that class, like he'd said."

She shrugged. "So? Maybe the instructor just wrote down the wrong day. I do that sometimes, get a day ahead or behind of the calendar."

"Well, the day was way off, not just Tuesday rather than Wednesday. And you know what that means. If the captain didn't go to the class, he broke FAA rules on recurrency training. Every flight he took without completing the recurrency class was an FAR violation, and you know how the FAA feels about those. It pisses them off pretty good. LifeLine'd get fined for *every* violation, and that'd be some serious money." He looked at her, and nodded at her grimace when she started calculating the dollars involved. "If the pilot and the instructor cooked up this cheating scheme together, they'd both be in a shitload of trouble. They'd probably get fired for compromising the reputations of both companies, LifeLine and the training school. Carter had spotted the discrepancy in the records and was going to check into it. I'd bet his death had something to do with what he found."

"You really think the two are related?" She narrowed her eyes. "I mean, even if he pissed somebody off by looking into those discrepancies, why would they care enough to murder him? Him discovering that they were doctoring up the records doesn't seem like a good reason to kill him." Taylor gnawed on her bottom lip, pinking the skin with the pressure of her incisors.

"Obviously you haven't dealt too often with the egos of most Lear captains." He smiled lamely and shrugged. "Other than me." He raised an eyebrow as though apologizing. "If some of those guys thought they would lose their jobs because they got caught pencil-whipping their training paperwork, they'd go ballistic. They wouldn't let that happen. Being a Lear captain is part of what makes me tick, one of the ways I identify myself to the world. It's really important to me, and I don't think I'm an exception to the rule. Other Lear captains feel the same way, I'm sure. It's not clear to me what I'd do if faced with losing my job—I doubt I'd do anything as drastic as shooting somebody—but there's others that might. Maybe Carter's killer didn't see any other way of quieting him."

"But what can we do?" Taylor wasn't sure she wanted to get

involved with harassing people who didn't have any qualms about killing coworkers. *Yikes.*

Suddenly an idea surfaced from the back of her mind. "Wait a second. We're going down to Aviation Safety for our recurrency tomorrow, we can do some poking around then. Maybe we can get someone to do the same thing to *our* records that Carter found on that other captain's paperwork. That'd be a first step in proving your speculation about Carter's death."

Then she had second thoughts. "But don't you think we should go to the cops with this information, too? Surely they'll figure out that Carter's death was no interrupted burglary as soon as they see the crime scene data and the autopsy report." She didn't want to keep potentially important clues to herself. What would that be, hindering prosecution?

"Well sure," Steve admitted. "We should go to the cops, but they'll just blow us off. They probably hate civilians gumming up their work. Plus, all we've got are my impressions of what kind of a person Carter was. That probably isn't enough to support an investigation." Opening the Suzuki's passenger-side door, he added, "I'll talk to somebody, anyway, see if I can make him believe me. I've got a high school buddy that was a cop last time I checked—I'll talk to him. Plus, I'll go to the office tonight and see if I can find the name of that other captain."

"Okay, sounds good to me. That'll help a lot." Taylor scanned the parking area as she spoke, and spied a thirty-something man climbing into a late-model Corvette on the other side of the lot. His expensive suit, his expensive vehicle, and his early departure for work marked him as a stockbroker. Wall Street's beginning bell rang at nine o'clock Eastern Standard Time, which equaled five Alaska Standard Time.

Taylor's grumbling stomach told her she was ready for breakfast, so she undid her seat belt and exited the car. "You got anything decent to eat inside?" she called over her car's hood. "Something beside cereal?" She knew, too well, his grocery shopping habits. He just bought what looked good at the time, regardless of what he needed or what was nutritious.

He stepped out of the Suzuki and walked around to her side. "I'm not too hungry right now," he confessed. Seeing a blood-spattered crime scene had probably upset his constitution, she figured, but her own gut had overruled her emotions. She had to eat something.

"Well, I'm starving. You got any of those frozen waffles I brought over? I brought over a tub of peanut butter, too, if I recall. Got any left?" She usually provided her own breakfast when she spent the night with him, since she had no intention to eat what he ate.

If he ate anything at all.

He wrinkled his nose at her. "How can you stand eating both peanut butter and maple syrup on waffles? Makes me cringe just thinking about it."

She smiled, undisturbed by his censure. "Hey, what can I say? Breakfast of champions."

SIX

Two days later, Taylor was staring out from a window seat in a Boeing jet cruising north toward Anchorage from Seattle. She had finally finished her recurrency work and was good for another six months of flight duty. That relieved her. She always felt tense in the classroom at Aviation Safety, knowing that the security of her job revolved around her performance there. If she'd flunked the checkride that followed the class she'd have gotten fired, or at least demoted. She sighed. Things had gone well this time, but in another half year she'd go through the worry again. It had been easier when she was a copilot—*everything* had been easier when she was a copilot—when she only needed recurrency and a checkride annually.

Steve had left Seattle before her. He, too, had taken his semi-annual checkride but LifeLine's shortage of Learjet captains had prompted Nate Mueller to call him back to Anchorage as soon as he had finished. No dawdling in Seattle for him. She hadn't talked to him before he took off, so she didn't know how he'd fared in duping an instructor into falsifying records. He was supposed to talk to Don Sosa, the instructor for Ed Guralnik, the Lear captain who'd wanted his records altered. Steve had located Guralnik's name during a late night paperwork search he'd done before leaving for Seattle. If Guralnik's instructor had agreed to more tampering, they'd have another piece of the puzzle surrounding their coworker's murder.

Taylor wasn't surprised Guralnik's name had surfaced as being part of the record-falsifying scam. And she certainly wouldn't doubt it if the man emerged as a suspect in Carter Masterson's death. From the day she'd first met him, she'd disliked him. A slender, tall man with a beaked nose and a tattoo on his wrist—one he thought hidden by his long-sleeve shirts—he was almost predatory-looking. With dark-red hair and a graying pencil-thin moustache, he oozed surliness. Even his truck—a dark-blue Chevy half-ton with a gun rack in the rear window—screamed misfit. His antisocial attitude made Taylor wonder how he'd gotten hired by LifeLine. He must be a good pilot, she'd thought at the time.

Like Kai Huskisson—who had called him a *macho jerk* the other morning—she had no good words to say about Ed Guralnik. He definitely rubbed her the wrong way. She had seen him strutting around the office too many times, crowing about his skill with the Learjet. Stories had circulated of him telling questionable tales to the female locals when a medevac called for out-of-town duty. He used his Lear captain status like a pheromone, verbally waving it around to attract the opposite sex.

But could he kill to prevent the loss of something so dear to him and his way of life?

Tired of wondering about depressing subjects like that, she peered out the window. As it always did, the beauty of nature outside easily distracted her. Below her sat a myriad assortment of islands, a crystal-clear afternoon sky scattering sunbeams across them. Geologists called it the Alexander Archipelago, but people who had seen the resemblance on a map had renamed it the Alaskan Panhandle. The string of islets dotting the ocean wasn't very wide—perhaps one hundred miles across the south end, narrowing to as little as thirty miles at the north—but from its tip the rest of the state extended west another seventeen hundred miles and north another nine hundred miles. At 591,000 square miles it was easily the largest of the fifty states, a fact Taylor delighted in telling anyone who wanted to hear about it.

Marveling at the kaleidoscope of color below her, Taylor pressed her face to the glass. The deep green of spruce trees abutted the blue of ocean; pristine, white snow smothered the tops of the gray peaks; aquamarine glaciers swept down their faces. The land looked like a crazy quilt.

Taylor never tired of admiring the endless beauty of Alaska, and that was one of the many reasons she loved her job with LifeLine. Her old job in Bethel had allowed her to sightsee on the flat, tundra-carpeted Yukon-Kuskokwim Delta—for what *that* was worth—but LifeLine's territory covered the entire state of Alaska.

That was a lot of sightseeing.

Even as enthralled as she was with the spectacular terrain below, the sounds of a flight attendant pushing a food cart down the aisle caught her attention. The grumbling of her stomach suggested that she should attend to more mundane needs, so when the food cart stopped nearby she glanced over hungrily.

"Let's see, you're eleven-A. You ordered the vegetarian meal, didn't you?" asked a young man, digging through one of the lower shelves on his cart. After a five-second search he extracted a lunch and placed it on the tray table unfolded in front of her. "Here you go. Thai stir-fry. I hope you enjoy it!" Wearing his eager-to-serve expression, he trundled a few more feet down the aisle and stopped his cart at the next row.

With a fork in one hand, Taylor dug into the savory-smelling dish. "Mmmmm," she murmured when the first bite hit her taste buds. She had heard that the airline's specialty meals—vegetarian, kosher, reduced calorie, no salt—were normally much better than the standard fare. Her mouth agreed.

An hour later, Taylor stepped out of the terminal into Anchorage's early spring effluvium. A light breeze propelled the unique scent of *break-up* past her nostrils, prompting her to cringe. Any longtime resident of Alaska recognized that odor: when the snow melted in April, everything buried for the winter became exposed and began to smell.

That made for an odd mixture of fumes, a sure sign that spring had sprung. The dog kennels were airing out; a winter's accumulation of roadside trash began to decay, even the past fall's rotted grass cuttings added to the unmistakable odor.

The feel of spring in the air combined with the warming temperatures to make Taylor decide to walk back to the LifeLine office. She knew it could be chancy—with no sidewalks on Old International Airport Road—but she set out after slinging her duffel over her shoulder.

Fifteen minutes later, after dodging puddles of melted snow and getting doused by the cars driving through them, she pushed the door open at LifeLine.

"Shit," she complained, staring at her pants legs. She fingered the mud that had been spattered on them by the passing cars. "That's the last time I try *that*. I should get hazard pay."

Nathan Mueller glanced up from his desk upon her entrance. "So, you're back." He squinted at her soiled appearance. "A little worse for wear, but still back." He looked up again. "You're dirtier, but do you feel any smarter?"

"Hey, my head is just swelling with knowledge, Nate. Either that, or I have sinus congestion." She unzipped her brown, leather flight jacket and hung it on the rack. "I was looking for Steve. Is he around the office? He left Seattle before I did, and I didn't get a chance to talk to him."

"Yeah, Taylor, Steve's in the hangar doing the revisions for the Jepps in the Lear." Nate lifted a small, brown binder of Jeppesen aeronautical charts from the desk and offered it to her. With a sly grin, he said, "And you get to do the revisions for the King Air. That's what you get for walking in the door at the wrong time."

She shrugged her shoulders. "Oh, I don't mind doing revisions, Nate. That's part of my job, right?" *And it will give me a reason to be in the hangar talking to Steve,* she thought. She needed a progress report. Dropping her duffel in the corner, she turned toward the hangar. "I'll go get busy."

The airstair door on the Learjet was hanging open when she entered the hangar, so she walked across the cement floor toward it. Once she climbed the steps she peeked around the corner into the cockpit. Steve sat in the captain's seat with a pile of approach plates stacked on his right knee; on his left knee he supported a duplicate of the binder she held.

"You cut out early on me, Steve," she complained from the cockpit entrance. "I never got a chance to find out if you got any of the info we wanted. I hope things worked."

Startled by her voice, he swiveled around abruptly and grabbed at the stack of approach plates sliding off his knee. "Taylor, I didn't hear you walk in. Gave me a start." He bent over to collect the crumpled papers as he balanced the binder on his other knee. "Sorry I took off without any word, but I had to catch—"

She broke into his apology in midsentence, full of questions. "Yeah, yeah, yeah. I know. But tell me what happened with Sosa. You must've gotten what you were looking for, huh?

How'd you work it? Did you get him to say something incriminating, do something illegal?"

Her head spun with thoughts of how they could present their findings without implicating themselves in somewhat unethical behavior. If they were police officers, their sleuthing would have been called entrapment. "That was pretty easy, figuring this out. Good thing we decided to check into it."

Steve interrupted her chatter. "Taylor, Taylor, wait a second. You didn't let me finish." He gestured for her to sit in the copilot's seat, and she climbed into it expectantly.

"I didn't get anything," he confessed. "I tried before Nate called me back, but it just didn't work out." He sighed disappointedly. "I thought I had gotten somewhere—I mean, Sosa even reached for my records kinda slyly, like he was going to change them—but then he seemed to backtrack. I guess he must've gotten spooked, because he set the paperwork down. He said,"—Steve changed into a nasally tone, imitating the Aviation Safety man—" 'I can't falsify your records. That'd be illegal and I could lose my license. And I certainly wouldn't want to lose this job, or screw up the school's good reputation.' " He smacked the pile of pages on his knee. Two fluttered down to the floor, and he reached for them. "Damn! I was this close, Taylor! He almost slipped up."

"Didn't you tell him that you knew he'd pencil-whipped somebody's records before? You could've acted like it was no big deal, make him trust you." She would've tried nearly anything in order to prove the suspicions they held about the reason for Carter's death.

"Of course I told him that. Not directly, though. I didn't want him to figure out what I was doing. But I alluded to it. I tried everything, okay?" He glared at her. She figured he felt as if she was accusing him, so she backed off.

"Okay, I'm sure you did everything, Steve. You gave it your best shot. I wasn't getting on your case." She squirmed out of her seat and wriggled through the narrow cockpit door. Once in the slightly larger cabin, she swung around and crouched on her heels as she looked back into the cockpit. "I guess we're back to square one on this, aren't we?" she sniffed, sulking.

He nodded. "Uh-huh. We better look at other possibilities. Maybe it *was* a failed robbery, Taylor. The cops may have pegged it right. After all, they're the ones with the experience in solving crimes." Then he shook his head and reached to tidy

the stack of paper in his lap. "We might have jumped to conclusions, wanting to figure out how Carter got killed. I suppose
we didn't want to believe that this was a random act of violence
because then we have to believe it could happen to us."

"Hey, that's the way the human brain works, Steve. We try
to invent sane reasons for insane events because the insanity
scares us. Don't worry about being human. Anyway, it may be
for the better." She rubbed his shoulder and stood. "It *was* kind
of harebrained, thinking some pilot would kill a coworker because he was scared about losing his job. I mean, come on."
She felt kind of foolish for even thinking there was any reason
behind the senseless death. "Well, I have to go do the revisions
on the King Air's Jepps. Nate snagged me for that when I
walked in the door. But hang around, maybe we can go get a
smoothie or something later."

"Yeah, a snack sounds good right now. I'll hang around, talk
to Nate or something until you finish."

"All done with the Jepps, Nate. Anything else?" Taylor closed
the hangar door soundlessly behind herself.

Steve perched on the edge of the desk across from Nate, who
was leaning back in his chair, his arms crossed behind his head.
"Nah, that's it," the office manager said. "Go ahead and take
off."

Grabbing her jacket and beckoning for Steve to follow, she
slid her arms through the sleeves. The front door swung open,
and she looked up, halting midway. A burly man of average
height stepped in, his own well-worn flight jacket draped over
his shoulders. He wore a gray baseball cap bearing the logo for
LifeLine; a few strands of closely cropped brown hair poked
out from beneath its brim. His broad smile swept from Steve
to Taylor, where it stopped briefly, then continued toward Nate.
"Hi, Nate. Hi, Steve," he beamed.

"Hi there, Robert," Steve greeted him.

"How've you been?" Nate asked. "I haven't seen you for a
while." Pushing forward from his relaxed position against the
chair back, he looked at Taylor and gestured at the other man.
"Taylor, this is Robert Berndt, one of our Lear captains. Well
actually, he's an ex . . ." His voice trailed off, then he changed
conversational tracks. "Robert, this is Taylor Morgan, a King
Air captain."

After making the introduction, Nate peered around Robert to

view the parking lot. His eyebrows lifted in surprise. "I don't see Julie out there, Robert. How'd you get to the office? Did you get your driver's license back?"

"No, I haven't gotten my license back. I took the bus." Robert's gravelly voice sounded hesitant to Taylor, and somewhat slurred. She started when she heard it—she had heard similar speech patterns coming from retarded adults, and the same intonation coming from a former pilot perplexed her.

The grin on Robert's face widened. "I read in the paper that you lost a Lear captain. You'll be looking for another one, right? I'm all ready ready to go back to work, so sign me up. I've had enough of this prolonged vacation."

Nate's expression of discomfort resembled that of a person biting into a *really* sour dill pickle. He picked up a pencil and began drumming the eraser on the desk. *Tat-tat-tat.* "Where'd you read that, Robert? We don't have any help wanted ads running for pilots."

"I read about Masterson getting shot. It was in the Metro section of the *Daily News*. The police blotter part. I knew you'd have to get a new captain with him gone, and that's why I came over. I can step right into his boots, I don't even need any training." Robert headed for the door to the locker room. "I'll just get my Nomex coveralls, take them home, and give them a good washing so they're clean. I don't want to look grungy, you know, when I start flying again. Go ahead and put me on the schedule starting tomorrow."

Nate glanced at Steve in puzzlement, then stared at Robert. "What are you talking about?" he stammered. "We've gone over this before, Robert. You can't fly anymore. I know you remember your injury, what it did to you. There's no way I can put you back into the Lear."

The mellow cast to Robert's face seemed to melt away. Angrily he sputtered, "There's nothing wrong with me, Nate, I keep telling you that! Why don't you believe me? Yeah, I was hurt in the accident, but I'm fine now. I'm all mended. The doctors are just wrong if they're telling you anything else!" He stomped his foot on the floor like he was a two-year-old throwing a temper tantrum. With a swipe he knocked a row of books off Nate's desk. Steve recoiled from the impact when they hit his leg.

Taylor gaped at Robert's behavior and glanced at Steve, who vigorously rubbed his injury. She wanted to run over to him, make sure he was okay and ask him what Robert was doing. However, she didn't dare move or voice her question. She didn't know what was happening.

Reaching out toward the angry man, Nate attempted to comfort him. "Robert, listen, calm down! You know that you can't fly the Lear. It wouldn't be safe for you or for anyone else. All you're doing is getting yourself worked up, and that can't be good. You're going to hurt yourself!"

"But I *know* you need another captain, and I'm all ready to take over! Just give me a chance! You won't be sorry. I'm fine!" The tone of Robert's voice rose as he screeched, and his face flushed beet red. His fists clasped and unclasped, seemingly without any conscious command.

When Nate sadly shook his head, Robert glared at him as though he wanted to kill him. The younger man cringed as if he wanted to disappear when he saw the ex-pilot's violent expression.

"Don't worry about us needing a new captain, Robert," Nate placated him. "That'll be taken care of. I've got a bunch of resumes to choose from."

Robert's gaze narrowed as he ran his eyes over Steve, then he scowled at Nate. "But you don't know anything about those guys! They're probably not good enough for the left seat! Not as good as I'd be!" When he received no encouragement, he snarled, "Damn you, you can't do this to me!" With a guttural croak, he whirled and raced for the door. He jerked it open roughly, then slammed it on his way out. The door shook under the force.

The picture of Robert clumsily running across the parking lot left Steve, Nate, and Taylor speechless for a few moments.

"What the hell was that?" Taylor trained her eyes on Robert's disappearing form. "I can't believe it. Does he think he can get his old job back, especially after pulling a stunt like that? He was all set to get his stuff ready for work tomorrow."

A sigh from Nate filled the room. "He's done this a couple times before, coming in wanting to get rehired. No matter how many times I refuse, he keeps trying. He's not thinking logically, and he really believes he's just fine. His doctor said he might act like that as a result of his head injury. He said it was something called ano . . . , ano . . . What was that name, Steve?"

"Anosognosia." Steve stood up from his seat on the edge of

Nate's desk and crossed his arms over his chest. "The doctor evaluating Robert said that anosognosia occurs once in a while when a certain part of the brain is damaged. That was his diagnosis for Robert. With those brain cells not working, he can't recognize that he has been seriously injured. Either that or he can't understand that his injury would make any difference in his life and the things he used to do. Robert sincerely thinks his ability to fly is okay. It's obvious to us that it's not, but not him. He's pretty mad because we won't listen to him when he says he's all right." Steve glanced out the window at the parking lot with a pained expression. "I feel sorry for him."

Shuffling over to retrieve his jacket from the coatrack, he grasped at the door handle. "Well, what about that smoothie you promised me, Taylor? I could use a diversion after what just happened."

Taylor snatched up her duffel and hurried to follow Steve out the door. Robert's outburst had shaken her.

"Got your beeper on, Steve?" Nate quizzed him. "You're still on duty, you know. And you too, Taylor."

"Yeah, I know." Steve patted the small pager clipped to his belt and rolled his eyes. "I'm wired for sound, don't worry. So's Taylor. We'll see you tomorrow, or later today if we get called for a flight. Later!"

Slurping noisily, Taylor finished her raspberry smoothie and grabbed a napkin from the holder to wipe her mouth. Not too many customers filled the Tastee-Freez, so she stretched her legs out on the bench where she sat. She glanced at two teenage girls at a nearby booth who chattered and giggled nonstop as they gobbled their hamburgers.

The scene made her remember her high school days, but she didn't recall ever going to the Tastee-Freez for burgers and a gabfest about boys. And she was sure they were giggling about boys.

Breaking away from her perusal of the teenagers, she turned back to resume her talk with Steve. "Yeah, I agree. I can see why you feel sorry for Robert. I don't even know the guy, but I sympathize with him. It must be awful thinking that you're all right, when the truth is so apparent to everyone else. Ugghh." She shuddered in response.

"Well, let's change the subject. I don't like to think about it, it makes me feel terrible." Undoubtedly Steve saw the same possibility Taylor did.

Steve took another swig of his milk shake. Even though Taylor had finished her drink, he had been sipping his only half-heartedly, doing more talking than swallowing. "Sitting in the Lear with those Jepps," he continued, "I did some more thinking about what happened in Seattle. You know, we went at it all wrong. We were expecting that instructor to do something that no sensible person would do."

"What do you mean? I don't follow you."

"He *must've* heard about Carter's death, and he must've put two and two together. First, he falsifies pilot records. Next, he gets a call from the holder of those records saying that the chief pilot is looking at them, and he's nervous. A day or so later, the chief pilot turns up dead. Coincidence? I doubt the instructor would think so.

"If he thought a murder investigation was going to follow—with the detailed look at everything Carter had done recently—I doubt he'd falsify any more records." After one more gulp from his shake, he squinted at her. "No wonder the guy in Seattle was toeing the line. We should have been surprised if he had done anything else."

"So we picked the wrong way to get clues about Carter's death, huh?" It had become obvious that they hadn't really thought about the situation logically from the criminal's point of view. Some detectives they were. "Then what can we do to get clues? We're not doing such a hot job so far."

A strident *wheep-wheep! wheep-wheep! wheep-wheep!* sounded from the pager in Taylor's jacket pocket, interrupting her speculation. Her eyes lit up as she glanced at the little black box. The text on the small display read: Morgan/Wisdorf/Medevac To SNP.

She glanced at Steve. "Oh, boy. SNP. That's St. Paul Island," she commented as she jumped up from the table.

"Yeah." He grinned. "Pretty long flight. Have fun." He pushed his milk shake mug away and stood. Languidly, he grabbed his jacket.

"Okay, come on, come on. Don't dillydally. I gotta get to the hangar." She tugged urgently on his sleeve, attempting to hurry him.

"God, do you get this worked up every flight? Calm down.

Getting to the hangar thirty seconds faster won't make much difference."

"Hey, humor me. You know how I am. You've seen this before." The beep of her pager always meant a call to duty, and set her heart to racing. She loved her job—being an integral part of an injured or sick person's rescue was a wonderful feeling.

"Well, yeah, I have seen you act like this before, Taylor. But every time it surprises the hell out of me. You're going to sprain something one of these days, running out the door somewhere." Steve chuckled at her anxiety and strolled on behind her as she dashed to her car.

SEVEN

Five minutes later, Taylor's Suzuki squealed off Old International and she leaped from the driver's seat. Steve sat in the passenger's side, lazily unbuckling his seat belt and ignoring her hurry. As she'd said, he'd seen her go into *medevac mode* before.

She glanced at him taking his own sweet time and shook her head. The adrenaline rush that always accompanied a duty call could not be ignored, so she turned away from the car. She wasn't going to wait for him to follow her—especially if he wasn't going to match her urgency. "Hey, I'll call you later," she yelled over her shoulder as she dashed across the parking lot.

She burst through the LifeLine door doing about eighty. "Got the page, Nate. On my way." Then she skidded to a halt and squinted at the office manager. "Wisdorf's name was on the dispatch along with mine. What's he coming along for? He's a captain, too. We got a sick copilot, nobody else around to fill in?" Normally, flights didn't call for two captains, and John Wisdorf had seen St. Paul Island before. He wouldn't just be sightseeing.

"Nah," Nate said. "John's got a route check coming up, I figured I'd send him on this flight for it. That okay with you? You're the one that has to sign him off."

She shrugged. "Fine with me. Just give me some check forms."

Nate grabbed the paperwork from his desktop and passed it over to her. She glanced at the sheets, nodded, and darted to the locker room. "Later!" she called. "Long flight, gotta get going!"

As one of her duties as LifeLine's check pilot, Taylor had to give annual route checks to the King Air captains. Not only did the senior pilots need to be proficient in the type of aircraft they flew, they also had to be proficient in the kind of flying they did in them. So she observed them on an ordinary flight to see if they conducted it properly. Like the one to St. Paul.

Approximately three and a half hours after leaving Anchorage— after a quick refueling stop in Bethel—the burgundy-and-silver King Air approached St. Paul Island. Taylor Morgan sat relaxed as she observed John Wisdorf from the copilot's seat; the two flight nurses in the cabin gazed periodically out the windows at the white-capped water below. The nine-mile-long speck of land to which the aircraft flew lay in the middle of the frigid Bering Sea, more than three hundred and fifty miles away from the nearest landfall. Another small island, St. George, protruded from the blue-gray ocean about fifty miles to the southeast.

Those two fragments of rock made up the Pribilof Islands. As the only solid surfaces found in thousands of square miles of water, the islands were de facto sanctuaries for sea mammals and seabirds, and were well known for their unique flora and fauna. If Taylor had been on the ground, instead of thousands of feet in the air, she could have heard the grunts and squawks of the numerous animals that called the Pribilofs home. The angular bluffs and cliffs of St. George housed nests used by red-legged kittiwakes and colorful puffins; the low sandy beaches of St. Paul were more suited to the sea lions and walruses that crowded its shoreline.

As John Wisdorf started the King Air's descent to St. Paul Island, Taylor glanced over her shoulder to check on her passengers. Rachel Warford held a paperback novel in front of her, and Stephanie Dufour sifted through the medical supplies arranged in containers in the plane's cabin. "You guys okay?" she asked from the cockpit.

Both of the nurses looked up and nodded. "We'll get our belts on when we get closer," Stephanie said. "Holler when we're five out."

With a mock salute, Taylor replied, "Will do. Should be a

couple more minutes." As she reached down to tighten her seat belt and shoulder harness, she pondered what waited for them upon reaching St. Paul, then tossed a question over her shoulder. "Hey, Stephanie, what happened to this guy we're picking up? How serious are his injuries? Is he losing blood? I hope he's not going to be in trouble if we get delayed by the weather and get caught somewhere."

"Not likely, Taylor, but the health aide on St. Paul *was* concerned enough to call for a medevac. When they dispatched us they said the guy had a compound fracture of the femur. That is kinda bad, but none of the major arteries were severed by the smashed bone, so he'll be okay."

A shiver always crossed Taylor's spine when she heard about the injury that necessitated the medevac she was on, but her heartbeat accelerated as well when Stephanie reported on the St. Paul situation. She couldn't even conceive of how helpless she would feel if she got badly hurt so far away from a hospital.

What would it be like, lying there on an island in the middle of the ocean, waiting for someone to rescue you? Relying on someone *else's* skills to deliver you to lifesaving medical help? She shuddered inwardly, grateful that she played the *rescuer* role in the medevac rather than that of the *rescuee*.

"How on earth did that compound fracture happen, Stephanie? Isn't that sort of an odd injury for out here? He must've wrecked his three-wheeler or something."

A wrapped roll of sterile gauze crinkled as Stephanie rearranged the box holding it. "No, that wasn't it. I heard this guy was part of a fishing party. They'd just come home for the day with their catch and were lugging this heavy wooden boat out of the water. One of the men lost his grip on the boat, and it fell. Crushed some guy's leg. I guess the bone splintered and parts of it were poking right up through his pants leg. The health aide stopped the bleeding, but there's no way anybody could handle a compound fracture out there on St. Paul."

"Well, I'm glad the weather was good enough to get out to pick the guy up." Taylor took note of the picture of St. Paul growing in the King Air's windshield and estimated the plane was about five miles away from landing. "Seat belt time, ladies. We'll be heading down in a second."

A settlement of about seven hundred people sat on a spit on the south shore of the island. The residents' crackerbox houses sat in rows, some still with lights on, even at the late hour. A seven-hundred-foot-high hill, the highest point on St. Paul, jutted up from the west shore.

When it came into view, the sight of the five-thousand-foot runway impressed Taylor, as it always did: the airstrip had nearly as many lights bordering it as the runways at Anchorage International. White sequenced flashing approach lights combined with red-and-green Visual Approach Slope Indicator lights in a brilliant display set off by the dusky sky. She knew that the high-tech array of lights were required because of the nasty weather that held the island in its grip more often than not. Illumination was needed to guide aircraft in from the midst of the soup.

Once a pilot had crossed 350 miles of open water, he wanted to be sure he'd be able to land. The lights just made the odds a bit better for the pilots fighting the weather. Taylor gulped at the thought of the flights she'd made to St. Paul when she'd battled clouds and poor visibility all across the vast stretch of water. The nearly clear skies that had accompanied her flight that day had relieved her.

"Okay, Taylor, let me strut my stuff here," boomed a baritone from the left-hand pilot's seat, breaking into her private thoughts. "There's no way you can flunk me on my route check when you see this *perfect* touchdown. The way only a *guy* can do it."

She grinned. She liked John Wisdorf, with his comical antics. They had traded good-natured jabs at each other ever since they had first met, both of them calling the other a sexist pig—and other names—for different reasons and at different times.

"Okay, John. I always thought you were a hammer-hand with lug nuts for brains. Prove me wrong." When he leered at her, his expression reminded her of the day of their introduction. While shaking his hand in greeting, she had to mimic a coughing fit to muzzle the burst of laughter rising in her throat. She couldn't help herself. John Wisdorf was a dead ringer for Marty Feldman, the comedian whose bulging eyes had brought him fame.

"Well, Taylor, here we go," he said as he reached for the aircraft's control yoke and the power levers. "Looks kinda bumpy down there, but I'll see what I can do. If I do less than perfect, I plan on blaming the wind."

A quick pass over the wind sock indicated landing to the north, so he set up for that. After reducing the power to the twin Pratt & Whitney PT6–50 turbine engines, he spoke to Taylor, all business now. "Autofeather's armed, flaps forty." She followed his directions without question and pushed the proper levers into position.

"Gear down and flaps to one hundred," he added after he noted the decrease in the plane's airspeed. A quiet hum was heard when she lowered the wheel-shaped lever that extended the landing gear and flipped a switch to lower the flaps. As she withdrew her hand upon completing the task, he nodded. "I want to stay out of the bumps."

A subtle nod from Taylor acknowledged his choice. "Fine selection. You need all the help you can get. And don't let the *pressure* to be perfect bother you." She knew her jibes likely wouldn't distract him, but for the sake of their amiable jousting she had to try.

The King Air glided down the final leg of the approach, though occasional gusts knocked it from its smooth path. Fifty feet, thirty feet . . .

The runway loomed ahead, the ground rose to meet the plane, then . . .

A *crackle!* and a *ping!* sounded in the cockpit as the aircraft settled down onto the rutted gravel runway and scattered the small dislodged stones. The airplane thumped and rumbled as it ran over the deep craters worn into the runway, and even though he had set up his landing perfectly, the pocked surface made the touchdown feel awful.

She lifted her eyebrows and grinned at John. "Perfect, huh?" she cackled. Picking up the route check form, she pretended to mark on the Unsatisfactory column for one of the testing criteria. "Maybe I'll give you another try, when we get back to Anchorage. See if you can land on asphalt. That's not too hard, even for a *guy*."

Replacing the check form in the map pocket next to her, she unfastened her seat belt. That done, she glanced out the windshield and scanned the area. "Where's the health aide and the patient, anyway? Shouldn't they be here by now?"

A cloud of dust on the road from the settlement three miles away answered her question. She saw a battered station wagon heading in their direction, and her heart beat faster. Jumping from her seat, she dashed to the rear of the plane, leaving John to deal with shutting down the aircraft systems. Behind the last of the passenger seats, she saw the nurses struggling with the heavy airstair door. She knew they were in a hurry to get the injured man on board.

That was her cue; no time for dawdling. She sucked in her breath and put her own weight into opening the door.

Once the station wagon reached the loading area, the nurses trotted down the airstair to meet it. They accompanied the village's health aide and several others in easing a stretcher from the vehicle: a quietly whimpering teenage Alaskan Native boy lay on its canvas sling.

Taylor's stomach convulsed when she caught a glimpse of a bloody bandage wrapped around the leg of the teenager. The gauze formed a cylinder of odd proportions, and without being told she knew the protruding bone splinters accounted for the distortion. That picture prompted a sense of urgency to erupt inside her, and she ran back to join John in readying the King Air for the stretcher.

Quickly, they unlatched and raised a wide, six-foot by six-foot hatch, which opened a large aperture in the King Air's fuselage. Rachel Warford and a villager climbed into the airplane's cabin and guided the hoisted stretcher through the opening, setting the stretcher on a narrow, rectangular berth fastened to the cabin wall. Stephanie clambered up the airstair and made her way to the head of the berth. The two flight nurses busied themselves in buckling the stretcher down and rigging IV tubing.

As Stephanie and Rachel attended to the injured youth, Taylor scrambled back into the plane and hastily latched the door behind her. As soon as she crawled back into the copilot's seat, John had the King Air ready to go. He seemed as antsy as she was.

In seconds, the aircraft's twin engines were singing their throaty song and the plane taxied away from the small crowd left standing under the fading light. With a roar, the King Air accelerated down the runway and leaped into the air.

An hour and a half later, when the King Air approached landfall at the western coast of Alaska, a large white sphere gleaming dully under the dusky sky attracted Taylor's attention. The huge manmade globe was anchored on the top of a craggy peak, the highest of several that were part of a cape jutting into Kuskokwim Bay. Hidden from view by the angular granite faces were a steep gravel runway and a small group of buildings.

Taylor smiled when she spied the white radar dome: it was a familiar sight from her days as a pilot working for Tundra Air Charters. She remembered flights taken to the compound on Cape Newenham, where the white globe served as part of the Air Force's Defense Early Warning system. The DEW site sounded the alarm if it detected an invasion force approaching the United States from anywhere on the Pacific Ocean. She had taken several flights down to the cape from Bethel, usually picking up or dropping off personnel due to transfer in or out of the station.

Looking past the DEW site on Cape Newenham, Taylor saw that the plane's current position placed it only twenty miles west of the leading edge of a weather front. In a matter of minutes, she knew the King Air would disappear in the wispy gray clouds blanketing the terrain ahead. They would conduct the remainder of the flight on instruments only; no ground references would exist once the clouds swallowed them.

That didn't alarm her. Both she and John were well qualified for piloting aircraft in zero-visibility weather, and she even liked flying through the soup at night.

Instrument flight seemed so peaceful, so soothing, slipping through skies the color of charcoal and the consistency of pudding. The air was usually smooth in the clouds, and she rarely had to worry about turbulence when skating through a stratus layer. The soft amber-and-white glow of the annunciator lights on the aircraft's panel relaxed her, and the lack of distracting scenery allowed her to concentrate on the job at hand.

She swung around in her seat and surveyed the dimly lit cabin. "Everything okay back there?" she asked, unconsciously grimacing when her gaze fell on the blood-spotted bandages wrapping the stretcher occupant's leg.

Stephanie glanced up to check the flow of the IV line running down to her patient's arm. "Everything's in control. Where are we, anyway? It's too dark to see anything."

"We're coming up on the top of the Alaska Peninsula. Coupla hours to go." Taylor turned back to the instrument panel and did a quick scan of the gauges. With all of their readings correct, she folded her arms behind her head and peered out her window into the dark clouds. The King Air was on autopilot, following the proper course, and she had nothing else to do. The form used for a route check had been filled out—in triplicate—and she didn't even need to monitor John's handling of the aircraft. That gave her a chance to let the quiet of the cockpit calm her—she still felt tense from the dash out of St. Paul—and she wanted to let her mind wander.

Ever since she and John had taken off from Anchorage International on the medevac, she had been impressed—as she always was—by how the whole progress had energized her. The power of the aircraft excited her; the urgency of the rescue flight stirred her emotions to an intense level. She had experienced similar sensations when she had flown medevacs in Bethel, but they hadn't been nearly as keen as when she was in the King Air. Must have been something about having a multimillion dollar machine willing to do her command, she decided.

She could imagine how heady it was for someone like Steve: not only was he performing medevac flights, playing a part in saving an injured person's life; he was doing those medevacs in an aircraft like the Learjet.

That jet was very powerful—almost like a dangerous predator, in the way it required such vigilance from its pilots. It brooked no mistakes; an error made during a flight could be fatal. Those considered skillful enough to fly the Lear were in the top echelon of aviators, and Lear pilots knew that everyone recognized that.

What an ego boost that must be, flying the Lear! Captaining the King Air on a medevac was a thrill, and she was sure commanding the *Learjet* for the same duty was ten times as good. She remembered the intoxicating adrenaline surge that had pulsed on and off through her system that night. What a rush . . .

She wondered what other people did for a high as potent as that. Drugs? Kinky, dangerous sex? Bank robbery?

Tickled by that thought, she leaned back in her seat and crossed her arms behind her head. Then something odd clicked into place in her head. What about maintaining a powerful high? Would anybody *kill* to preserve a rush?

Several days ago she would have said no. Several days ago, when Steve had suggested that a Lear pilot might have killed Carter to silence him, to save his job, she had hesitated in agreeing.

What kind of motive for murder was that? It seemed a petty justification for such a heinous crime. Why would anybody chance a murder conviction because they feared the loss of their job? It would ruin their lives.

Then she recalled newspaper stories she'd read, stories telling of deadly overdoses and arrests for drug possession. She shook her head, her gaze narrowing as she stared at the blackness outside. How much more evidence did she need to prove that people would destroy themselves during the search for the next high?

And they would kill for it, too.

From the crack user that intentionally kills during a holdup, to the inebriate that unintentionally kills when he climbs into his car for the drive home, murders were committed every night across America in the name of addiction.

And it would be even easier to kill when your drug of choice was legal. If you obtained your high straight from doing your job.

As a Lear pilot.

Steve's hunch that a coworker was implicated in Carter's murder suddenly took on a frightening likelihood. Her head buzzed as she digested the possibility of that thought being correct.

The hum of the PT6 engines did little to steady the thumping of her heart. She silently begged for the calm, dark skies to reassure her, to tell her she couldn't be right.

EIGHT

Rat-a-tat-ta-tatatatatataTaTaTATA . . . Bump-bump!
Bump-bump! Rat-ta-ta-ta-bump-bump! The raucous
pounding of bongos burst from the clock radio at Taylor's bed-
side, and her eyelids flew open. She blinked rapidly as the beats
reached a crescendo and Sergio Mendes hammered through the
beginning of his "Fanfarra." Still half asleep, several seconds
passed before she oriented herself well enough to smack the
clock's TAPE OFF button. Silence hung over the loft the instant
she stifled the insistent rhythm.

Glaring at the clock's red LED digits—which read 6:00
A.M.—she dropped back onto her rumpled pillow. She closed
her eyes and blindly fumbled for the pager on her nightstand.
Once her fingers connected with it, she flipped its ON switch
and buried herself back under the covers.

"New tape . . . Gotta get a new tape . . ." she mumbled in-
coherently and went back to sleep.

Four hours later, a bleary-eyed Taylor swung her bare feet out
of bed and onto the beige carpet of her loft. She had splurged
recently to make the cabin more comfortable by purchasing a
Berber rug for her sleeping quarters. Rubbing her toes in its
thick pile, she decided it had been worth it. Even when she
remembered puncturing her thumb on the carpet strips when
installing it.

She scuffled across the loft—the cool air hardening her

nipples underneath her XXL T-shirt—and climbed down the ladder toward her warm bathroom. It wasn't *really* any warmer in there, but the peachy paint on the walls made it appear so, and her subconscious was willing to let an optical illusion fool her that morning.

As she peered at her face in the medicine cabinet mirror, she smiled wistfully. At least the subtle rose tint reflected back on her face camouflaged her pallor. After her late-night return from St. Paul, she figured she'd look as if she spent the night in an alley. Losing sleep always did terrible things to her complexion. She was no night owl.

After running a comb through her hair, she pursed her lips and slapped her cheeks to add a little color to them. Not entirely satisfied with the result but too sleepy to do anything else about it, she padded to the kitchen across from the bathroom.

It took her about a minute to prepare her breakfast—oat bran with brown sugar and frozen raspberries mixed in—and deposit it in the microwave to cook. The sounds emanating from her belly reminded her that she hadn't eaten since well before leaving on the medevac late yesterday afternoon, and she was ready for some relief. While the machine hummed energetically, she poured a large glass of orange juice. When the oven dinged, she withdrew the cereal bowl, stirred it, and dumped some Cheerios on top of the oat bran to add a little texture.

As she carried her breakfast to the table she mused about what she would do that day. She was on call, so she may as well go to the hangar. Maybe Steve would be there. She wanted to discuss some things with him.

Like what had disturbed her the previous night. Then, it had taken her nearly an hour to unbend after the excitement of the medevac, and during that time she continued to ponder Carter Masterson's murder. The way the night had affected *her* made her positive that a real excitement junkie could bring himself to kill to prevent losing that feeling. If he thought someone stood between him and his job, he'd decide to silence that person. Permanently.

Steve's reasoning was probably right, she concluded. Carter's murderer could've been the Lear pilot he had suspected—Ed Guralnik.

If Guralnik was that kind of person—and she thought he was, based on knowing him—he could be dangerous. If he conspired to have Carter killed, or actually did it himself, they had to prove it.

Scooping up a spoonful of hot cereal, she absentmindedly arranged its sprinkling of Cheerios into a design and stuffed the artwork in her mouth. She looked out her living room window and contemplated the indifferent weather outside as she chewed.

The Suzuki Sidekick wheezed and coughed well after Taylor turned off the ignition, so she popped the clutch to still it. The vehicle jerked forward a few feet before the engine died. She shrugged and looked around the half-full parking lot sheepishly. The car needed a tune-up, but she was such a cheapskate she didn't want to pay for one. Maybe she could talk Colin Stuart, the LifeLine mechanic, into helping her do it herself.

The picture of Nate leafing through April's *Professional Pilot* greeted her when she reached the office and shoved the door open. Steve was there, too, bent over the computer in the corner with a stack of flight logs near his elbow. Both men looked up upon her entrance.

"What's this, banker's hours?" Nate snickered.

Taylor waved at Steve and turned to squint at Nate. "Hey, I don't have to be in the office the whole time I'm on call, so I slept in. I didn't get home until after *one o'clock* this morning." She unzipped her flight jacket and hung it on the coatrack. "Anyway, I turned my beeper up right at six this morning, so you could've gotten me if a medevac had come up. This isn't fair, you know, being on daytime call and getting a medevac that keeps you out until past midnight. You should've given the call to the nighttime crew. Made them come in early, instead of keeping me out late."

"Yadda, yadda, yadda," Nate teased. "You've gone through this before, Taylor. You know there's no way you can schedule medevacs. They're rarely convenient." Nate tossed his magazine to the side of the desk and leaned back in his chair with a grin.

Taylor rolled her eyes for Nate's benefit and headed for the hangar door. Halfway there she stopped at the computer in the corner. "Morning, Steve," she greeted him. "Come with me to the hangar, okay?"

Nate snickered immediately. "Oh, come on, Taylor. You guys were only apart for one night. Do you have to go feel each other up as soon as you get back together?"

"Yeah, Nate. And if *you* had a girlfriend you'd know how that goes," she retorted jokingly. She hoped that was all he thought they were doing. She didn't want him involved in their murder investigation.

Steve lifted his eyebrows, stood up, and cracked his knuckles. He appeared to know what Taylor wanted. Turning toward Nate, he nodded in her direction. "I'll be in the hangar for a few minutes, but I'll get those flight hours plugged into the database right afterward. Okay?" He swung around to follow her through the door.

Just as the two pilots were disappearing into the hangar, the front office door swooshed open. A tall figure stepped in. Taylor swung around and glanced over her shoulder to see who it was. Her heart seized when she recognized the man: Ed Guralnik. The LifeLine hat he wore shaded his eyes, giving him an even more sinister look. A day's worth of stubble on his chin didn't help, either.

She wondered where he'd learned his personal appearance and grooming techniques—Hannibal Lechter?

Not wanting to be party to a conversation that included him, she turned away without a greeting. It was bad enough thinking about him; she didn't want to *talk* to him, too. Just as she was reaching for the doorknob, she halted. An idea had just come to her. She changed her mind about talking to him, and spun around to speak. "Hey, Ed! Good timing. Steve and I were just heading for lunch. Want to join us?"

Steve gaped at her. She knew what he was thinking. Had she forgotten that Ed was the main suspect in Carter's death? Why would she want to have lunch with a murderer?

Trying to silence Steve with a pointed look, she smiled at Ed. "We were going over to the watering hole. Meet us over there, huh?"

Ed's eyebrows rose. "You look like you're heading the other direction," he muttered, nodding at the hangar door Steve was holding open.

"Nah. I just have to get my flight case out of the King Air before we leave." She waved nonchalantly in the direction of the aircraft and stepped inside the hangar. "We'll see you in a minute." She motioned for Steve to follow.

"What are you doing?" he squawked as soon as the door closed behind them. "I don't want to have anything to do with

Ed until we know he's not part of Carter's murder."

"Hey, I thought we could find out some things if we got him talking. He doesn't know we suspect him, and he might say something without realizing it would hurt him. It's worth a try, isn't it?"

Scratching an eyebrow, Steve hesitated, then nodded. "Okay. But let me do the talking. If he decides to go after one of us because of what we know, I'd prefer it was me."

She frowned at him. She had no intention of sitting on the bench for this play. If push came to shove, even literally, she wanted a piece of it. However, she knew better than saying so right then. "All right. Let's head for the Clarion. Let's take separate cars, though. That way, if one of us gets beeped, the other one can stay with him."

Ten minutes later, that's exactly what happened. As Taylor's Suzuki and Steve's Camaro sat nose-to-tail at the intersection of International and Spenard, waiting for the light, she heard him honk. Glancing at her rearview mirror, she saw him lift his pager and gesture to his left toward LifeLine.

When the light turned green, she continued down Spenard while he made a U-turn toward Old International. "Well, now it's just me," she murmured to herself as she saw him disappear. She didn't like the idea of being alone with a potential murderer, but actually there would be plenty of other people in the room. She'd be safe.

Still pondering how to get something incriminating out of him without arousing his suspicion, she swung into the parking lot at the hotel near Lake Spenard. Ed Guralnik was already there, standing by the side entrance to the bar-restaurant with his hands stuffed in the pockets of his Levi's. He looked uncomfortable.

Parking her vehicle next to his truck—and noting a rifle perched in the gun rack—she clambered from it. "Ready for lunch, Ed? I'm starving," she lied. She'd eaten only two hours ago, but he didn't need to know that. If he thought the meal was a setup, there was no telling what he'd do.

Without acknowledging her comment, he scanned the lot. "Where's Steve? I thought he was coming." His eyes showed mistrust. Was he on to her? she worried. Or had he only accepted the invitation because the other Lear pilot was coming? Would he back out because of that?

She didn't want him to duck and run, now that she'd hardened her nerve. This could be the best chance she'd ever get to talk to him. "Oh, he got beeped right as we were leaving. But we can still get something to eat. Come on," she pleaded. "I hate eating alone." She smiled sweetly at him, though her guts were telling her something entirely different. She wanted to smack him, sure that he was the one that was responsible for Carter Masterson's death. Directly or indirectly. "Let's go get a table," she offered and headed for the door.

He followed in silence.

Seated in a booth near the windows that overlooked the lake, he stared at her intently. No words passed between them for several minutes. She didn't like his expression—it made her *extremely* nervous. Finally he spoke. "Why'd you invite me for lunch? I know you don't like me. For that matter, I don't like you, either."

She gulped. Talk about cutting to the chase. She'd better have a good line.

"Well, you're right. I don't like you." There was no way she could bluff her way into him thinking she enjoyed his company, so she stuck to the truth. A *modified* version of the truth. "Actually, I wanted to talk to you."

His eyes narrowed and she felt her heartbeat skyrocket. It's now or never, she thought. "I gave a route check the other day. When I was putting the paperwork away, I noticed something. Some discrepancies in your records."

Ed froze. He never bothered to deny what she'd said—he looked as though he was well aware of what the *discrepancies* were. He had only one question for her. "Who else knows?" he asked, tight-lipped.

Well, who else *did* know? she wondered. Should she tell him Steve was in on it also, or make him think it was only her? Maybe if he only had to deal with one person, an unthreatening woman, he might be less guarded, more likely to say something he'd regret. "Oh, it's just me," she cooed. Then she played her trump card. "I thought maybe my silence would be worth something to you. Something in the five figure range, maybe?"

She hoped bluffing about taking a bribe would open his mouth. If he thought she was a schemer—as *he* was—he might be less reticent. He'd think her less likely to go to the authorities with anything he said if she had her hand in the cookie jar, too. She doubted he'd mention the murder, but maybe something would slip to give her a clue to his involvement.

His reply to her request for money was not what she had expected to hear, however.

"Nah, I think not," he drawled. "I think you'll just keep your mouth shut because things could get real uncomfortable for you if you don't. Get the picture?" He leaned forward and leered at her, sweeping his arms under the tablecloth at the same time.

Beneath the table she heard a *click!* and felt a stinging sensation spread across her kneecap. Something cool and wet began trickling down her shin.

The skin over her cheekbones drew back. She gaped at Guralnik, aghast. "You just cut me," she stammered, breathing hard.

He appeared startled by her reaction. "Hey, it's not deep—I didn't want you to scream." Then he looked as though he'd just remembered something. "I guess I don't have to worry about that, though. Surely you realize that screaming would result in something much more unpleasant happening farther down the road." His glare hardened.

That made her freeze. What had she just done? Carter Masterson had been the only person who knew of the record tampering, and he was dead. Now she had told Ed Guralnik that she, too, knew of it. Would she be marked for *elimination* too? A final silencing?

The look on her face must have told him everything he wanted to know, because he grinned a feral grin. "Yeah, I thought so," he snarled. "This'll be our own secret, won't it?" His retracted the knife's blade and tucked it back in his pocket.

With his words roaring in her ears, she nodded vigorously. She couldn't answer—she was speechless.

Her attempt to wring secrets from him had backfired. She had just set herself up for something, and she had no idea what that *something* would be. When a waitress headed for their table, menus in her hand, Taylor shoved her chair back and dashed from the restaurant.

That evening she sat at the small dining room table in Steve's condo, drumming her fingers. Several bags of Chinese takeout oozed delicious-smelling steam from their perch on the center of the round slab of butcher block. Glancing at her watch, she grimaced. Nate had said her boyfriend had gone to Prudhoe Bay to medevac an oil field worker back to Anchorage, and would be home by six. It was six twenty-five. He hadn't gotten home yet.

Tapping her toe, she pushed the food bags around on the table. She was anxious about telling him of the conversation with Ed Guralnik. He'd be furious with her when she told him what she'd done, but surely he could see how she'd gotten useful information from the scary encounter.

A rattle of keys signaled his arrival, and she jumped from the table to meet him. When he swung the door open she blathered, "Steve, Steve! I have to tell you something!"

He unzipped his jacket, one eyebrow raised. "No 'Hello, Steve. How was your trip?' Just 'I have to tell you something'? Jeez, Taylor. Give me a chance to get my coat off, would you?"

"Okay, okay." She reached out to tug his jacket off his shoulders and sling it into the hall closet. "There. Now you're done with that. Can I talk to you?"

He shook his head, and smiled in acquiescence. "I got no choice, do I?" When he saw how frantic she looked, he erased the grin from his face. "What? What is it? You didn't have lunch with Ed without me, did you? I figured you just brushed him off when I got beeped, ate by yourself later."

"Oh, come on. I'm not going to waste a perfectly good opportunity to talk to him just because I have nobody to baby-sit me." She planted her feet, arms akimbo, and glared at him. She didn't like *fragile woman* treatment from anybody.

Especially from Steve. He knew better.

He glared right back, though. "Hey. I thought we decided *I'd* do the talking, Taylor. You're so stubborn. You never listen to me."

"Well, you weren't there," she retorted. "Anyway, I figured he'd talk to a woman. In his world, women aren't smart or tough enough to give him any trouble." Then she cringed at what she'd said. Guralnik's opinion of women had rung true with her that afternoon. She'd tucked her tail and ran as soon as he'd threatened her. Of course, a switchblade to the kneecap was no subtle hint; but even so . . .

Trying to forget her chicken-hearted duck-for-cover move, she stood tall, attempting to look imposing for Steve's benefit. She unconsciously slid her right knee behind her left one to conceal what her impetuosity had resulted in, even though there was no way he could have detected the cut on her kneecap.

She'd had the sense to change pants before she went to his place.

"There's more, though," she added. When Steve cocked his head, uncertainty clouding his eyes, she knew he'd go ballistic when she told him the rest of the story. She'd better be careful of what she mentioned.

"Hey, I'm not sure I want to hear this," he conceded. "What else do you have?"

"He threatened me when I told him I knew about his pencil-whipping of the records. He said it'd better remain 'our own secret,' or it would get *uncomfortable* for me." She only mentioned the verbal portion of the threat, sure the actual physical threat would prompt him to forbid any further investigating.

When Steve gaped at her, she could see the fright in his expression, mixed with incredulity. She was glad she hadn't told him about the cut. "He what?" He choked on the words. "That's exactly why I wanted to do the talking, Taylor! God! What have you gotten yourself into now?"

"I haven't gotten myself into anything, Steve. He won't do anything if I don't get anyone else involved in this. And as far as he knows, I haven't."

"Did he say anything about the murder?"

"Naw. He's not *that* stupid. But I'd say that the threat is a good indication that there's more than just record-tampering going on here. Wouldn't you agree?" She hoped looking at the puzzle of Carter Masterson's murder would distract him from his anger with her.

And it did.

Nodding, he scratched his head as he thought, his mind far away. "Yeah, I'd say so. We guessed right about him; didn't we? But what do we do now?"

"I don't know. All I got was a threat, but he said *nothing* about killing anyone. We sure can't do anything with that." Her face contorted. They were closer to a solution to the crime, but had nothing to pin on anybody. That was frustrating. "You got any ideas, Steve? You want to take a run at him yourself?"

"I don't know. Looks like we're going to have to play this by ear." He walked into the living room and sat down on the sofa. "Maybe I can talk to a few of the copilots. He might have said something to one of them. Couldn't hurt, could it?"

"As long as you don't make it obvious what you're looking for. Doesn't make any sense to give anyone else an idea of what we're doing. No telling who's involved with him."

He scanned the room as he pondered the situation, then caught a whiff of the Chinese takeout. Looking at Taylor quizzically, he asked, "That dinner? Why don't we discuss this as we eat? I think better with a full stomach."

"Yeah. Me too. That's why I got the stuff."

NINE

In the early morning of the next day Taylor found herself returning from Homer, a small town at the southern tip of the Kenai Peninsula, 150 miles from Anchorage. Her cut knee had worried her when she'd set out —she didn't know how it would hold up through a day of flying—but the liberal application of Bactine to the thread-thin wound had done the job. The cut wasn't deep, and the knife's blade had been razor-sharp, so it had sliced clean. The thought of that razor-sharp blade against her throat made her shiver, though.

Next to her —riding shotgun in the right cockpit seat—sat John Wisdorf. "This is like déjà vu all over again, huh?" she cracked to him. "Except this time *you're* the copilot."

"Yeah," he grumbled. "My bad luck the sick guy I'm filling in for isn't another captain. Now I'm at a disadvantage. Not only do I have to sit in the right seat next to you, I'm not even sitting in the right seat because I'm giving you a route check or something."

"Well, that's the way it goes. You'll get your turn to be a hard-ass check pilot one of these days. And I pity the first guy you give a check to." She grinned at him, hoping that would soothe his annoyance.

At times like that when she was flexing her authority over other captains—like during a check ride, or when circumstances called for them to act as her copilot—she didn't know if she should act apologetic. She had every right to exercise

control over them at those times, but she knew occasionally—
even though they never openly begrudged her—it had to get to
them. Not only did she have less time as a LifeLine employee
than some of them, she was younger than some, as well.

Furthermore, she was a *woman*.

For a man raised in a male-dominated world, where macho
ruled, that had to sting.

Before her guilty conscience got to her, she was brought back
to the work at hand by the air traffic controller working six
miles away. "Lifeguard four-three-three-lima-lima, Anchorage
tower," a mellifluous male voice intoned. "You're cleared to
land runway six-left, wind zero-three-zero at eighteen, gusting
twenty-eight, low-level wind shear advisory in effect. Traffic is
a JAL heavy exiting runway six-right, holding short of six-left."

"Lifeguard three-lima-lima copies cleared to land on six-left,
traffic in sight." Taylor released the radio's push-to-talk button
and tightened her grip on the King Air's yoke.

The view of the Chugach Range filling the windshield jerked
up and down, side to side, as turbulent air hammered the plane.
The approach to Anchorage had corresponded with an increase
in gust intensity. When the medevac flight had left Homer half
an hour earlier, nothing but a slight chop in the air existed. But
upon reaching the top of the Kenai Peninsula they were definitely experiencing more than that.

"I guess I should have expected this turbulence, huh?" she
complained to John Wisdorf. "As soon as I saw lenticulars
above the Chugach when I left the house, I should've been
ready for a butt kicking."

"Well of course," he acknowledged, then leered at her. "Now
it's my turn to ask you if you can handle it. Let's see how a
girl does." He grinned smugly, now that she was in the same
position he'd been in during his route check the other day.

"Okay, I've got it. Prepare to be dazzled." It was rare to be
pitted against one of her peers in a game of one-upmanship,
but when it happened she just grinned and took it. Came with
the territory. She figured she deserved it, anyway. Teasing John
Wisdorf during his route check—even though he'd played
along—may have been unprofessional.

Turning back to business, she concentrated on the long asphalt runway two miles ahead. Out of the corner of her eye she
spotted froth tipping the waves washing across the gray waters
of Turnagain Arm to her right. Turnagain Arm, a narrow off-

shoot of Cook Inlet lined by jagged cliffs and mountains, worked to magnify the effects of the wind by constricting the airflow like a funnel. The whitecaps displayed the physics behind that in a way no one could mistake.

Certainly not Taylor, who fought against the grip the gusts had on her airplane.

"Whatever happened to March coming in like a lion and leaving like a lamb?" she contemplated out loud. "This is April, but it looks like we're still in the lion phase. This wind isn't too lamblike."

John just shrugged without replying.

As the King Air passed over the west shore of Cook Inlet, she peered down at Point Woronzof's bluffs and the gray mudflats bordering them. "Not much snow left down there," she mused. "Summer should be coming soon."

"Hey, quit sightseeing," John teased. "Isn't it time to call for some flaps? And gear? God, do I have to baby-sit you? I thought *I* was the copilot."

"Yeah, I guess you're right. I better get busy." She reduced power and set up for landing. "Autofeathers armed, please. Give me flaps forty, and the gear."

She couldn't believe she had let herself become distracted by the sights around her. That was a half-million dollar piece of machinery she shepherded through the sky, and the winds were gusty enough that it could get away from her if she was daydreaming.

Glancing over her shoulder, she saw Rachel Warford secure her seat belt. A nearby IV bottle swayed from side to side on its support, and Stephanie Dufour reached out to steady it. Taylor didn't envy the flight nurses a bit right then; she knew that they were feeling the effects of the turbulent wind. Not only did the wind make it difficult to perform their jobs; it had to be uncomfortable dealing with airsickness at the same time. It was much easier for the pilots to combat queasiness; when they concentrated on their duties they had no time to feel sick.

"You guys doing okay back there? We'll be down in about two minutes," Taylor reassured the nurses. Swinging forward, she sneaked a peek to her right, where John relaxed in the copilot's seat, contentedly gazing out his window at the overcast skies. "How can you sit there so calmly? Don't these gusts bother you? If I didn't have my hands full, I'd be turning green."

"You must have a more sensitive inner ear than I do," he replied. "Rough air doesn't do anything to me."

She wrinkled her forehead and bent back to her work. Under her direction the King Air battled the gusts all the way down its final approach and planted itself firmly on the runway.

Even though the landing had been hard—as required by the gusts—it had been square and properly timed. The best anyone could have done under the conditions. "That good enough for you?" she smirked once the wheels squeaked upon meeting the asphalt.

"Well . . ." John couldn't say anything else, so he clammed up.

Minutes later, the silver-and-burgundy aircraft taxied up to the LifeLine hangar where an ambulance waited.

As Rachel and Stephanie prepared their patient for exiting the airplane, Taylor gently maneuvered past them toward the rear cabin door. Her heartbeat had accelerated the minute she rose from her cockpit seat, and even as she struggled to lower the airstair against the wind she could feel the pulse throbbing in her neck.

It wasn't until the paramedics loaded the patient into the ambulance and drove off toward the hospital that her heartbeat slowed. "I don't know about this, John," she said as the other pilot trotted down the airstair to join her. "These medevacs get me so wired. Steve said I'd get used to it, but I've been doing them for years and that hasn't happened. Maybe it never will for me."

"Well, it still gets to me once in a while, and I've been flying medevacs for about six years." He set his flight bag down and unlatched its top, then bent over to rearrange its contents. "But I kinda like that adrenaline rush you get, don't you? I wish I'd get a chance to fly the Learjet. I know the rush must be even better with that ship."

Another excitement junkie like me, she chuckled to herself.

"Well, you certainly know your way around the medevac routine, John. Every check I've given you went really well," she praised him. "I bet your chance for an upgrade'll come pretty soon."

"I don't know, Taylor. LifeLine hasn't offered me anything yet, and they've had plenty of opportunities." He finished with his flight bag and stood up with a distant expression on his face. The gaze from his goggle-eyes narrowed. "Maybe it's because I don't have a college degree, or something else like that. It kinda ticks me off, but I'll stick with the King Air if I can't have a seat on the Lear."

She nodded, sympathizing with him, but wondering why he was saying anything about his upgrade status then. She'd known him since her hire date, and he'd never mentioned his disappointment before. "If they wanted you to have more education before they offered you a Lear job, couldn't you sign up for some college classes? That's what I'd do. You could even keep working during the semester since you don't have to be here if nothing's going on."

John shook his head at her idea. "I'm not too good with book learning, Taylor. Even the recurrency training classes give me a fit." He glanced at her slyly and gestured toward the hangar with his head. "If I'm lucky, maybe one of the Lear pilots will unexpectedly run away to Pago Pago and I'll have to step in for him. Or maybe something else could befall him. Ha-ha-ha!" He winked at her.

Then he shelved his grin and grabbed her elbow. "Anyway, let's go on in. I gotta take a leak."

A bit taken aback by his last remark, Taylor set off right behind him.

I guess I'm only one of the boys, she thought as she reflected on John's candor about bodily functions. He probably wouldn't say anything like that in front of the nurses.

Then she frowned about the rest of his comment. He had wished a Lear pilot would disappear so he could take his place. That sounded too much like what had just occurred. Is that why he was mentioning his disappointment, because Carter Masterson's death had reminded him of it? Or did he want to unburden a guilty conscience with a *harmless woman*?

Fifteen minutes later, John had gone home, leaving Taylor mindlessly shuffling around the office. She didn't have any reason to stay—nothing to do around the hangar—but she didn't want to leave, either. Talking to Steve about Wisdorf's curious upgrade comment was what she *really* wanted to do. She figured she'd wait for him to return—the Lear was due to arrive soon. He'd left his condo before her for a flight to Barrow, but even a trip to the northermost settlement in Alaska didn't take too long in the jet. She'd loiter around until he got back.

Across the room, Nate Mueller busily scribbled on the pilot

schedule for the next week, humming tunelessly as he worked. "You're up for the night shift next week, Taylor," he said. "No problem with that, hmmm?"

"Nah. But when have I ever had a choice, anyway?" As Nate snickered, the room was filled by the grinding noise of the big hangar door opening. She nodded at the sound. "There's Steve with the Lear. I guess I'll go wander into the hangar. Kai's with him, right?"

When Nate nodded, she pushed away from the desk. Her chair became stuck on the carpet runner below it and nearly toppled over, but she grabbed it before it fell. She said, "Whoops!" for Nate's benefit and scampered for the hangar door.

The tug had detached itself from the Lear and was *putt-putt-putting* off as she approached the jet's parking spot. Steve and Kai were climbing down the airstair, both carrying flight bags and talking. Wearing their identical Nomex coveralls, the two men looked like copies of each other with dissimilar coloring.

Blond and dark, she thought. Just like catalog pictures that show the same outfit in different shades. What a pair.

Every time she saw the two of them together her heart went pitter-pat. Even though Kai was a few years younger than Taylor, he still garnered her full attention. She could imagine nibbling on his full moustache, ruffling his shaggy hair, running her hands down his . . .

Yikes. She always had to remind herself that *Steve* was the only man in her life. She'd better watch her imagination.

The men drew near, and Taylor appreciated the casual saunter in Kai's gait. She was sure it wasn't conscious, but nonetheless it was definitely an appealing quality. So was the firmness of the rest of his body. No middle-age spread there.

Damn, she cursed as she studied Kai. One more man she'd have to ignore. What was it with these Lear pilots, anyway? Even Carter Masterson had been handsome, in a more mature way.

When she focused on her use of the past tense to refer to Carter she suddenly sobered, and met Steve and Kai with a polite smile on her face rather than the leer she felt like making.

"Gentlemen," she greeted them, motioning with her hand and bowing. "I presume you had a pleasant flight?"

Steve halted in front of her. "Taylor! Glad you're here!" He gave her a quick peck on the cheek.

That surprised her. They never traded affection at work. Was he picking up on her attraction to Kai, and feeling a bit possessive? Marking his territory?

Kai definitely recognized the signals, and gave Steve a sideways glance. "Well, I'll get out of the way so you two can talk. Or whatever. I've got paperwork to do." Nodding a greeting at Taylor, he strode off.

Taylor watched him walk across the hangar, then squinted at Steve. "You guys have a little boy talk on the way back from Barrow? I hope you didn't say anything about what we've learned about Carter's murder."

"Naw, nothing about that. You and I promised we wouldn't say anything to anybody until we were sure." He looked at her curiously. "Anyway, what are you doing here? You weren't waiting for me, were you?"

"Yeah, I was. I brought the King Air back about a half an hour ago, had a medevac to Homer. Some guy with a ruptured spleen. He decided to celebrate spring's arrival by drinking about a case of beer and tearing around town on his Harley." She grimaced, her nose wrinkling. "Unfortunately, the combination of alcohol and motorcycles was a bad one. When he hit a patch of leftover winter ice and ran into a fence he impaled himself on one of its posts. Internal organs don't handle sudden stoppage like that particularly well, you know?"

"Yeah, I know. Springtime does weird things to people." Steve's features twisted, too, surely imagining how the drunk's injury must have felt. "Springtime does weird things to the weather, too. How'd you like landing in that wind? You were in it, weren't you?"

"Yeah, it started before we got back to town. Blowing eighteen, gusting twenty-eight. I was flying with John Wisdorf—he took over for a sick copilot—and he was needling me about making a good landing in the wind." She looked sheepish when she shrugged. "The same way I needled him during his route check the other day. I guess he wanted me to flub it, and I would've deserved it if I had." She glanced to her right at nothing in particular, then looked back to meet his gaze. "I wanted to talk to you about that. Not the wind, but John."

"What, you don't like flying with him?"

"No, that's not it. He said something that's bothering me, though." She sighed and thrust her hands in her Levi's pockets.

"You know how we've been focusing on Ed's fear of losing his job as a reason to kill Carter?"

"Yeah, but what does that have to do with John?"

"Give me a second here, Steve. What if it wasn't someone scared of losing his Learjet job, but someone who *wanted* a Learjet job?"

Steve looked at Taylor blankly and shook his head. "What do you mean? Did John say something to you that made that come up?"

"He didn't say anything intentionally, but I can read in between the lines." She encapsulated the conversation with John, telling Steve about the other pilot's indignant tone of voice when he discussed being overlooked for a promotion. Then she narrowed her gaze into a question mark. "See?"

"See what? What does that have to do with Carter's murder?"

"Come on, Steve, you're getting tunnel vision. You're so sure that Ed plotted the murder that you can't pick up on clues that point toward someone else. What John said, and the way he said it, makes me think maybe he's involved in the whole gruesome business. He might have killed Carter to make room for *himself* on the pilot's roster for the Lear." She looked anxiously at Steve to gauge his reaction to what she'd said.

But Steve wasn't buying it. "One big problem, Taylor. John couldn't have had a captain's job like Carter's anyway. You know that. He'd have to do time in the right seat first before getting upgraded to the left. He'd need some copilot time. LifeLine doesn't hire Lear captains unless they have Lear time already—"

"Yeah, I've thought of that. I know that LifeLine fills pilot vacancies from within the company, if possible. John must've figured that Carter's slot would be given to one of the current copilots. That'd leave an empty right seat position and he could slip in that way."

"Well, why didn't he kill a copilot? Why Carter, a captain?"

Shaking her head, she held her hands out, palms up. "I don't know. That's one thing I couldn't figure out. Maybe it was just chance. Carter was the easiest Lear pilot to get to. It wouldn't matter if a captain or a copilot died, anyway; the same thing would happen."

"I don't know. I'm having a hard time seeing John Wisdorf as a murderer. He's just too nice."

Taylor gaped at him. "You think nice people can't do nasty things if they're pushed? I know I could do a lot of unpleasant things if it meant getting bumped up to Lear pilot. The idea of flying that airplane trips buttons in me that I didn't know I had!"

"You could kill for that?" He stared at her incredulously. "I guess I don't know you at all. Here I thought I did."

"Hey, I never said I'd kill for a seat in the Lear, but I'd sure work my tail off to get there. Even fly with real jerks if it led to a job like that. I can see why John is pissed off because LifeLine won't give him a chance in the jet. Maybe that was enough to set him off, make him think he had to do something drastic to get an opportunity to prove himself in the Lear."

Steve shook his head. "Nah. John's not smart enough to pull Carter's murder off. At least, do it without getting caught right away."

"What do you mean? He's certainly smart enough to captain a King Air, and he's a good pilot. The route check I gave him was really good. He seems smart to me." She puffed up with a peeved expression on her face. "What is it really? Don't you think I have enough intuition to detect the feelings underlying an innocent statement? I know what I heard, and I think it's enough to warrant a second look. I certainly don't want to think John could kill somebody, but I also don't want to accuse Ed if he's not to blame. We just can't be sure yet."

"Cool down, Taylor, I'm sure your intuition is good, I just know more of the story than you do. Think about what he said to you, that he wasn't too good at book learning. That's why LifeLine didn't offer him a seat on the Lear. He understands mechanical things well, he's good with the King Air, but he just doesn't think fast enough to handle the Lear." He cocked his head and fiddled with the zipper on his coveralls. "The company's looked hard at John, and they like the way he works with the King Air, but he doesn't seem like he could perform the way they want on the Lear. For the same reason, I don't think he could devise a plan to kill Carter. Whoever did it was smart enough to know how to cover his tracks, how to disguise the crime as a burglary. . . ."

Taylor pursed her lips and ran a hand through her thick bangs. Steve's reasoning made sense. More sense than *hers*. Looked like it was time to back off. "Yeah, maybe you're right. We could have found the right suspect already; it could be Ed.

Maybe we'll spot the clue that wraps this up sometime soon." She averted her face to peer at her toes, then brought her face up with a devilish grin on it. "I know, maybe we should be looking for somebody who watches *Murder, She Wrote*. They'd know how to plan the perfect murder!"

"Yeah, right. I think you watched too much TV during your days in Bethel." He rested a hand on her shoulder and steered her toward the office.

TEN

"Give me some of that paperwork, Kai." Steve sat down across the desk from the other man and extended a hand. "I'll finish it up for you."

With a flourish, Kai made a stroke with his pen and shoved the flight log toward a basket. "All done. Sorry, I didn't realize you liked paperwork that much. If I had, I would've let you do all of it. I've got a hot date to go to, and it would've been nice to blast out of here right away." He stood up from his chair and tucked a melon-colored polo shirt into well-worn jeans.

Taylor appraised his change of clothes, and decided the Nomex coveralls hadn't done much for him. He looked better in street gear. Not that he didn't catch her eye in his official LifeLine garb, but the jeans he'd changed into were tight enough to get a red-blooded woman like her perspiring. Too bad she couldn't do anything about it.

"You got a hot date? It's barely eleven o'clock." Steve wriggled his eyebrows at Kai appreciatively. "It must be going well with that new girlfriend you were talking about. She sounded pretty enthusiastic to me. You got a nooner planned or something?"

"Or something," Kai retorted, grinning.

A big gulp traveled down Taylor's throat. *Kai had a girlfriend? And anticipated an exciting afternoon with her? Damn,* she didn't need him and Steve talking about things like that; her imagination was difficult to rein in as it was. The thought of him doing what she assumed he'd do later got her hormones raging, and the thought of him doing it with another woman made her jealous.

Reaching across Steve's chest to retrieve the King Air flight log, she started fumbling with it as though she was ignoring them.

"Taylor's standing right next to you guys," called Nate from the neighboring desk. "Keep your comments to yourselves." The amused look on his face indicated to her that he was not above such talk himself; maybe he had just guessed how she was taking it.

"Sorry, Taylor." Raising his eyebrows, Kai grabbed his scuffed leather jacket off the coatrack and stepped toward the door to the parking lot. His glance whipped from her to Steve and back before he shoved it open and exited. He seemed to know how his talk of a hot date had gotten to her. "Later!" he yelled over his shoulder and hiked off.

"He's got the right idea," Taylor acknowledged as she gestured at Kai's disappearing form. "Why don't we go do the same thing, Steve?"

A puzzled look crossed Steve's face, then he laughed. "Oh, I get it," he chortled. "When you said 'go do the same thing' you probably didn't mean a nooner. You meant go get lunch."

"Well, yeah." Taylor squinted at Steve. "I can't believe you'd think I'd say something like *that*; I'm not as crude as you guys." And she didn't like broadcasting the personal side of their relationship to the rest of the world.

Steve shook his head, though. "Unfortunately, Taylor, you're out of luck. I could've gone for a nooner"—he smirked at Nate—"but not lunch. I brought a sandwich in a few days ago and forgot about it; I have to eat it today or it'll go bad. I'll share it with you, though. Deal?"

Wrinkling her nose, she thought about that. She couldn't handle his eggs-and-bacon breakfasts, and she didn't think she could tolerate his lunches, either. It was probably something like bologna on rye. Or worse.

Although she hadn't ever eaten a lot of meat during her life, recently she'd decided to become a strict vegetarian, a vegan. As she approached the big four-oh it was getting harder to remain trim, and the saturated fat found in animal products didn't help. Plus, the thought of cutting into Bessie or Oinker during dinner didn't sit well with her anymore.

Even so, she thought she'd ask what he'd brought. She was pretty hungry, and he might have forgotten his carnivorous ways and brought in a BLT, hold the B. Stranger things had happened.

"So, Steve, what'd you bring for lun—"

The *bleep-bleep . . . bleep-bleep . . . bleep-bleep* of Steve's pager interrupted her. "Oh, damn," Steve groaned. "We just got back! And we're getting called again? That never happens." He stared at Nate, as though he could do something about the un- wanted medevac call.

Nate hiked his shoulders. "Hey, it's out of my hands, Steve. You know you can't plan these things. At least you were here to begin with when you got beeped. Think about poor Kai— he's going to have to break his hot date. He might not have even made it to the restaurant yet."

Taylor smiled at the thought. Whatever Kai and his girlfriend had planned, it was off now. Even if it had been a nooner. Somehow that made her feel better, until she realized how catty that was. She shouldn't let jealousy affect her just because an- other woman could enjoy him and she couldn't.

When she saw Steve reach for the phone to report in with the hospital, she called out to him before he dialed. "Hey, I'll come help you get ready to go, okay?" Maybe she could con- sole Kai when he got back to the office in a few minutes. Surely he'd be depressed because his afternoon plans had gone down in flames, and letting him cry on her shoulder was the least she could do. She headed for the hangar.

A half-hour later, Taylor was back in the front office. Steve Derossett and Kai Huskisson had left with the Learjet for the town of Kotzebue, a mostly Native settlement twenty miles north of the Arctic Circle on the west coast of the state. They needed to medevac an eleven-year-old Alaskan Native boy to Anchorage for repair to a lung punctured by an errant rifle shot. The youngster had been flown from his home village of Sela- wik to Kotzebue, and waited there for the Lear to rush him to a hospital.

Taylor thought that only urban dwellers without gun-safety experience shot their friends by accident, but it still happened in the remote Native villages where weapons were a part of the subsistence life. Often, if you didn't own a rifle, you didn't eat, and she assumed having a large number of arms in a village made all of the residents ultra-careful when allowing children to carry them.

Not so.

Letting the door swing shut behind her, Taylor marched into the locker room from the hangar. She remembered the lunch Steve had mentioned, and she was hungry. She'd check it out. "You want anything from the fridge, Nate?" she yelled as she peered inside the small dorm-style refrigerator. "Can of pop or something?"

"Nah," the office manager replied from the other room. "Still nursing one here. Thanks, though."

"Okay." She pawed through the contents of the refrigerator. People were always leaving things in there and then forgetting about them. The accumulation was dreadful—somebody's cheese sandwich had a growth of hair you'd need a lawn mower to trim.

Finally she spied the brown paper bag with Steve's name on it. Inside she found a store-bought sandwich. "Don't even *think* about eating this!!" declared a stern warning stenciled on a strip of masking tape affixed to its Saran Wrap cocoon.

She looked at the preparation date on the Carr's Quality Centers stamp: "Apr 4." Two days ago. Not too bad. Regardless of the dire warning it sported, she started to unwrap the sandwich. "By the time you get to this, Steve," she said under her breath, "it'll have gone bad. I'm doing you a favor by eating it."

After tossing the Saran Wrap covering in the trash can, she spread the slices of bread apart. The sandwich had been made on whole wheat bread—a good start—but the filling disappointed her. Roast beef. She wouldn't eat that. Peeling the meat away, she lofted it at the trash can, too. "Oh, well," she grumbled, "maybe the rest of the sandwich is edible."

Surprisingly enough, it was. A generous helping of not-too-wilted lettuce, a thick tomato slice, and some pickle chips rounded out the sandwich. When she peered into Steve's lunch sack she found more treasures: two small packets of mayo and mustard, a quarter-pound tub of potato salad and a bag of tortilla chips. "Hey! Jackpot!" she chirped. The stripped-down sandwich might not satisfy her entirely, but the other stuff would help.

"What?" Nate yelled from the front office. "D'jou say something?"

"Naw, not really. I was just commenting on the buried treasure I found in the fridge."

"Well, you're braver than I am. Some of that stuff in there is scary. Be careful."

"Don't worry, my self-preservation instinct will kick in before anything in here bites me."

Regardless of her bravado, she looked at Steve's lunch again, more carefully this time. The sandwich had spent two days in the cooler. Would it be okay?

Shrugging, she decided it would be. She'd thrown away the pieces of roast beef, which were the parts most likely to spoil. Everything else was packaged with preservatives and could probably survive a nuclear holocaust.

Squirting some mayo and mustard on the remainder of the sandwich, she used the condiments' plastic wrappers to spread them on the vegetables. She realized the disemboweled sandwich probably wouldn't last her very long, but beggars couldn't be choosers. She was hungry *right now*, and the rest of the lunch would help stave off starvation for a bit longer.

But even her hunger couldn't excuse the taste of her first bite into the sandwich. It nearly curled her hair. "Gack!" she squawked, as she swallowed it. "Boy, has *this* gone bad!"

A second later she felt her mouth and her throat begin to burn, like she had swallowed a fistful of cayenne pepper. Her eyes widened dramatically—she hadn't ever experienced anything similar. Adrenaline surged into her system; she knew something was wrong. She'd never eaten a rancid sandwich before, but she didn't think it created symptoms like that. "Nate?" she croaked, realizing she needed help.

By the time she heard him rise from his chair, alerted by the tone of her plea, acute nausea was sweeping across her body. The sensation was ten times worse than the most virulent case of stomach flu she'd ever experienced.

And then her head began to pound as the room swam around her. She couldn't believe vertigo could attack her as she stood on solid ground.

"Oh, God, Nate!" she stammered, right before she gagged and pitched over. Holding on to the edge of the trash can for support, she vomited into it again and again. "Nate!" she mewled.

Suddenly, he was at her side. "Taylor! Taylor, what's wrong?" His strong grip tightened around her shoulders as he held her over the trash can. She continued to vomit, even though she'd emptied the entire contents of her stomach. Nothing else was left but drips of digestive acid, then the vomiting spells became nothing but dry heaves.

"The sandwich," she whispered.

"You ate a sandwich? Had it gone bad?"

Unable to form words anymore, she just nodded weakly. Spasms continued to wreak punishment on her body, and she could sense her heart beating faster and faster.

"Ambulance!" Nate cried, his voice trembling. "I'm calling for an ambulance! Hold on, Taylor!" He eased her onto her side on the locker room floor. Saliva ran from her mouth, and her torso rocked as the dry heaves persisted.

The sound of his voice changed pitch and volume in her head as he spoke to her, and her vision started to fade and blur. The comforting pat of his hand on her arm disappeared as he dashed for the phone on his desk. "Hold on, Taylor. I'll be right back."

The last thing she could make any sense of was an ironic thought: even though she flew medevacs every day she'd never ridden in an ambulance. Would any of the paramedics recognize her?

ELEVEN

By eleven o'clock that evening, Taylor had returned to her Upper Hillside cabin. She had trudged directly to her sofa and climbed up onto it, cocooning herself in the corner with an afghan. Knowing that sleep should be a priority for her, she thought about heading up for bed, but her nerves were still frayed. She couldn't bring herself to climb up to the loft yet. Too much to think about.

She had refused the overnight observation recommended by the ER doctor. Her distaste for hospital settings—an odd attitude for a medevac pilot—had prompted her to flee for the comfort of her own home. She'd take her chances with the possibility of complications.

The fruit smoothie she slurped as she reclined on the sofa helped to soothe her sore throat, but nothing could diminish the shaky mental state she found herself in. She finally realized, only too well, that if she had eaten those slices of roast beef rather than chucking them in the trash, she'd be dead.

A sobering thought.

Once the ER doctor had discerned that Taylor's brain was operating well enough to understand things again, she told her what had happened: food poisoning. But not in the form of a sandwich that had gone bad in the fridge, but in the form of a deadly toxin added to its ingredients.

When the ambulance had arrived to transport Taylor to Cook Inlet Medical Center, Nate Mueller told the paramedics of the

sandwich she had just eaten, and pointed at the roast beef remains in the trash can. He'd assumed she'd ingested some of
them, so one of the rescue workers picked a slice up and sniffed
it as a test. He wrinkled his nose—it smelled like a cigarette
butt.

That was an obvious clue.

Immediately, he threw the slice away and turned to bark at
his coworker. "She's got severe nicotine poisoning! She'll need
gastric lavage, right away!" Lifting her onto the stretcher, they
carted her to the ambulance and raced off to Cook.

In the ER, nurses performed the necessary gastric lavage on
her. The gastric lavage—stomach pumping—had caused the
raw throat that plagued her, for obvious reasons. The lavage
began with inserting a half-inch rubber tube in her esophagus.
As she gagged and retched, it was threaded down to her stomach and flooded with water that was then sucked out. That was
done several times before the nurses and doctor were satisfied
with the cleansing of the stomach. Afterwards, activated charcoal was administered to absorb any remaining nicotine in her
system.

The doctor had been surprised by Taylor's quick recovery
from the severe nicotine poisoning, until Taylor told her she
hadn't eaten any of the roast beef. The paramedics had detected
the strong smell of cigarettes on the meat slices—from which
they diagnosed nicotine poisoning—but fortunately she'd
tossed the roast beef in the trash. The remaining part of the
sandwich, the bread and lettuce and tomato, hadn't been as
liberally dosed with the nicotine, and she hadn't noticed a cigarette odor until she bit into a wedge. The doctor deduced the
young pilot had only gotten a small dose of the toxin that had
leached into the bread, but not the lethal dose smeared on the
roast beef itself. It only took one to three milligrams of nicotine
to cause death, the doc had said.

Becoming a vegan had saved Taylor's life.

That thought whirled around her head as she tucked the afghan around her neck. No wonder she couldn't bring herself to
go to bed—she was scared shitless.

But then a second thought hit her—who would've spiked
her food with a deadly toxin? Nobody knew that she was going
to eat Steve's sandwich. If nobody had known that, then the
poison wasn't aimed at her, but at *him*.

But who would have targeted him?

The first solution to the whodunit question was obvious—Ed Guralnik was number one on the list. But why would he have poisoned Steve? She was the one Guralnik had threatened with harm, not her boyfriend.

However, Ed knew she had damaging information on him. If he also knew that she and Steve were an item—more than likely, regardless of their attempts to hide the relationship while at the hangar—he would assume that she had shared her discovery with her lover.

Had Guralnik decided to hedge his bets, do Steve in before he could even consider spilling the beans?

That, in itself, was a clue. If Ed had elected to do something as radical as kill Steve, she figured the sinister-looking pilot was covering up for more than a little pencil-whipping of his records. Was he also Carter Masterson's murderer, she wondered.

Her suspicion of him made more and more sense—he seemed to be digging his own grave with his actions. Her other suspect in Carter's murder, John Wisdorf, seemed to pale in comparison.

Surely the secret poisoner was the same person who'd killed the Lear captain —who else would be so worried by an investigation to attempt murdering Steve? And she couldn't connect John Wisdorf to either her looking into Carter's death—of which he had no knowledge—or her brush with the Grim Reaper. Wisdorf didn't know she'd eat her boyfriend's sandwich.

As she mulled over the suspects in the poisoning, an unpleasant idea cropped up. Had she been the target of the lethal spiking of the sandwich, after all? It was possible that Ed Guralnik poisoned it to get at Steve, but it was also possible that someone else had poisoned it to get at her. *She* was the one investigating Carter's killing.

However, the only person that knew she'd eat that sandwich was Steve himself. He was the only one that could have poisoned her.

She froze when she digested that thought. *Damn!* That was right. Steve knew she'd eat his sandwich because he'd offered it to her. Right before he'd conveniently left on a medevac.

Shrewd move. Nobody would suspect him of poisoning his own sandwich. He only had to offer to share his lunch with her—as he'd done—and figure out a way to get out of there before he actually had to eat some of it himself—which he also had done.

Eyes widening, she wrapped her arms around her knees and pulled them closer to her chest. The poisoner had to be the same one who had killed Carter. Could her lover be involved in the murder of a coworker? And *her* murder as well? It gave her pause.

Seconds passed, then she emphatically shook her head in disagreement. He was one of the most gentle men she knew. He couldn't be a cold-blooded killer; that wasn't part of his nature.

Then she started when she thought of something else. What about Steve's links to Carter's murder? Like his access to keys for the dead man's apartment and a loaded gun by his bed?

For that matter, what did he think about the times she'd admired Carter's physique? How did he like her telling him that if she were available she'd relish the idea of trying out a seasoned, older man? Could he have become jealous because of those innocent remarks?

Her disturbing thoughts continued. She wondered how he liked Carter being the chief pilot for the Lear when he was just a line pilot.

Furious because she could even invent such awful thoughts, she pounded on her thighs. "No!" she yelled to the still air. "He couldn't kill somebody for those reasons! And he couldn't kill me because I might expose him."

She jumped from the sofa and headed for the loft ladder. If she tried really hard, she could ignore the terrible thoughts she'd just pondered. Maybe going to sleep would allow her to forget—those wretched images couldn't invade her dreams. Her nightmares, yes, but not her dreams. Surely she'd have nightmares that evening, but not about Steve wielding a gun.

Firmly ensconced in her bed, snuggled under her down comforter, she heard the rattle of keys in the lock on her front door. She froze. It was Steve, back from his medevac. Would he be surprised to see her? Naturally, he'd think that his nicotine-tainted sandwich had done its grisly duty, but she would be living proof that it didn't.

"No," she insisted again to the empty cabin. She wouldn't think that way. With the comforter slipping from her chest, she sat up in bed and waited for his arrival.

The cabin's door swung open. "Taylor? Are you home?" Steve questioned from the doorway.

Taylor could see him from her bed in the loft, and she studied his expression. Was he really looking for her, or was he just checking to see that the coast was clear? As soon as she thought that, she mentally slapped herself. *Cut that out. He didn't do anything*.

Clearing her still sore throat, she rasped, "I'm up here, Steve." When he heard her voice from upstairs he jerked his head up to survey the loft. The change in his expression set her at ease—he had appeared worried, but relief shone in his eyes when he spied her.

Seconds later, he bounded up the loft ladder. "Damn! I was scared for you, Taylor!" He sat on the edge of the bed near her head and studied her. "Why didn't you stay at Cook for the night? Didn't they offer that to you? Observation?" Steve glared at her. "Complications could have developed. Then what would you have done? You shouldn't play Russian roulette with your health, Taylor. Nate filled me in when Kai and I got back, and he said you got food poisoning from something you ate. That could've been bad."

"You're right about that," she snarled. "But it was more like food tampering. I got nicotine poisoning—somebody doused the sandwich with nicotine! I had to get my stomach pumped!"

Gaping at her, he unconsciously stroked his throat with a beefy hand. He obviously knew what gastric lavage entailed. "Nicotine poisoning? God, Taylor. I didn't know you could get nicotine in liquid form."

She arched an eyebrow. "Sure you can. It's easy. The ER doc told me you can get it at any garden supply store. It's used as a pestici—"

He interrupted her, satisfied with her answer, and asked a more important question. "But, Taylor, who'd do that to you? Go out of his way to find nicotine like that?"

As soon as he asked the question, he provided his own answer. "Oh, no. It was Ed Guralnik, wasn't it?" Another pause ensued as he appeared to examine that reply. "But why is he following up on his threat to hurt or kill you? I thought he only used that as a warning, to prevent you from notifying anyone else about what he'd done. As far as he knows, you *haven't* told anybody. Or did he find out about me somehow, and assume you told me after you talked to him?"

"Right assumption, wrong victim." Taylor arched an eyebrow. Her eyes narrowed. "Whoever spiked the sandwich with nicotine wasn't after me. They were after *you*." She saw his puzzled expression, so she explained. "It occurred to me when I was thinking about it—I ate your sandwich today. Nobody knew *I* would eat *your* sandwich. The poison was aimed at you."

Steve blanched when he realized the implications. "But why would Ed be after me? Even if he'd learned of my knowledge of his record-tampering, why didn't he go after you, like he'd said he would?"

Snorting, Taylor shook her head. "Who knows? Maybe you were easier to get to, or maybe he wanted to shut both of us up by shutting you up. Anyway, you can't hold a criminal to his word, Steve." She hiked her shoulders. "But I don't think it was Ed Guralnik anyway, as much as I'd like to believe it."

Steve stared at her. "Who else could it be? He's the only one we've pegged as a possible suspect in that pencil-whipping, and Carter's subsequent death."

"But look at the pattern here. We're not sure if Carter's discovery of the record falsification got him killed, but we do know that he got killed for some reason. It wasn't random. He didn't surprise a burglar." She focused on Steve, forcing him to look at her. "We've got one dead Lear captain, and another one—you—that's supposed to be dead. Somebody is knocking off the Lear captains. That's the pattern. And do you remember who besides Ed I suspected of having a hand in Carter's death?"

Steve nodded reluctantly. "John Wisdorf. But if I recall correctly, I didn't believe you."

"Well, just a few minutes ago I didn't believe me, either. I had just taken him off the list of suspects for Carter's murder because I thought the killer had to be the same person who was behind the poisoning. At first I thought I was the target for the poison because of my looking into Carter's death. However, that's something John doesn't know about, so there's no way he'd want to kill me because of it. But now, once it appears you were the target, and you're another Lear captain, John jumps to the top of the suspect list. Over Ed. Ed would have no reason to kill other Lear pilots—he already is one."

"Now wait a minute here, Taylor. Remember, I doubted John's ability to get away with a murder. I didn't think the motive you suggested made much sense, either. That hasn't changed, as far as I'm concerned."

Taylor sniffed. Steve was pretty hard to convince sometimes. "Well, then look at it this way. If he'd killed Carter to make a hole in the Lear roster, like I suspect, he realizes now that it didn't work. And I wouldn't think he'd quit trying to open the list, give up and face the possibility of a murder conviction without getting the Lear seat he'd killed for. Why take a big risk and quit before you get the rewards from it?" She leaned back against her pillow, pulling the comforter up to her chin. The cabin was a bit chilly for someone clad in nothing but a large T-shirt. "Killing you is the next logical step, Steve, if anything about a murder plot could be called logical. *You're* a Lear captain. You may have moved up one notch on his list when Carter's death didn't do him any good. You could be the next hit."

"Oh come on, Taylor." He looked at her in exasperation, his voice carrying a note of frustration. Her conclusions seemed to be getting to him. "How stupid would that be," he asked, "committing another Lear captain murder and trying to cover it up? Somebody would get real suspicious when we start dropping like flies. I can't believe you're even contemplating that."

"Oh, give me a break." She squinted at him, angered by his retort and his tone of voice. "If he was dumb enough, and psychotic enough, to murder Carter, why wouldn't he be dumb enough to try it again? There's no logic in either move."

"But that still doesn't explain how he could come up with a smart plot to kill Carter. I still don't think he has that kind of mind. The most devious I've ever seen him is when he filled his cup with root beer at Taco Bell when he paid for water."

She couldn't help herself. When that image entered her mind she had to laugh. She had to laugh even more when she remembered something she'd said before. "Well, if you don't think he could come up with a viable plan of his own," she cracked, "perhaps what I said about watching *Murder, She Wrote* isn't so crazy. A murder mystery fan would certainly know all of the murder strategies that work well. If the super sleuth doesn't solve the murder until the last minutes of the show or the last chapter of the book, the villain's scheme must've been pretty good." She grinned, realizing how lame that comment sounded.

"So, Dr. Watson," she chimed in a dulcet English accent,

"are you acquainted with Mr. Wisdorf's reading habits? If not, perhaps we should investigate that."

Steve lifted an eyebrow. "You're not serious, are you? I mean, that was a funny crack, but that's all it was, right? We don't really have to find out if he has a library card."

"Yeah, don't worry, I was joking. I'm not losing it." She patted the bed next to her. "Why don't you get undressed and hop in here with me? I feel a remission coming on—I may need mouth-to-mouth resuscitation. You're a medevac pilot, don't you know how to do that?"

Then she squinted at him slyly. "But no French kisses—my throat is still sore."

TWELVE

When Taylor rolled over in bed the next morning, she stared at the empty space next to her. The sight of her bed sans Steve made her feel a bit guilty, since she'd utilized some rather duplicitous methods to get him out of it the previous evening. The last thing she'd wanted then was for him to spend the night.

He had made a convenient assumption when she'd asked him to leave only an hour after he'd arrived. "Is that because I refused to make love to you?" he asked. "That was for your own good, mind you, but you're still kicking me out? Damn."

She couldn't blame him. It looked like she was using him as nothing but a sex toy that had to earn the right to share her bed. If he passed on the sex, out he'd go.

She tried to soothe his wounded feelings. "That's not it, Steve. You were right to refuse sex. I'm still recovering from the poison fiasco, and getting all revved up by playing with you might not serve me well. You know what you do to me." She reached out and stroked his cheek, smiling lasciviously to punctuate her comment. It didn't hurt to play up to the male ego, especially after unwittingly whacking it a good one. "But by the same token, I need to sleep alone tonight if I really want to get the most out of my rest. Having you here wouldn't help."

"Okay," he acquiesced, seeming relieved to hear that she thought he was too much of a stud for her to handle at the moment. He slipped out of bed and began to dress.

"So, I'll probably see you at the hangar tomorrow?" he mumbled as he dragged a navy-blue waffle-weave pullover over his head.

"I guess. I don't know what time, though. Nate said I could take it easy. He offered to give me a few days off—sick leave, I guess—but I said no. I'll be okay if I get a good night's rest tonight." She snuggled farther down beneath her comforter and tried to look sleepy for Steve's benefit.

"All right." Fully dressed, he bent to give her a light kiss. "Sleep well, then." He climbed down from the loft and exited the cabin.

As soon as she heard the sounds of Steve's Camaro disappear, she flung the comforter off and leaped from her bed. She had work to do, and it was getting pretty late. The conversation with Steve concerning the possible suspects in her poisoning had her genuinely puzzled, and she had to make some decisions.

Both Ed Guralnik and John Wisdorf had strikes against them—some items pointed at them being Carter's murderer, but others didn't. It warranted some investigation. Their employment records seemed a good place to start, and that meant a late-night visit to the LifeLine office. Though it appeared that John was the primary suspect—if the kill-the-Lear-pilots-to-make-room-on-the-roster plot was correct—she couldn't disregard Ed. After all, he'd done *something* worth threatening her over.

After shedding her XXL T-shirt in exchange for a heavy gray cotton sweater and Levi's, she left her cabin. After a quick scan of the surrounding area—force-of-habit for anyone who lived in virtual wilderness—she satisfied herself that no bears or moose menaced from the woods. She trotted to her Suzuki and zipped out of her yard.

Twenty minutes later she'd returned to the empty LifeLine office. She parked near a rear corner of the building to hide her Suzuki from Steve, just in case he drove past. Chances were remote that he would—why would he be motoring around the airport at one in the morning?—but she still felt paranoid and guilty about the way she'd duped him earlier. If he learned of her trickery he'd be mad, just as he'd be mad if he knew what she was doing back at the office. She wasn't going to press her luck.

In a way, though, that was kind of nice. He was always

watching out for her, keeping her in line. She had a tendency to act on ideas before she really thought them out, and it was reassuring to know that somebody was covering her butt when she got herself into trouble. His conservative personality *did* complement her own impulsive one.

But sometimes it dragged her down. Like when she had to hide her actions from him, fearing his reaction. As she'd done at the cabin.

Once she'd parked and let herself into the vacant LifeLine office, she'd headed for the employee records. Maybe a look at the past employment of Ed and John could give her some clues. It was worth a try. Pulling out the old resume for her King Air coworker, she scanned it.

"Hmmm," she hummed. "Aleutian Air. PIC in a Cessna 207. Then copilot, and captain on a Metroliner. Pretty fast run up the ranks." She glanced up. That was interesting, and it was something she could verify. She knew guys with Aleutian—as she knew many people in the small world of Alaskan aviation—and they could be a good source of information. If they'd been working there with John Wisdorf, they could tell her a lot about his flying habits and the reason why he'd quit.

Or gotten fired, if that had been the case.

Running her finger down the page, she found the first employer he'd listed. Her eyes widened appreciably. John Wisdorf had worked as a nurse at a small medical facility in Idaho, where he'd grown up. She peered out the dark office window, her eyes unfocused. How did he go from nurse to pilot? she wondered. That was a pretty abrupt change. Like going from bus driver to concert pianist. She found that odd, but shrugged and slid his resume back into his file.

Next resume to come out was Ed Guralnik's. Only one previous employer listed for him, but it was a big one. The United States Air Force.

She frowned. Unlike the excess of contacts she had in civilian aviation, she knew nobody in the military. That could hamper her check into Ed's past.

As she read down the Air Force entry on his resume, she started. He'd been a jet jock, on the F-15s. She sucked in her breath. No wonder he was so addicted to jet flying that he'd *threatened* her when she'd approached him about his record tampering. He wouldn't want to lose his pilot's job he'd learned to savor the rush he'd gotten from the F-15s, and the only civilian plane in which he could duplicate that rush was something like the Learjet.

But could he have murdered Carter to conserve that feeling? She pondered that for a moment, then decided yes. He had the kind of personality that could warrant killing another person if he'd been trained to fly a deadly machine like the F–15.

Of course, society condoned that kind of killing. During wartime, it wasn't called *murder*, it was called *neutralizing the enemy*. But it wouldn't require much to warp a mind enough for it to sanction shooting somebody that didn't threaten the country's security, but his own. *That* was something to think about.

Even so, the other pieces of the puzzle didn't fit together well for Ed Guralnik's involvement. The person who'd poisoned Steve's sandwich must have had some stake in Carter's death and their investigation in it. As far as she knew, the other Lear captain only had knowledge of *her* entanglement in the affair. It didn't make any sense that he'd targeted her boyfriend, unless he went after her through him.

Well, even though she didn't like to think John Wisdorf was part of Carter Masterson's death, she'd concentrate on him first. She'd go see her friends that flew for Aleutian Air, see what they could tell her.

And that's what she was doing that morning.

Easing into the same pair of Levi's and sweater she'd worn the previous night, she clambered down the ladder. She needed to find out when the Aleutian Air flight from Dutch Harbor arrived in Anchorage, and who was crewing it.

The trip from the Upper Hillside to Anchorage's International Airport had served as a break from thinking too hard. No rain-slick streets to negotiate, no traffic jams to navigate through, no school buses to maneuver around. The morning's broken clouds had changed to scattered clouds and the day had the looks of sun and spring. Nice weather.

After leaving the Suzuki in the three-story airport parking garage, she walked over to Concourse C where many of the intrastate flights boarded. That part of the airport was what had remained of the original terminal, and plans were in the works to demolish it and replace it with a more modern structure, more fitting to the high-tech world of twentieth-century air travel. She sighed as she wandered down the hallway, looking at the prehistoric-seeming boarding areas. She missed the old part of the terminal already—it had character.

Swinging into Gate C3, she approached the check-in counter where a twenty-something woman peered at a computer terminal. Behind the attendant set a tall board holding pushpin letters that identified the arriving and departing flights. Taylor could see that Flight 2378, from Dutch Harbor, had gotten in at 9:34 and was scheduled to leave again in about forty-five minutes. Her call to the Aleutian Air counter earlier that morning had told her that Ben Koechlein, an acquaintance from happy hour (which was a mandatory stop for all of the airport people at some time), was part of the crew for that plane.

"Morning,"—Taylor looked at the agent's nametag—"Sheri. Are the guys out in the plane?"

"Yeah, they are," she muttered, still glued to the monitor. "But you can't go out there." Breaking away from the screen, she looked over the counter at Taylor, who pointed at the airport identification badge clipped to her shirt collar. "Oh," said the woman. "I guess you can. Well, be my guest. They're out in the Metroliner. They may be busy—they're due to leave soon."

"Okay, I won't be long." Taylor scooted around the counter and walked to the door to the tarmac outside. There were no tunnel-like jetways in Concourse C; only glass doors that opened directly to airplanes sitting on the asphalt ramp area thirty feet away. Maybe, if you were lucky, a utility-grade line of carpet led from the terminal exit to the airplane's lowered airstair. But not usually.

On her way to the Aleutian Air aircraft, she scanned its sleek body. The Fairchild Metroliner, glistening white with red stripes running down its fuselage, gleamed in the morning sunlight. Its narrow shadow formed the shape of a caterpillar on the ground, with the silhouette of its extended airstair taking on the appearance of some oddly shaped tentacle. She smiled. The airplane certainly had earned its nickname: the Lawn Dart. The Metroliner was a lot longer than it was wide, and looked almost anorexic. "Go off your diet," she snickered at it as she stepped up the steps to the cockpit.

"Hi there, Ben," she greeted the dark-haired thirty-five-year-old man sitting in the Metroliner's left-hand pilot's seat. "Did you get upgraded to captain, or are you just sitting in the left seat while he's out getting coffee?"

Pushing his wire-framed glasses up the bridge of his nose, Ben Koechlein looked up from the magazine he held in his lap. "Hi, Taylor. Didn't you know I got upgraded? It's been months."

"Well, yeah." She looked a bit sheepish. "Now that you mention it, I think I did know. I just haven't seen you in your new uniform. The number of stripes on your sleeve threw me."

The tall thirtyish man sitting in the right-hand pilot's seat grinned at her. "You would have known he was the captain if you'd looked at *me*." He pointed at the clipboard resting on his thighs. "Ben's got a magazine in his lap. I've got all the work in mine." His dark moustache danced over his upper lip as he laughed. Holding out a hand, he shook hers. "Rob Ribitzki. Pleased to meet you. You're Taylor—"

"Taylor Morgan. I fly for LifeLine, and I'm a friend of Ben's. I always run into him at happy hour at the Clarion. He's the only one except me that drinks orange juice at a bar."

"Yeah, well," Ben conceded, "I still haven't learned to drink alcohol. Tastes like mule piss. Brrr." He shuddered. "So, what brings you over to my side of the airport, Taylor? Not enough dead or dying bodies to keep you busy?"

She flinched at his joke. Considering why she came to talk to him, his remark struck a nerve.

Ben noted her expression—probably misjudging the reason for her discomfort—and promptly retracted his words. "Sorry," he apologized. "Bad joke. You medevac guys don't like black humor, huh?"

She had to shake her head. "Not true, Ben. I've heard some pretty macabre jokes around the hangar. Some of those Lear pilots can get pretty gross." She squatted on her heels just outside the cockpit and balanced herself against the bulkhead. "I've got a question for you. Do you know John Wisdorf? He used to work for Aleutian. Metro captain when he left."

Ben Koechlein narrowed his eyes in thought, then snapped his fingers. "You mean that guy that looks like some deep-sea fish that got dragged up to the surface from twenty leagues down? Him?"

Cracking up at Ben's imaginative verbal sketch, she nodded. "I've never heard him described quite that way, but I guess it fits." Her coworker's protuberant eyes *did* resemble the bulging eyes of some ocean monster. She'd always thought of his looks in other ways, but Ben's take on them did it better. "Anyway,

LifeLine's thinking of upgrading him to the Lear, and they've got me out doing some checking on him. You know, how his past jobs went, how well he flies . . ." She hoped her reason for inquiring about Wisdorf sounded right. It was the only thing she could come up with on short notice. "Did you ever fly with him when you were a copilot and he was a captain?"

Rob Ribitzki looked at Ben goggle-eyed. "You were a co-pilot? That's not what you told me. You said you got hired as a captain, that you didn't know how to do copilot stuff."

"Oh, I was just kidding you." Caught in a lie, Ben blushed furiously, and tried to backtrack to cover it. "You were brand new, and you acted so naive I had to give you a hard time. You know how it goes, right, Taylor?"

"Well . . ." She arched one eyebrow at him. She'd done things like that as well—manufactured a few stories for people who wouldn't know better—but she hadn't been caught at it. Yet. "Anyway, did you fly with Wisdorf?"

"No, I didn't. He had left for his job with you guys before I got hired. But I've heard about him, and I've seen him around the airport. What I'd heard was pretty good. Talented pilot, never missed work, loyal to the company. That what you wanted?"

"Yeah, kinda." She wanted more, but didn't know how to ask for it. Maybe what she needed would just surface on its own, she hoped. She tried another tack. "Is that why he got upgraded to left seat of the Metro? Because he was good? He went through the pilot roster pretty quick, according to his resume. Was it really that fast? He went from a 207 to the left seat of the Metro, boom-boom boom." She wanted to catch her coworker in a lie on his resume—that would tarnish his nice-guy image with her, and make him seem more able to be a murderer.

Of course, murder was a far shot from lying on a resume. But still . . .

Ben shrugged and flipped the magazine closed. The front cover of his April issue of *Alaska Magazine* showed a close-up of blueberry thickets on the hills near the Arctic Valley ski slope. "I don't know about the 207—I hadn't heard anything about that—but the upgrade from right seat to left seat in the Metro *was* fast. He was good enough for an upgrade, but I doubt he would've gotten the chance to prove it if it weren't for his captain dying from a heart attack during a flight."

Taylor gaped at Ben. A captain had died while flying with John Wisdorf? Yikes! "The guy had a heart attack? In the air?"

The Metro's copilot joined Taylor in staring at Ben Koechlein. "I hadn't heard about that. What the hell happened?"

Ben held his hands up as he shrugged. "I'm not sure. All I was told was that the captain—Shafer was his name, I think—had a heart attack in the air on a dead-head flight from Bethel back to Dutch. Wisdorf put the plane on autopilot and did CPR, but couldn't revive the guy. He had to get the Metro back on the ground by himself, do everything with no help from another pilot. I guess management figured he did such a good job in a panic situation that they gave him Shafer's captain slot. Nice outcome from such a grisly event, huh?"

Yeah, I guess so, Taylor thought. *Too* nice.

"How old was Shafer?" Ribitzki asked. "Did he smoke? Was he overweight?"

Taylor could see the anxiety in the copilot's eyes as he spoke. She figured he was probably worrying about losing the captain on one of *his* flights and being responsible for handling the plane on his own. The thought made her shiver, too: an inexperienced copilot stuck with a monumental job like that.

Ben Koechlein cocked his head at Ribitzki's question. "That was one of the weird things about it. Shafer wasn't too old, just thirty-nine. He had none of the warning signs for heart failure—no concrete arteries, no enlargement of the heart muscle. The autopsy showed nothing." He shook his head at the mystery, then glanced up when he remembered something. "There was something kinda odd, though. They found coke, a lot of it, in his bloodstream."

Taylor frowned—Shafer had been coked up? That *was* unusual. Very few of the pilots she knew abused drugs, and *none* of them flew stoned. "Don't you guys get drug tested, Ben? We do at LifeLine. I thought everyone did that."

The Metro captain nodded to reassure her that that was true. "Yeah, we do get drug tested. But I don't think the FAA was requiring that when Shafer was flying. Plus, the guys that told me about him said they'd never seen him high on anything worse than caffeine." Ben knurled his eyebrows as he peered at his magazine with vacant eyes. "Maybe Shafer was tired for some reason and took a big hit of coke to bring himself up for the flight. I don't know." He pondered for a few more seconds, then stashed his reading material in the sidewall pocket to his left. He turned back to her, his expression signaling the end of the conversation. "Anyway, Taylor, we need to get going here. We'll be leaving in a few minutes, and I need to go get the passenger manifest. I'll walk you back to the terminal."

Both she and Ben stood, and she backed away from the cockpit door to let her friend exit first. Waving at the copilot as she moved toward the airstair, she offered a farewell. "It was nice meeting you, Rob. Maybe I'll see you at happy hour some time soon. Tell Ben to bring you along when he goes. We'll have better stories then, less gruesome than the one you heard today."

"I hope," Rob Ribitzki muttered as he bent back to his clipboard.

As Taylor left the airport's garage—after paying two bucks for her parking—she pondered what she'd just heard. "So John had a captain die of a heart attack on a flight with him, huh?" she repeated to the empty cab of the Suzuki. "Someone who didn't have any signs of heart disease? Odd." She pulled out of the lot onto International Airport Road, heading for the LifeLine office, deep in thought.

THIRTEEN

"So how was your post-sandwich visit to the ER yesterday? Is your throat still sore?" Nate teased when Taylor stepped into the office and shut the door on the morning's springtime air.

Stopping dead in her tracks, she tried to wipe the surprise off her face. "Who told you about my throat? Was it Steve?" she asked nervously, thinking it could have been someone else. Maybe the hospital had called about her ER bill and mentioned the stomach pumping due to the nicotine poisoning. The hospital didn't have any way of knowing she'd object to Nate being privy to that info; she'd prefer he didn't hear about it. No sense worrying him.

"Of course it was Steve." Nate squinted at Taylor and shook his head. He appeared to ponder that question for a moment, then forgot about it and shrugged. "Anyway, didn't I tell you to watch it with the food in that fridge? Who knows how old some of that stuff is?" He made some grumbling noises deep in his throat, miffed because she hadn't listened to him, then lightened up. "You're feeling okay now?"

"Yeah, just peachy. Good night's sleep and all that." Taylor relaxed, encouraged because Nate didn't seem to know about their suspicions concerning the nicotine spiking of the sandwich. She slipped her jacket off and hung it on the coatrack, fingering a stain on the sleeve she hadn't seen before.

Nate glanced at the cars lined up in the parking lot outside and chuckled. "Steve barely had time to tell me how you were doing, since he had just gotten beeped—"

"He got beeped? He isn't here?" Rats. She wanted to tell him what she'd discovered about John Wisdorf. She was prepared to ignore him as he ranted at her for continuing to snoop on her own, then planned to tell him where to put his comments. Enough was enough. "Where'd he go? When's he coming back?"

"Oh, he said he'd be back around five or six. The flight was only another transfer to Seattle, wouldn't take too long."

"Did Jude and Colleen go with him? Or are they just doing some other work in the hangar? I saw their cars in the parking lot when I drove up." She hoped they hadn't left on the same medevac; she wanted to discuss John Wisdorf's RN past with them. And the nature of heart attacks.

"Well, Jude went on the Seattle flight, with Julie Malcolm backing her up. But Colleen *is* in the hanger, restocking the cabinets." Nate cocked his head at the locker room, where the door to the hangar was located.

"Good. I gotta go talk to her." She marched off, leaving a curious Nate Mueller staring at her disappearing back.

Taylor pushed the door open and stepped into the hangar, scanning the enormous structure. Both King Airs stood sturdily in their slots, though the Lear was on a flight. At that time it was probably somewhere over the northern Pacific en route to Seattle. Small noises echoed over the concrete floor from the corner and attracted her attention. Obviously Colleen was in there, and the pilot could see the nurse fumbling around in the tall cabinets next to a wall.

"Hey, Colleen!" Taylor called, heading for her.

The other woman turned and watched her coworker approach, hiking boots squeaking as the Vibram soles scraped over the floor. "Got a few questions for you," Taylor announced. "Got a moment?"

"Morning, Taylor. I sure do. I'd welcome a few questions to liven up this drudgery. Too bad these shelves don't stock themselves." The thirty-something woman ran her fingers through her blond pageboy and swept a hand across the face of the cabinets. Generic medical supplies—rolls of sterile gauze, cleansing solutions, rubber IV tubing—dotted the metal racks inside.

"That must be a drag," Taylor conceded, "making sure you

never run out of all the little stuff. It's easy to remember if you've got a working defibrillator on hand, but all the bandages and things would be hard to keep track of."

Colleen shrugged, looking resigned to doing grunt work. "You do what you can," she sighed. "So, what's your question?"

"Several, actually. I just heard that John Wisdorf used to be an RN before he started to fly. Did you know that?"

"Well, yeah," Colleen said, acting as though that was old news. "We talk about it a lot, him and me. He said that's why he wanted to get a job flying medevacs. He saw them coming into the hospital he worked at in Idaho and thought that'd be an exciting way to work in the medical field."

Taylor raised an eyebrow quizzically. "But why didn't he just become a trauma nurse, like you, rather than a pilot? He already had the training to do nursing stuff."

"He already had the training to do pilot stuff, too," Colleen acknowledged. "He got his first pilot's license before he went to nursing school. Flying was really his first love, anyway, but he had to earn a living. He didn't think he could do it as a pilot. So he went to school to be a nurse instead. He'd had to care for his elderly parents when he was younger—get their meds, check blood pressure, all that—so it made sense to go that way for a profession."

Taylor nodded, absorbing those facts. "So, I guess you guys talk all the time about the medical stuff going on with the medevac patient. And he knows all of the lingo you use, huh?"

"Of course. Sometimes he helps us in back, let's the copilot—if he's experienced—take care of things up front. I'm surprised he didn't talk to you the same way."

Taylor shrugged her shoulders and made a face. "I rarely flew with him when I was a copilot, and now that I'm a captain, all I do with him is give him check rides. No time for talk then." She scuffed her boot toe on the floor, then ventured into the next topic she wanted to cover with the nurse. "To change the subject, Colleen, now I've got a really odd question for you. How would you trigger a heart attack in a healthy person?"

The startled expression on the flight nurse's face made Taylor hesitate. Had she said too much? Would Colleen think *she* was trying to plan a murder? The heart attack question was a pretty odd one to ask completely out of the blue. She attempted to account for her interest in the subject, and manufactured an excuse. "I was reading a murder mystery last night, and I'm trying to decide 'whodunit' before the author lets me know at the end of the book." The funny look from the other woman made her roll her eyes. "I know, I know, that's cheating, but you know me. I gotta have the answers before anyone else. So sue me." She laughed, holding her hands up, palms out.

Colleen shook her head, puzzled. "You're a weird trout, Taylor, but let me think about what you asked." She knurled her eyebrows and chewed on her lower lip. "The easiest way to do that would be potassium, I think," she decided. "Just shoot it into an IV line and it'd do the job right away."

That answer didn't satisfy Taylor; it didn't fit the circumstances of the heart attack suffered by the Aleutian Air captain of whom Ben Koechlein had spoken. No potassium had been found during the man's autopsy, and he certainly didn't have an IV line attached at the time of his death.

"I don't know, Colleen," Taylor said, squinting. "Nothing's been said about potassium so far in the story. I mean, nobody's even eating a lot of bananas." Her wry expression served to apologize for the lame joke. "Are there any other ways to prompt a heart attack?"

"Well, there's the obvious one. Cocaine. People die of heart attacks after overdosing on that. I'm surprised you didn't think of that yourself; it's one of the first things we ask when a medevac patient has had heart attack. Did he, or she, use recreational drugs?"

"Yeah," Taylor drawled. "I'd forgotten." Then her gaze narrowed. "But those are *accidental* overdoses, and the patients are habitual users. Or *abusers*. In the story I'm reading the heart attack is planned, and the victim isn't a druggie."

"Okay, then. The cocaine was injected by someone else." Colleen balanced against the cabinet's door, cocking her thumb and index finger like she was squeezing a syringe. "That's all it takes with certain people. One good hit. The first time it enters their system, it's lights out."

Hmmm. That was starting to sound right, Taylor thought. Shafer hadn't been known as a user, but he *did* have cocaine in his bloodstream. He must have been the kind of person who had a fatal aversion to the drug, and one injection had been enough to kill him. But how had John Wisdorf gotten him to stand still for the sting of a syringe? While they were flying? She'd have to think about it more. Just as she turned to thank

Colleen for her very educational answers, Nate Mueller's voice bounced off the hangar walls.

"Hey, Taylor!" Nate yelled from the locker room door. "You want to come in here? Somebody wants to talk to you, a guy from APD." He ducked back inside the office.

Anchorage Police Department? What was that about? Were the cops there to arrest her for the *misinformation* she'd fed the officer guarding the crime scene at Carter's apartment? *Yikes!* Taylor's eyebrows arched as she pondered the reason for a police visit, and her heart started to pound.

Leaving Colleen to her sorting, Taylor walked to the half-open locker room door. Scooting around it, she stepped into the front office where a suited man sat across from Nate. The stranger rose upon noticing her and offered a hand to shake. Taylor extended hers and his large paw enveloped her fingers.

"I'm Detective Franklin," the man said, "Anchorage Police Department, homicide division. Pleased to meet you." He released Taylor from his firm grip. When he didn't appear ready to throw cuffs on her, she relaxed and began to study him.

His simple act of standing had alerted Taylor to how tall and burly the man was: his moves were slow and measured, and the fabric of his suit coat sleeves stretched tautly across his upper arms.

Looking at his stout build, Taylor imagined him as a patrolman. Certainly he hadn't had any trouble convincing criminals to accompany him to police headquarters; they surely thought twice about attempting to escape *his* clutches.

She contemplated that for a moment, then decided that if he'd nabbed her and she wanted to give him the slip, she'd just knock his glasses off and kick him in the knee. Then she'd run like hell. Someone that big didn't strike her as a sprinter.

"Mr. Mueller says that you knew Mr. Masterson," Detective Franklin boomed. "I'm interviewing all of his coworkers as part of the investigation into his death." The question posed by his blue eyes seemed to ask, "Will you help?"

Taylor thought, *Hey, I'm already on it,* then she asked out loud what she could do to aid the police.

"Mr. Mueller said we could use the next room to chat a little. Could we do that?" Franklin pointed toward the pilot's locker room and grabbed two chairs. The strain of hauling one chair per hand didn't seem to bother him in the least as he casually strolled across the office.

She shrugged for Nate's benefit, and followed the gigantic investigator into the room.

A half-hour later, Taylor preceded Franklin out of the interview room. The detective was slipping a small spiral notebook into the inner lapel pocket of his blue pinstripe suit, and a thoughtful, even speculative, expression covered Taylor's face.

"Detective Franklin," Nate addressed the man. "Looks like you're all done talking to Taylor. I hope she was some help." The office manager raised his eyebrows at her as though to ask her if she'd been a good interrogation subject. When she didn't reply, he turned back to the policeman. "So, is there anything else we can do for you?"

Nate's face had competent-professional-at-your-service written all over it. She figured that the police involvement in Carter's death was the most excitement he'd seen for a long time.

"Well, Ms. Morgan was most helpful," Franklin declared. "Now I need a list of all of your employees, including how I can contact them." The other man pointed at the pilot roster on the wall and stepped toward it. "Is this the list?" he asked as he pulled his notebook back out of his pocket.

Nate scanned the list. "Yup, that's it. Pilots on top next to the aircraft they're qualified for, nurses below that, mechanics on the bottom. Telephone numbers follow all the entries." His eyes ran down the roster to the list of nurses, where it halted. "Of course, the flight nurses are technically not employees of LifeLine; they work for the hospital. We just like to keep track of everyone."

"Is this everyone that knew Masterson from work? Anyone missing?"

"No, I don't think so." Then Nate wrinkled his forehead as he thought of someone. "Well, there's one more. He's no longer an employee, but he stops by periodically. Name's Robert Berndt."

"Robert Berndt?" Franklin's gaze narrowed as he scribbled on his pad. "He knew Masterson, then? What happened to him, anyway? Why isn't he an employee?"

"He doesn't work for us anymore because he was involved in a serious car wreck. Got a pretty bad head injury. As a result of that injury, he's not competent enough to command the Learjet, the plane he was assigned to. We were told he probably couldn't handle any kind of aircraft, not even a small one." The discomfort of discussing Berndt's dismissal from LifeLine was obvious on Nate's face; Taylor could see it.

Franklin seemed to sense it, too, and his matter-of-fact questioning tone mellowed. "So he *did* know Masterson." He poised his pen over his pad, ready to jot down details.

"Well, sure, he knew Carter. They both flew the same aircraft." Nate grimaced; Taylor figured that he was remembering something especially disturbing about what had happened to Berndt. "However, the accident was three years ago, and he hasn't been around here since then. Not regularly, at any rate."

Franklin studied Nate's face. "Then he wouldn't have talked to Masterson any time near the night of the shooting?"

When Nate said, "No, I'd say that didn't occur," Franklin drew several lines across his last entry and popped the notebook back into his pocket.

"Then sir"—the detective glanced at Taylor—"and ma'am, I'm all done here. I can contact the other employees from the precinct headquarters. Thank you for your help." He bobbed his head and turned for the door.

Taylor watched Franklin disappear around the building's corner, then glanced at Nate. "Well, at least they're not concentrating on a failed robbery as the motive for the shooting," she growled. "They're starting to look at fellow workers, like they *need* to."

A puzzled expression passed across Nate's face as he stared at her. "What do you mean, like they need to? What do *you* know?" His eyes seemed to plead for information, as though she'd left him out of something.

She grabbed up some paperwork out of the IN basket on Nate's desk and shuffled through it aimlessly, then met his expectant look and set the papers back into the tray. "Okay, here goes. Steve and I thought the cops were way off track when they suspected Carter's killer was a startled burglar. There are too many coincidences in the whole scenario, plus Steve knows some things the cops don't that cast a different light on the murder. The day before he got killed, Carter told Steve a few interesting things . . ."

Taylor began a sketch of the information that lead them to their own investigation into Carter's death. Within a few minutes of chattering, disrupted by several questions from Nate, she came to the food poisoning. She hesitated, then, and contemplated not telling Nate of the nicotine, but decided she had to come clean. She made it brief.

"So that's it," she concluded. "That's what Steve and I think about the nicotine on the roast beef. Somebody—somebody involved in Carter's murder—spiked it. Find the poison, and we find the murderer. And vice versa."

"I can't believe you decided to take this on yourselves and didn't notify the cops." Nate's wide-eyed gaze made her uneasy. He was making too much of it, and that could mean trouble. "The police should have been brought into it. What if the nicotine had killed you, and they didn't know what was behind it? They wouldn't've known it was related to Carter's murder."

"Oh, calm down, Nate." Taylor reached out to pat him on the shoulder. "We've never had hard evidence about any of this; it's all speculation or innuendo. And the cops would have figured it out eventually. Anyway, I told Detective Franklin what Carter'd told Steve, and the APD can look into it if they think it has merit. But from Franklin's expression when I told him, I doubt they will. He just jotted something down in his notebook while I talked and started on another avenue of questioning when I was done."

She propped her hip on the edge of Nate's desk. "So, are you with us?" she said. "Can we count on your support? We've got to figure out if it's Ed or John—or both of them for all we know—that was behind the *seasoning* of Steve's sandwich. Any ideas from you? We've got to figure this out before the warnings get more successful. Obviously someone either wants us to call off the dogs, or is willing to continue murdering Learjet captains until he gets what he wants. Either way, it's bad news."

A loud *whoosh* echoed across the office as Nate forced air through his pursed lips. He scowled at Taylor, but then seemed to make a decision and his glare mellowed as he shifted in his chair. "Looks like Franklin was on the right path," he agreed, "when he wanted to contact all of the LifeLine employees. I assume that he'll call them. Maybe that's something you should do, too, see if you can discover some relevant tidbits about Ed and John that another pilot knows. Even one of the nurses could be a good contact. Get Steve to help when he comes back from Seattle tonight." He surveyed the roster board and his eyes lit up. "You can kill two birds with one stone here." He pointed.

"Go see Julie Malcolm. She lives with Robert Berndt. You could quiz both of them at the same time."

Taylor cocked her head, quizzically. "Julie lives with Robert? I didn't know that." She shook her head. "Good thing I've got the office gossipmonger on my side. I'd never hear this stuff if it weren't for you. Sheesh."

Turning back toward Nate after glancing at the roster, she reached for the phone. "So then the same number works for both of them? I'll just call to see if I can stop by, maybe tomorrow. That approved, Generalissimo Mueller?"

"Wait, wait, wait." Nate chuckled and grabbed his Rolodex. He began flipping through it with an index finger. "You need their Girdwood number. The one on the board is their town house in Anchorage and they're not there—they're spending some time at their ski chalet. Julie commutes to town while Robert putters around the house all day, but tomorrow's her day off so she'll be there as well." He bent back to the Rolodex. "Julie says the off season is really nice in Girdwood. No winter traffic to fight on the way to Alyeska, nothing but the small number of year-round residents to compete with at the bake shop for lunch. Should be a fun trip, driving out there on a spring day." He extracted the proper card from the Rolodex and handed it to Taylor.

"What am I going to say to them about why I'm going out of my way to track them down?" Taylor peered at the card in her hand and turned it over to see the other side. It was blank. She arched an eyebrow. "Do you think they'll clam up if I tell them why I'm there?"

"Why should they?" questioned Nate. "It's not like we're investigating *them*; we're following the paths of Ed and John. Don't tell them that, but allude to the fact that they're not the ones being looked at." He laughed, and added, "If Carter had been killed by a lethal injection, then we'd be looking for one of the nurses. Then Julie could be worried."

"Hey, I bet Robert'd be delighted to talk to you," Nate added. "Just say you're helping the APD, and he'd jump at the chance to talk to you. He's always had a liking for solving mysteries. This would be right up his alley. And it would be the truth, sort of, in a roundabout way. You *are* helping the APD. They just don't know about it yet."

Both of them laughed, and Taylor bent to dial the phone.

FOURTEEN

After wolfing down a submarine sandwich at the Carr's Quality Centers deli, Taylor moved to another part of the store and started thumping melons. She didn't like making her weekly trip to the grocery store while she was on call—if she got beeped she'd have to abandon a cart full of food in the middle of the aisle—but she needed to kill some time until Steve's return from Seattle. As little as she relished the prospect of him berating her for what she'd done that morning, she still wanted to tell him what she'd found at Aleutian Air.

By four-thirty, with her weekly ration of vegan TV dinners fighting a few cantaloupes for space in the cart, she had reached the head of the checkout line. A plump, redheaded woman rang up her groceries, and a teenage boy hauled them out to her car. The view of his tight sixteen-year-old butt reminded her that Steve had rejected her initiation of sex the previous night because of her nicotine hangover. What a drag. She hoped that was a one-time occurrence, that her obvious health would assure him amorous activities could continue once more. Controlling her libido around him wasn't easy when her hormones were on a rampage; he really got her motor running.

While the teenager loaded her car, she glanced at the sky. As was typical of Alaska, the weather had changed again. What had started out as a soon-to-be-sunny day had transformed into a more-of-the-same-gray day. The old Alaskan sourdough adage,

"If you don't like the weather now, wait five minutes," was true.

She would've hated being a meteorologist in Anchorage, or anywhere else in the state—the weather forecasters were wrong more often than they were right, and everybody enjoyed making fun of their prognoses. Blaming them wasn't fair, though. Alaska was huge, with three completely different weather environments—no wonder it was difficult to predict.

Swinging into the parking lot at LifeLine, she glanced to the east. Silhouetted against the Chugach Range, she saw a sleek silver-and-burgundy shape emerge from the gray flannel overcast blanketing Runway 24R. The Learjet's landing lights flashed on, adding a bright mote of white to the gloom of the sky.

"Oh, boy," she murmured as her gaze shifted from the sky to the slot near the office into which she guided her Suzuki. "There's Steve. Did I time this right, or what?" Unbuckling her seat belt, she jumped to the puddle-pocked asphalt and scampered to the building's front door. A light drizzle had followed her back to the office from Carr's, darkening the surface of the parking lot and pinging on the vehicle's top.

With the door swooshing closed behind her, she greeted Nate. "Getting ready to go home?" she asked rhetorically as she watched him scoop papers into a pile. She shook her head when he plopped the entire stack into his IN basket. "Is that how you organize your stuff?" She gaped in disbelief. "Just toss them all in the same basket?"

"Hey, I'll sort 'em tomorrow. I just don't feel like doing it today." He shrugged and squinted at her. "What are you doing back here? You waiting for Steve?"

"Yeah. He was about halfway down final when I pulled into the parking lot. He should be taxiing up right about now." Just at that moment, as though she'd cued it, the growl of the hangar door opening echoed through the office. She smiled. "And here he is." She saluted the office manager and headed toward the lockers. "*Hasta la vista . . .* baby," she cracked in her best Arnold Schwartzenegger voice and disappeared into the other room.

By the time she had entered the hanger, the view through its open runway-side door was showing a handler attaching a tow bar to the nosewheel of the Learjet. Steve Derosset and Kai Huskisson were trotting down the airstair, their flight bags dangling from their arms. The aluminum clipboard containing flight paperwork gleamed from the copilot's other hand.

Taylor sighed when she saw the attractive, sexy form of Kai Huskisson. She wished that the younger man didn't get assigned to fly with Steve quite so often. Every time she saw the two handsome pilots together she had to slap her imagination into submission, and that was getting harder and harder to do. What was a red-blooded American woman to do?

"Hey, guys. How was Seattle?" she yelled as she jogged the remaining fifty feet between her and the two men. The sound of her hiking boots hitting the cement floor ricocheted across the hangar.

"How was Seattle?" Kai repeated when she converged upon them. "It was great. I couldn't believe it. Raining here, but real sunny in Seattle. Talk about a turnaround." He motioned for her to follow him and Steve across the hangar.

"Yeah, it was a real drag coming back to Anchorage. I wanted to walk around in the sunshine." Steve knit his brow in disgust, then brightened when he wrapped an arm around her shoulders. "Good thing I've got somebody to come back home to. Somebody to keep me warm on a rainy night." He gave her a quick peck.

Cocking her head in surprise, she glanced up at her tall beau. He was doing it again, she thought. Marking his territory. He must really be worried about Kai if he's breaking their unspoken rule dealing with affectionate gestures at work. She had never spoken of her attraction to the young copilot, but Steve was picking up on it. Must be her tone of voice.

Clearly uncomfortable with the intimate display between his captain and Taylor, Kai upped his pace toward the locker room. "I can see you two want to be alone," he acknowledged. "I'll get out of your way." He strode off.

As soon as Kai disappeared, Steve dropped his arm from Taylor's shoulders. The exhibition was over. "So, what'd you do today? Anything interesting? I guess you're rested up"—he raised an eyebrow as though unsure of the truth of that statement—"so Nate must've put you back on the board. Did you get any medevacs?"

Taylor shook her head. "Naw, nothing going on. Certainly no trips to Seattle. You're so lucky, getting to go to all those exotic places."

"Well, Seattle isn't *exotic*--"

"Oh, yeah? What about Magadan? Russia's pretty exotic."

"Yeah, I guess so, but we don't go there all the time. I have to go to Seattle just about every week, sometimes several times a week. It *does* get boring."

She sniffed. "Hey, flying the Lear's a lot more exciting than the King Air. You get to go all over the place."

"You'll get your turn at the Lear one of these days." Steve smiled and ruffled her hair teasingly. "Just be patient. You'll get upgraded soon."

"Well, I wish I could hurry things up. Patience is not my strong suit." As she shoved the locker room door open for him, she blanched. Her last comment about accelerating an upgrade reminded her of what she'd discovered that morning. She needed to run it past her big partner in crime, get a second opinion. Given that the room was empty—fortunately, Kai had already left—she resolved to own up to her snooping. "Hey, Steve?" she called to him as he tossed his flight case into his locker.

Peeling his flight suit off, he looked up. "Yeah?" he grunted as he struggled to extricate his arm out of the Nomex sleeve. The navy-blue cloth was snagged on the denim of his shirt, and he was tugging on it. "What?" He glanced at her quizzically.

"I *did* do something this morning that was pretty interesting. Went over to talk to a guy I know at Aleutian Air."

"Why'd you do that?" he asked, most of his attention directed at getting out of the Nomex uniform. The suit wasn't meant to be put on over street clothes, but most of the pilots wore them that way anyway. "You looking for some part-time work? Need more money?" he cracked.

"Yeah, right," she shot back. "Us King Air pilots don't get paid like you jet jocks do." She hoped to add a bit of levity to her remarks before she focused on what she'd done. He'd be mad. She sucked in a breath. "No, I went to Aleutian because that's where John Wisdorf used to work before here."

Steve spun around, staring at her intently. "How'd you know that?" he quizzed, then narrowed his eyes. Making the connection, he stopped tugging on his Nomex suit and faced her head-on. "You looked at his job application last night, didn't you? When you kicked me out, saying you needed to get some sleep." He leveled his gaze on her, his eyes getting beady. "You're still investigating him, aren't you? I thought we agreed that you wouldn't do that alone." His expression firmed into granite.

"Hey, we never agreed to that. That's just what you assumed." She puffed up, trying to look more formidable. "I'm a big girl, I can watch out for myself. Anyway, don't you want to solve this murder? You could be the next one up!" If she'd been targeted for extermination, she'd be pretty interested in finding a suspect and bringing him to justice. *Jeez.*

Snorting, he shook his head in frustration and lowered himself onto the locker room bench. "Well, of course I want to see the murderer caught, but I'm not going to do it myself. That's what cops are for." He ran a hand through his shock of blond hair. "God, what am I going to do with you? You never listen to me." Sighing, he puffed out his cheeks in resignation. "At least you didn't get in trouble this time." Then he looked up expectantly. "Did you?"

"No, I didn't," she acknowledged. "But I did find out some really interesting stuff. Regardless of what *you* say, the trip was worth it." She sketched out her talk with Ben Koechlein, including her discovery of Wisdorf's nursing background and the convenient death of the pilot who'd flown with him. Steve's features creased when she detailed the heart attack and her coworker's subsequent upgrade to captain.

"So," she concluded, "if he wanted to get rid of his competition, he could've done that easily. Wait for a deadhead flight with no one on board but the two of them, then whack Shafer up the side of the head and inject a wad of coke in a vein. Enough of the stuff to trigger a heart attack. He was a nurse; he'd know how much cocaine to use, and wouldn't have any trouble figuring where to inject it. And cocaine was the perfect thing to use—when an autopsy is done, all the medical examiner sees is an overdose of a recreational drug. They assume Shafer was a cokehead." She rolled her eyes and plopped down on the bench next to Steve. "Not only do they not suspect Wisdorf; he turns out looking like a hero for getting the ship back on the ground while he's trying to do CPR on his captain."

"So, you think John killed Shafer to get a Metro captain's seat." Steve nodded slowly. "And you must think he did the same thing with Carter Masterson to get a Lear copilot's seat." When she held her hands up, palms flat in a what-do-you-think gesture, he narrowed his gaze.

"But why did he shoot Carter to get rid of him?" he asked.

"If he knew so much about injecting deadly drugs, why didn't he do that?"

She squinted at him, attempting to trigger the right response. "Think about it, Steve." When he shrugged, she shook her head—he wasn't connecting the dots yet.

"He flew with Shafer all the time," she reminded him, "but never with Masterson. He had the opportunity to get close to Shafer, close enough to drug him, but not so with Masterson. If he couldn't get close to Carter, he needed a different weapon to kill him. A handgun can do the same thing as a hypodermic needle, but at a longer range. He *had* to shoot Carter."

The blood to Steve's cheeks was starting to drain away as he realized what she was saying. "This is getting kinda scary, Taylor. The threat from Ed Guralnik was bad enough, but now we're seeing that John Wisdorf could be just as dangerous. We don't know which one of them is responsible for Carter's death and that makes the stakes just too high." He grasped her head to force her to look at him. "I've stuck with you so far, Taylor, but I think it's time for us to step back. I don't care what you say, you're going to get yourself in trouble. Why don't you listen to me for once, and cool your jets? Let the cops handle this."

"Well, it looks like they're trying to, now," she assured him. Clasping his hands, she dragged them away from her face. He appeared to interpret that move as dissent, so she attempted to mollify him by telling him of the morning visit of Detective Franklin and the officer's interest in Masterson's coworkers. However, she didn't reveal her subsequent conversation with Nate Mueller about checking in on both Ed Guralnik and John Wisdorf. There were still strikes against both of them, and she couldn't leave holes in the puzzle. That wasn't her style.

"Yeah," she concluded, "it looks like the cops are starting to look at Carter's death as more than an interrupted burglary." She squirmed around on the bench and stared at the floor, her posture implying she was giving up.

At least she hoped it implied that.

"Well, there you go," Steve advised. "Leave it alone now. Okay? Promise?"

"Hmmmph." She nodded her head once, which seemed to satisfy him, though *she* wasn't satisfied. She still planned to make her trip to Girdwood the next day.

One nod of the head and a guttural squawk didn't constitute a promise, did it?

FIFTEEN

By noon the next day, Taylor was motoring down the Seward Highway on her way to the town of Girdwood. The small settlement of several thousand year-round residents huddled at the base of 3,939-foot Mt. Alyeska and supported all of the activities of the mountain's ski resort. Girdwood's population tripled during the winter months, when ski chalet owners from Anchorage descended upon the town, and the day-trippers added to the confusion from nine A.M. to ten P.M. Only thirty-five miles from a large metro area, Alyeska Ski Resort was popular with Alaskans, as well as Japanese tourists who flew across the Pacific for a visit.

Fortunately, no hordes of ski fanatics crowded the Seward Highway that spring morning. The next influx of congestion on the road would be from the tourists that visited Alaska in the summer, but not many of them had arrived yet. It was just her and the asphalt that day.

The trip to Girdwood would take her to the cabin of Julie Malcolm and Robert Berndt, and she was looking forward to it.

At least she was looking forward to the drive out there.

As far as the visit was concerned, Taylor's initial introduction to Robert hadn't been all that delightful, and she felt uncomfortable about meeting him again. She still recalled his emotional explosion at the LifeLine office and didn't want a repeat performance.

Considering those factors, she had no idea how things would

go. She hoped Nate was right, that Robert would enjoy talking to her when he knew she needed answers to questions. "He's a real mystery buff," Nate had assured her. "He loves solving riddles, so play up to that."

Not sure if Nate's comment should relieve her, she chose to ignore the possibility of disaster and allowed herself to dwell on the beautiful drive ahead of her.

Twenty miles from Anchorage, well out of the residential areas, she drove past Potter Marsh and slowed slightly as the Seward Highway changed from four lanes to two lanes. Movement on her left caught her attention, and she smiled at the binocular-wielding bird-watchers standing on the boardwalk that encircled the marsh. Obviously these bird-watchers had wanted to get a head start on the tourist season, when the marsh swarmed with visitors admiring the many ducks and geese that called Alaska their summer home.

Fortunately for the bird-watchers, they had beaten the rush. No one else was there. Unfortunately, though, they'd miscalculated the arrival of the waterfowl season and not a single duck was there, either.

Turning her view back to the road ahead, Taylor buzzed past the disappointed bird-watchers. She could imagine their conversation over dinner that night: surely they'd resolve to visit Potter Marsh again, though not before they consulted their animal habitat books more closely.

A half-mile past Potter Marsh, Taylor slowed again when the highway began to curve abruptly. At that point the road was nothing but a narrow stripe of asphalt tracing a line along the bases of sheer granite cliffs. The Seward Highway had been built by blasting through the foothills of the Chugach Range, resulting in the steep rock faces that towered over the highway. The nearly vertical slopes dropped precipitously to the surface of the road, then dropped again to meet the treacherous mudflats of Turnagain Arm.

It was not a road where she cared to lose control of her car.

If she did, she would face two possibilities: smash into solid rock faces like a bug hitting a windshield, or sail off the edge of the highway and ricochet off the train tracks before slamming into the deadly ooze of the tidal flats.

Trying to ignore thoughts of riding her car to Valhalla, she leaned forward to peer through the car's windshield and scan the nearby cliffs. She hoped to glimpse some of the Dall sheep that grazed on the vegetation covering the hills. Frequently they ventured within fifty feet of the highway, emboldened by the vertical rock walls that separated them from the humans below.

She remembered hearing of a visitor who had spotted an injured Dall sheep, a young ewe with a badly mutilated front leg. Apparently, the ewe had misjudged the roughness of the terrain she was scampering across and had taken a nasty fall. When her injury was reported to the Alaska Department of Fish and Game, the ewe was tranquilized and taken to a veterinary hospital for care. After amputation of her shattered leg, she became a ward of the Alaska Zoo where she joined other Dall sheep in one of the many exhibits of the state's indigenous animals.

Taylor smiled when recalling the happy ending to the sheep story. Surely the ewe would've died in the wild, unable to forage for food and in great pain, but now she got regular meals and a chance to work as an ambassador for the animal kingdom. The pilot felt that when city dwellers learned about wild animals, from visiting zoos or reading books, they were more likely to respond positively to protection of the wildlife.

With no sheep making an appearance on the hills, she went back to her driving duties and let her mind wander. She needed to review her plan for the upcoming talk, solidify her strategy. There was no wisdom in blindly charging into the conversation without an agenda.

She'd better stick to her original plan, tell Robert just enough of the facts to get him talking. There was no sense in telling him she suspected former coworkers of murder. Surely that would upset him and he would fall mute at that point.

No, she should do as Nate suggested, let his love of mysteries guide him down the proper path. He may not tell her the exact information she needed, but he could unwittingly make Ed a more likely suspect than John, or vice versa.

After all, he knew both men. Without realizing it, he could provide information that could verify the guilt of a murderer. A murderer he knew.

As she cruised down the Seward Highway, Taylor attempted to concentrate on something else. She had confirmed her strategy, but she didn't want to overanalyze it.

Out of force of habit, she glanced down at her speedometer and recoiled. The needle hovered around seventy-five, and she realized she had been zooming around the highway's narrow curves. She left off the accelerator immediately and let the car coast down to a speed more appropriate to the winding two-lane strip.

She scowled at herself, surprised by how easily she had become distracted by thoughts of murder. She drummed her fingers on the steering wheel and pursed her lips. It amazed her how the content of thoughts affected her actions.

Had it been the same way for Ed or John when they planned to kill Carter Masterson?

She shivered and checked her speedometer once more. *Whoops!* She was doing it again. Every time she thought about Ed, or John, or murder, she unwittingly pushed the accelerator an iota farther down. The frequent curves of the highway didn't really lend themselves to speed, so she'd better watch it.

The scenic wayside ahead caught her eye. A large wooden sign poked out of the ground near the guardrail bordering the turnoff. She knew what the sign said. It was similar to others posted along the highway at scenic points and described what people were looking at, and its historical significance, if any.

From the wayside you could see a receding tide, and the mud of the exposed tidal flats shimmered under a sky that was turning sunny. Another weather change. As she drove past the turnoff, the sight of silty water rippling along the low-tide line reminded her of the previous summer when the gray ooze had captured the attention of many Anchorage residents.

That day highway travelers were stunned when they saw a large pod of killer whales lying on the mud. The black-and-white Orcas appeared to be sunning themselves, like visitors to the beaches of St. Tropez, but in fact they were stranded high and dry.

The biologists summoned to aid the whales pushed through the crowd milling around the scene; a number of the onlookers had actually waded out through the treacherous tidal flats to help the whales.

Eventually the civilians were shooed off and only biologists remained to work with the whales. They watched their charges for hours, watering them down to protect their skin from the harsh summer sun, and just waited for the incoming tide to free the whales from the grip of the mud. When the tide came in, the whales were off, safe and sound.

Taylor smiled at the memory of the crowd cheering as the last orca struggled back into the water.

After bumping across a set of railroad tracks, she came up to the turn toward Girdwood. Just as she braked to swing left off the highway, her stomach emitted a growl like a kettle drum. "So, you think you know where we are, huh?" she said, peering down at her stomach with a grin. "Okay, I'll stop. Quit your blubbering." She cranked the steering wheel over to the right and stopped at the small mom-and-pop grocery on the corner. "Are you satisfied now?" she said to her stomach, and jumped out of the car.

Two minutes later, she climbed back into the Suzuki and proceeded to peel the Saran Wrap off an enormous Rice Krispies Treat. "Mmmmm. I'm glad they're still making these. I thought they only made them during the winter for the skiers," she said out loud. She patted her tummy affectionately. "Good idea to stop, I'm glad I brought you along." She snickered at her own wisecrack—she was such a wit.

Turning back onto the road, she continued toward Girdwood and the Alyeska Ski Resort. She stared at the mountains that made up the resort. They looked so daunting, so formidable, so . . . so *steep*. It was hard to remember she had covered every trail on those mountains, top to bottom, without even flinching. Had she been braver during the days when she actually had time to go skiing?

She hoped she could act just as resolutely during her visit with Robert and Julie. This may become a turning point in her investigation of Carter Masterson's death, and she needed to handle it skillfully. Possibly both of them could steer her in the right direction in the investigation if she was able to read their comments correctly.

SIXTEEN

As she entered residential Girdwood, she fumbled in her jacket for the directions to Robert and Julie's chalet. She glanced down at the scrap of paper she'd extracted from her pocket and squinted at the scribbles. "Let's see, drive past the turnoff to Crow Creek Pass Mine"—she studied a wooden arrow pointing to the north—"then take a right on Timberline."

Her eyes darted back and forth across the road for a few seconds before she reached a small thicket of spruce trees. Branches drooping off the trees nearly hid the white letters on a green street sign, and she slowed to read them. "Hmmmm. T-I-M-B . . . Here we are, Timberline."

With a tug on the steering wheel, she turned to the right off the Alyeska Highway. The Suzuki banged and rattled as it connected with the bumpy surface of the gravel road, and she downshifted to reduce her speed. Glancing down at her crumpled paper, she muttered, "Follow Timberline for a third of a mile, past Vail"—she nodded as she passed another sign—"turn right on Alpina. First house on the left, blue trim on natural cedar." She shoved the directions back into her jacket pocket and set her eyes on a small A-frame chalet directly ahead. "This must be it," she said as she swung into a narrow driveway.

The Suzuki puffed and snorted for a few seconds after she turned the ignition off, and she glared at it. "Time for a tune-up," she muttered, then looked up to scan the chalet.

It was beautiful, very typical of the vacation homes that made up Girdwood. Stained and log-oiled cedar covered its exterior, and windows filled the entire front of the A-frame. It was apparent that anyone inside the house could look right out on to the slopes of Max's Mountain, the centerpiece of Alyeska Ski Resort.

The A-frame seemed to form the vertical stem of a capital *T,* the rectangular addition behind the A-frame its horizontal top. The right arm of the *T* was a garage—a rarity among the seasonal homes—and the left arm sported even more windows. Though the chalet was small, it looked expensive and Taylor wondered how Robert afforded it now that he no longer made a Learjet captain's salary.

Maybe he had some kind of disability insurance, along with investments. Undoubtedly, Julie contributed her flight nurse's pay to the family coffers, too. A very contemporary arrangement.

Once it became obvious that she was wasting time by examining her surroundings, she forced herself to clamber out of the Suzuki. Hitching her pants up, she walked to the house and looked at the doorbell for a long second.

She had to assume the meeting would go well, but even so, she was still a bit apprehensive. She felt as though a lot rode on the success of her conversation with Robert and Julie. She might learn a great deal that could aid her investigation of Carter's death, or she could fall flat on her face by upsetting them for some reason.

The memory of Robert's volatile temperament, the one he exhibited the day he dropped by LifeLine, was firm in her mind. She didn't want to set him off, but she didn't even know what the trigger would be.

Summoning her resolve, she reached out and rang the doorbell.

Thirty seconds later the slender, dark-haired figure of Julie opened the door. "Hi, there," she greeted Taylor as she leaned on the doorjamb. The many silver bracelets encircling her wrist tinkled musically as she reached to wave the other woman into the house. "You're right on time. Most people miscalculate how long it takes to drive to Girdwood, and I was expecting you a few minutes later. I was just finishing up with a rocker I'm staining." The flight nurse swiped at her bangs with ochre-tinted fingers, and flipped her hand over to regard the telltale dark smudges. She looked up sheepishly. "I guess I pay for being a do-it-yourselfer."

Taylor gave Julie a reassuring smile. "Hey, I do the same thing. I hate paying good money for something I can do myself."

"Well, I guess so. Didn't you build your own house?"

"Yeah, but it's more of a cabin. Not too big. A little smaller than your place here." Taylor closed the door behind her, and when she did an odd odor assaulted her nostrils. It was a combination of Danish Finishing Oil, a smell she recognized from work that she'd done on her own furniture, and . . . salad greens? Weird combination.

"Come into the living room," Julie offered, gesturing at the glassed-in A-frame section of the house. "I'll get Robert. I've got some water on the stove, can I bring you anything . . . tea, coffee?" She walked toward the kitchen, glancing over her shoulder to catch Taylor's answer.

"Some tea would be nice," Taylor answered before she turned to peer through the big windows at the spectacular view. Julie's agreeable disposition was relaxing her; maybe the visit would be a useful one, and Robert wouldn't explode.

The sounds of Julie rustling around in a cupboard bled into the living room, accompanied by her call to another part of the house. "Robert," she yelled, "Taylor Morgan is here. I told you about that—you want to come in?"

A muffled voice answered in the affirmative, a door opened and closed, and the sturdy clunk of footsteps resounded nearby.

"So you're Taylor Morgan," said a hesitant, gravelly voice a second later. She swung around when she heard Robert. His voice was the same one she remembered from the office, though its slurred quality had lessened. He was pulling a canvas apron over his head, the logo for Home Depot stenciled on the fabric. His well-worn Levi's sported twin smudges of brown on the knees. The sleeves of his red-and-blue plaid flannel shirt were rolled.

He peered at her in curiosity as he hung the apron from a wall peg. "I've met you, haven't I? You look familiar."

She gulped. "Yes, you have. I was in the LifeLine office when you stopped by a few days ago. You were . . . You stopped by to—"

He interrupted her broken explanation and waved his hand irritably. "Yeah, now I remember." His features drew taut, then

ke into a more genial mien a moment later. He stepped into
e living room. "So, what can I do for you? Julie said you
anted to talk to us."

About that time Julie walked in from the kitchen and handed
a steaming mug to Taylor. "This is orange pekoe," she said. "I
hope that's okay." She offered one to Robert as well and sat
on a couch upholstered in a burgundy velveteen. "You were
going to tell Robert why you wanted to talk to us. I'm rather
curious about that, too. Your phone call was somewhat cryp-
tic."

Taylor looked at Julie, then back at Robert, and cocked her
head. Keep it simple, she said to herself. *Don't tell them any
more than they have to know.* Ed and John were the ones she
needed information on, not them. "Well, I'm kind of embarrassed by this," she said as she cupped the mug between her
hands. "I don't want you to think that I'm paranoid. . . ."

Julie laughed a dainty laugh. "Sometimes paranoia is warranted in these crazy days we live in. Don't feel uneasy."

The attempt to loosen her up was not lost on Taylor, and she
felt grateful. No wonder Julie was a nurse—she wanted to make
people feel better in many ways. "Okay, here it goes. I'm sure
you heard of Carter Masterson's death." She hesitated for a
moment before she picked up on the nods from both Julie and
Robert. "Also, you may have heard that the police thought he
was shot by a burglar he surprised."

"Yes, I was shocked when I read that in the newspaper," said
Robert in an ambivalent voice. "Anchorage is getting so violent. I'm glad we can escape to Girdwood from time to time—
it's a lot quieter here."

"I'm sure it is," Taylor agreed. "It's lovely out here." She
glanced out the front windows at the greening foliage on the
nearby mountains. "Anyway, a homicide detective stopped by
the office yesterday, wanted to talk to Carter's coworkers."

"What?" A look of puzzlement shone on Robert's face. "The
police are talking to the coworkers? Are the coworkers suspects? I thought you said it was a robbery, I can't imagine any
of the guys I know becoming burglars."

"Well, I'm assuming that the detective wanted to get some
overview on the case, get some clues to the robbery. I think
it's typical to interview everyone close to the victim: coworkers, family members, friends . . . Everyone is a suspect or a
source of information."

Robert nodded. "Yeah, I guess that's true." He raised ,
eyebrows and started rubbing his mug with a thumb. "If it
standard operating procedure to do that, it sounds like a wast
of time in this case. At least, talking to the coworkers woul
be. Everyone liked Carter, and people don't plan to burglarize
their friends' homes. Plus, none of the pilots would have a
reason to do that—they get paid well." He paused and seemed
to ruminate on that comment, then stared at Taylor. "You
would know that. Anyway, what's your connection to Carter's
death, anyway? Why are you so interested in it? I didn't know
you were a friend of his."

"Well, I am. Since you don't know me—I was hired after
you got hurt—you wouldn't know this, but I'd been friends
with Carter for several years. That's why I want his death in-
vestigated more diligently. I think the police are moving too
slowly. Their track record isn't too good so far—nothing had
happened with anything until yesterday, when that detective
poked around the office." Taylor breathed in the spicy aroma
of her tea and took a tentative sip. It wasn't too hot, so she
took another.

"I'd like to look into Carter's death," she continued. "I think
I'd bring a different focus on it. As a pilot, I'd know things
the police wouldn't know, things they wouldn't even know how
to find." She took another sip of tea and glanced over the rim
of her mug to see how Robert was taking things. He seemed
attentive and curious, but not anxious.

So far, so good.

"Of course, I have to do this looking around from the side-
lines. I doubt the police would appreciate help from an amateur.
In the same vein, I'd appreciate it if you could remain close-
lipped about our talk."

Robert turned toward Julie, who shrugged noncommittally.
"I can do that," she said, "especially if you can speed up the
process of finding Carter's killer."

"Yeah, I'd like that, too," Robert chimed in. A concerned
expression glossed his features. "Carter was a friend. He flew
with me as a copilot, then took my place after my injury. Of
course I want the slimeball that killed him tried for murder,
and I'll help as much as I can."

"Okay, great." Taylor felt herself relax. She had persuaded
Robert to talk to her, and it appeared that he didn't realize she
had a hidden agenda. She hadn't said anything about Ed or

John, or that she was investigating a planned murder, not a botched burglary. "So, that's why I wanted to talk to you. I was hoping to get some ideas about his death. I want to look into some things, talk to some folks he knew. That would speed up the investigation; perhaps the police could discover Carter's killer sooner. I sure don't like the idea of a killer going free—"

"Neither do I," retorted Robert with a scowl. He sat down next to Julie on the sofa and gestured at a nearby armchair. As Taylor sank into it, Robert tilted his head back to study the ceiling. "First thing we have to think of is who would benefit from robbing Carter. We need a motive." He lowered his gaze to look across the room to the other woman, and stared at her for a good ten seconds. "How about one of the rampers? They're always broke, they've got these gas-guzzling roadsters that must eat money like it's going out of style. That's a pretty good motive. I would think that a well-paid Lear captain would look like an easy target to them."

He pointed a finger at Taylor. "Plus, they knew Carter, they knew his schedule, they could plan a robbery for a time when he was gone and they were free. There's your opportunity. As for the means . . ." He absently fingered the stain on his jeans. "Guns are easy to find—most teenagers know where to get one. Means is obvious."

"Rampers, huh? Yeah, that's a thought." Taylor leaned forward in her chair. She could see Robert was falling into mystery fan mode, reciting means, motive, and opportunity like an expert. She was definitely going to play on that. "But what about evidence? The cops didn't find any fingerprints, they didn't find a weapon at the crime scene or anywhere else. All they found were things in the apartment that looked as though they'd been rifled through. Looked like a disrupted robbery, but they didn't have specific clues."

"Yes, I recall that," Julie said. "Don't you remember the newspaper report, Robert? There wasn't any mention of evidence."

"Hmmm, I'd forgotten." Robert entwined his fingertips in the classic Sherlock Holmes deep-thought pose. "No fingerprints or other evidence. That's odd. Those rampers don't impress me as sophisticated types. I doubt they would know to clean up a crime scene before they left. They probably didn't even know what kind of evidence the police collect." He leveled his gaze on Taylor and arched his eyebrows expectantly. "What does that suggest to you?"

Taylor shook her head. She wasn't going to play this game; she wanted *him* to talk. She wouldn't tell him what she thought.

With a snort, as though disgusted with her stupidity, he growled, "An accomplice! That's what you should be thinking—there was a clever accomplice! Don't you see that? There was someone smart enough to plan the robbery, supervise its execution, tell them not to leave any evidence at the crime scene. He'd let the rampers do the dirty work and take the risks, while he orchestrated everything from the wings. The rampers would get a share of the proceeds from the robbery, he'd avoid arrest, and everybody'd be happy."

Julie looked at Robert and nodded. "That makes sense, honey. Doesn't it, Taylor?"

Taylor could see that Julie was proud of him for figuring it out, but it only made *her* frown.

Robert was going off in a direction that didn't give her any of the information she needed. She had thought bringing up the lack of evidence would bring him to the conclusion that Carter's death was not related to a failed robbery. She hoped that would prompt him to examine something else, something that could confirm her suspicions of murder.

But, noooo. Damn.

"What do you suggest, then?" Taylor wanted to take another stab at it. "Who do you think this *leader* could be? Someone at work?"

"No, no," he groaned. "I already said that the other pilots don't have a motive for robbery; they make plenty of money. You should know that, you get a paycheck. The pilots don't even have a means, none of them own guns. At least, they didn't when I was around." His eyes got glassy and he crossed his arms across his chest. For a few seconds he seemed to be running down a list in his mind. Then his eyes regained their focus and he cleared his throat. "I can think of one person at work that *would* have a motive. Someone that could get co-operation from the rampers without any sweat at all."

Shifting in her seat, Taylor narrowed her gaze. Maybe Robert was going to say something about Ed, or John. They had occasion to work with the rampers when they needed an aircraft prepared for a flight. "Who do you think could be behind this, Robert?" she asked, on edge.

"Nathan Mueller," he said. "Nate." He hardened his gaze and started to count on his fingers. "First, means: he has a gun, I've seen it. He could've given it to the ramper for the robbery. Second, motive: Nate's always having money problems, has been for some time. I guess he can't budget his salary, or his tastes are too extravagant. Third, opportunity: he knows Carter's schedule forward and backward. He's the one who draws it up. He could put Carter on nighttime call, plan the robbery for when Carter's taken a flight."

Taylor peered at her toes to hide her face, sure it displayed her obvious disbelief. Then her head jerked up and she squawked, "Nighttime call! Damn! My schedule changed from day to night today, and I gotta get back to town!" She leaped to her feet and stared at her watch. "I have to make tracks. I've got sixty miles to drive before six o'clock! Damn!" She fumbled at the waistband of her jeans, and her eyes widened in horror.

No pager hung there.

"Oh, no, I don't have my beeper with me. They can't even get to me while I'm on my way to town. I can't believe I screwed up like this. I've never forgotten my beeper before." Making a desperate face, she ran past a startled Julie and glanced back at Robert. She thought she saw a subtle smile on his face as she dashed by. Surely every medevac pilot had gone through similar panic, and he was probably stifling his laughter.

This is making a good impression, she agonized.

Over her shoulder she yelled her thanks to Julie for the tea and vaulted out the door toward her car.

SEVENTEEN

The door of Taylor's cabin slammed open and she hurtled through it. Puffing from the sprint from her car, she lunged toward the small sofa's end table and snatched up her pager. In one fluid move she flipped its switch to ON and swung around.

Breathing hard, she focused on the display of her desktop stereo that sat across the room. Its red LED digits glowed at her like a bank's time and temperature sign, reading 6:02 P.M. When she realized she'd made it home to her pager nearly on time, she relaxed and collapsed on the sofa.

Blowing her bangs off her face with a noisy *Pphhtt!*, she slumped against the cushions. She'd lucked out. And she didn't want to go through that again; a close call probably wouldn't turn out as well a second time. To forget to preplan was bad enough, but to have the lack of preplanning result in heart-stopping anxiety was worse.

While she had ordered herself to slow down on the way out to Girdwood, she had been praying that no cops would stop her for speeding on her way home. As she raced down the winding two-lane highway, narrowly missing rocks that had tumbled onto the asphalt from the steep cliffs, she had implored the Suzuki not to break down if she nailed one. No car—certainly not her ninety thousand-plus mile vehicle—could withstand that kind of torture.

And she couldn't afford to be late.

But she'd made it. Several minutes after setting her pager back on its stand—and once she'd ceased to gasp—she stumbled toward the refrigerator. The panic that had accompanied her all through her dash home from Girdwood was gone, and more mundane anxieties had erupted.

Now she was hungry.

Her last meal had consisted of nothing but the giant Rice Krispies Treat she'd bought in Girdwood, and she needed some proper food for dinner. She'd better take care of her hunger; she'd require some energy if she got a medevac call that night.

Pulling the freezer section open, she peered inside. "Let's see. Three Bean Chili, Linguine in Marinara Sauce, Oriental Vegetables Medley . . . that's it? I gotta learn how to cook." At age thirty-seven, she still existed on pre-prepared meals, just like a teenager who'd been kicked out of the house at the age of maturity. Wrinkling her nose, she noted the sorry state of her refrigerator and decided to enroll in a cooking class for vegans.

If there was such an animal.

The box of frozen chili occupied the top of the pile, so she grabbed it and shoved it in the microwave oven. While the small machine hummed energetically she collected some utensils and poured herself a glass of juice. She stood in front of the oven as it purred, sipping as she mused about who'd actually invented the microwave. It was easily the most effective time saver developed in the twentieth century as far as she was concerned, and its creator must have become a millionaire from selling the plans. Two minutes later a metallic *ding!* interrupted her reverie, and she extracted her dinner.

"I'm not much of a gourmet, am I?" she confessed to the steaming carton of chili. Then she frowned as she contemplated the fact that she was talking to her food. Again. "Get a life, Taylor," she admonished herself.

With that thought banging around in her head, she sat down and applied her fork to her chili. No sense in putting the meal on a plate; she'd eat it right out of its container.

The aroma of spice and beans wafted up to her nostrils and she shoveled a fork full of them into her mouth. In mid-chew, the temperature of the chili reached her nerve endings and she gasped. "Yoow!"

Instinctively she reached for a nearby magazine and fanned her mouth vigorously. She figured it might be sacrilege to use

Professional Pilot as a pair of bellows, but what the heck. It worked for her.

As she ventilated her burning mouth she reflected on her visit to Robert and Julie's chalet. Her talk with them had confused her, and she wanted to discuss her afternoon with Steve. Without thinking about it, she reached across the table and yanked the phone closer so she could dial his number.

Seconds later she froze in magazine mid-wave, then cradled the receiver. She couldn't call him. He didn't know where she'd gone that afternoon, and for that matter she didn't *want* him to know. Certainly he had assumed that she would give up on her search for a killer, and she liked it that way.

However, the afternoon had left her wired. She still wanted to talk to him. Reminding herself to be circumspect about what she said, she dialed again. Since she was on nighttime call for the next seven days, they couldn't plan anything for that evening, but at least they could chat. He was still on daytime call, so he must be off duty by now and was probably sitting home watching television.

Waiting for *her* to call, wondering where she'd been all day.

She dialed, but after seven rings she hung up the phone. Looked like Steve actually had a life, which was more than she could say about herself. He was probably at an organizational meeting for that softball team he wanted to join. Softball season was starting soon; that'd make sense. She felt a bit disappointed because he wasn't home, since the idea of talking to him had sounded good right then. Making a face, she took another bite of chili.

Now what? She didn't feel like watching TV herself, and she didn't have a VCR, so videos were out, too. How else could she keep herself awake until midnight, when she'd dare to go to bed? If she didn't get a medevac call by then, chances are she wouldn't get one at all.

She'd already finished her magazine and hadn't gone to the library or the bookstore earlier for anything else. She didn't feel like going there now, she was at a loss. Maybe she'd run over to the hanger and sit around there for a while, kill a few hours before the *Jay Leno Show* came on at eleven.

Anyway, she needed to do some thinking, and she did her best thinking around airplanes.

•   •   •

Pulling into the LifeLine lot, she coasted into a parking space. Grinning, she noted that the lights were on in the office and Nate's car sat near the door. Oh boy, she thought. Here's someone to talk to about her afternoon trip. Her coworker had been the one to suggest the visit to Girdwood, so he'd probably want to know how it had gone.

Then she backtracked. She couldn't tell the office manager of her talk with Robert and Julie—the ex-pilot had implicated Nate in Carter Masterson's murder. She couldn't drop that bombshell on him; no way could she predict how he'd react. *Damn.*

Fuming, she exited her vehicle and plodded toward the office. *This was no fun.* She couldn't tell anyone what she was dying to tell *somebody.*

Turning the knob, she opened the door. Nate looked up instantly, as frantic as a deer caught in a car's headlights. "T-Taylor!" he croaked. "What are you doing here?" He pushed the papers he was holding back into the file cabinet where he stood. "You scared the hell out of me. I didn't hear your Suzuki."

She'd scared him? Why? What had he been doing?

"I parked in the middle of the lot, Nate," she explained. "That's probably why you didn't hear me. Anyway, what are *you* doing here? Heartburn keeping you up?"

Nate laughed and seemed to calm himself. "Naw. I'm just looking at the resumes we've got for Lear captains. We still haven't hired anybody, and the guys are getting tired of no weeks off. Gotta get somebody here soon." He shoved the file drawer closed. "All done for the night, though. I guess I'll get out of here."

Her eyebrows arched. "That was a fast visit. I just got here. Was it something I said?"

He shrugged. "No, it wasn't. I got here half an hour ago, and I can only look at resumes once or twice and I'm bored. I'm going to run some names past Dan Skinner tonight, though. *He's* the chief pilot; he makes the decision on hiring, not me. Maybe if he decides who to go with, I can make a few calls tomorrow. Get this whole shindig done with." He walked to the coatrack and grabbed his jacket. "Is that approved?"

"Yes, that's approved. And you're excused." She snapped off a salute to his departing form.

Alone again, she sighed and tossed her jacket over the back

of Nate's vacant chair. Wandering across the office, she stepped into the locker room and exited into the hangar. She wanted to sit in the King Air for a bit, align the disparate thoughts wadded into a ball in her head. Maybe the atmosphere inside the aircraft would be soothing enough to allow her to do that.

It usually did when she was flying; why not when she was on the ground?

She glanced at the pair of burgundy-and-silver-striped King Airs sitting on her side of the hangar and craned her head to spot the Learjet she assumed was behind them. Adjusting her trajectory to swing around to the King Airs, she decided to climb into the Learjet instead. Perhaps sitting there would feel better—that airplane pushed buttons she didn't know she had, and just the smell of its interior made her orgasmic. Maybe her brain would work more efficiently after a hormone boost.

When she angled around the King Air's nose, she halted. The Learjet wasn't there. She frowned in disappointment—she had been all primed. *Oh well,* she thought, *it's on a medevac. That's what it's for, anyway.*

Curious about where it had gone and when it would be back, she strode back into the office. The schedule would tell her the facts.

Back in the office, she glanced at the white surface of the data board. In Magic Marker Nate had scrawled the Learjet's crew, destination, takeoff time and estimated return. Steve Derossett and Thomas Lauder had left for the Alaska Peninsula town of King Salmon at fifteen hundred hours—three o'clock— and were due back at eighteen hundred—six o'clock.

Steve was still flying? No wonder he hadn't answered his phone.

Glancing at her watch, she realized the jet was late. Two hours late. Assuming the inevitable, she figured they'd hit a snag in King Salmon and would be back soon. Maybe a few minutes. Resigning herself to a short wait, she headed back to the hangar and climbed into the King Air. Once settled in the copilot's seat, she flipped up the master electrical switch and tuned the radio to the control tower's frequency. By monitoring the radio she'd hear the air traffic controller communicate with the jet when it approached Anchorage, and she could be waiting when it got home.

●　　●　　●

As she stood in the small opening next to the larger hangar door, Taylor spotted the sleek burgundy-and-silver form of the returning Learjet. It taxied onto the asphalt of the LifeLine ramp and swung over next to a waiting ambulance. Steve and Thomas jumped down the airstair once the jet had been shut down and aided the paramedics in sliding a stretcher out from the cabin. Two nurses—Jude Macabee and Colleen Everett— emerged from the jet and followed the procession back to the emergency vehicle.

Right before a paramedic prepared to shut the ambulance's rear door, Colleen reached out to stop him and jumped out of the vehicle. "I gotta get something out of the jet for this guy," she called over her shoulder. She ran back to the jet and scrambled up the airstair.

A second later, her head popped back out. "I don't see it," she yelled. "He said that asthma medication was in his jacket?" Jude shouted back from the ambulance in the affirmative, and Colleen disappeared again.

When she reappeared with a plastic vial in one hand, the lights on the ambulance began to flash in preparation to leave. She dashed across the tarmac and jumped into the vehicle. The door closed behind her, and the ambulance raced around the corner of the building, red strobes blinking.

Steve and Thomas watched the ambulance drive off, then headed back into the Learjet. A moment later they emerged from the jet, lugging their flight bags. They conversed animatedly together as they walked, then Steve tossed his head and laughed uproariously.

Taylor envied Steve for his ability to maintain some composure right after completing a medevac. She was usually so wired she couldn't think about anything else for some time.

"What are you laughing about?" she asked when she stepped away from the door.

Steve missed a step when he heard her speak, and his face darted away from that of his companion. "Taylor, what are you doing here?"

"Just killing some time." She shrugged. "How was King Salmon?"

"Same-o, same-o," Thomas replied. "Actually, more same-o than usual. We musta sat in the Lear for a coupla hours waiting for that patient. You know how that is."

Smiling, she nodded. She *did* know how that was. As the

two men approached, she remembered when she had recently watched Steve and Kai Huskisson do the same thing. Where her partner and his hunky copilot had looked like two peas from the same pod, the blond man and his current copilot didn't even look like they came from the same vegetable garden.

Thomas was older than Steve, portlier than Steve, balder than Steve, even shorter than Steve. Even though they had the same hair color and wore identical Nomex coveralls, that's where the resemblance ended. The thick lenses of the other man's glasses clouded the watery gray of his eyes, and pudgy fingers were wrapped around the handles of his flight case.

Whatever happened to her assumption that all Lear pilots were studmuffins?

"Well, I better get out of here, Steve," Thomas said as he prepared to head for the locker room and a change of clothes. "My wife is trying out the new kitchen grill and I want to be there when she sets the house on fire. I'll leave you two alone so you can do whatever you were going to do." Leering at them, he headed across the tarmac.

"What are you doing here this late?" Steve asked when Thomas had left. "I'm taking off as soon as they bring the jet in. I've been on duty since this morning. You want to come back to my place?" He gestured with his head at the hangar and resumed his walk toward it.

She glanced at the Learjet and swung around to parallel his path. "Okay. But I'm on duty tonight, so I might get beeped. My assignment just changed from days." She upped her pace to match his long-legged stride. "Anyway, tell me about the medevac you just came back from."

He shifted his flight case from his right hand to his left and started unzipping his overalls. "Come on in, I want to get out of this zoot suit. I'll tell you on the way." Their footsteps echoed in the cavernous hangar as they stepped through the door and crossed the floor.

"That medevac was to King Salmon," he continued. "Some guy fishing on the Kvichak River got worked over by a brown bear."

"Wow, ouch!" Taylor shuddered violently and crossed her arms over her chest as though she were protecting her breasts from a bear's teeth. "Did the guy get hurt badly? I know a big brownie can do a number on just about anything."

They strolled into the locker room. Laughing, he reached to

unlock his locker. "This guy really lucked out. He was looking for a bush to pee on when he surprised a sow and cubs—"

"A sow and cubs? You can't get any more dangerous than that! She must've had him for lunch!"

"Naw, like I said, he was lucky. The sow just wanted to threaten him long enough to give the cubs a chance to escape, so she only chewed on him a little before she gave up and took off. Once his buddies found him they dragged him back to their floatplane and flew him to the nearest town for medical help."

He stepped out of his coveralls. "The nearest clinic was in King Salmon," he added, shaking imaginary dirt off the fabric. "That's where we picked him up. The health aide there was able to stop the bleeding, but he needs some major restructuring of his arm and chest." He hung his coveralls from the locker's hook and picked up his flight case from the floor. Hoisting it into the locker, he dropped it next to his coverall's dangling legs. "This guy's going to have some scars that'll be real conversation starters at parties."

Taylor wrinkled her brow. "But if he was getting attacked by a bear, why didn't he use some bear repellent on her? You know, that cayenne pepper spray? I know that stuff works pretty good, didn't he have any?"

"Well, yeah, he *did* have bear repellent. Unfortunately, it was in his jacket, and the jacket was lying on the stream bank three hundred yards away." Steve chortled at the irony. "He'll probably wear that repellent can around his neck like a Saint Christopher medal from now on." He slammed the door of his locker and leaned back on it.

"Yikes. I guess so." Of the many injured people she'd flown back to Anchorage, she'd never had anyone mauled by a bear in her plane. That was because most victims of savage bear attacks didn't survive. The fisherman had been luckier than he could ever imagine.

The thought of rapier-sharp claws tearing into living flesh made her shiver, and she abruptly changed the subject. "Anyway, do you remember when you told me that I'd get my turn at the Learjet one of these days?"

The chuckle from Steve indicated that he remembered the comment, but might have regretted making it. "Yeah, I remember, but the operative words there were 'one of these days.' You're not too far off from an upgrade, but we're hiring a new captain right now, not a copilot. Don't get so impatient."

"Well, I've got to amuse myself until about midnight. Better here than your condo. Maybe you can humor me by giving me a short Lear tutorial," she begged.

She hoped her supplicant look and tone would make him relent. Even though she hated to resort to feminine wiles to get her way, she would do it this time.

This was important: she was dying to get her hands on that jet. She knew she'd never get to do anything but sit in it and look over the cockpit, but that was enough for then. There was something to be said for hangar flying.

Smiling, Steve shook his head as to say "I can't believe I'm doing this," then swept his hand toward the hangar. "Okay, I've got a few hours. Let's go see how you do."

EIGHTEEN

Muzzling a grin, Taylor marched off toward the Learjet. The sleek jet's shiny exterior gleamed under the hangar's dull lighting, and its airstair poked out of the front of the fuselage like an odd appendage. Upon reaching the steps near its nose, she climbed them and peered into the jet's cabin as though for the first time.

In a way, it was her first time. She had never entered the Learjet for the explicit reason of learning something about it. Taking the first step in exploring it was a miniadventure in itself. Before she had been nothing but a passerby, but now she felt like more.

Only dim illumination flowed into the jet's cabin, but that was enough for her to navigate inside. While scanning the medical accoutrements, she spotted a red nylon jacket thrown over one of the rear seats. Shaking her head and smiling, she walked over. She grabbed it, then began to paw through its pockets.

"Is this the jacket that got left on the stream bank, the one with the bear repellent in it?" she asked Steve when he climbed through the airstair door.

"Yeah, I guess so. Where'd you find it?"

"It was hanging back here. I guess it got left behind."

Steve snorted. "Looks like the owner of that jacket isn't too concerned about it now, once he doesn't need to get to that pepper spray."

Digging into one pocket, then the other, Taylor gazed up

with a puzzled expression. "I don't see any spray in here. Do you suppose he never had the stuff with him to begin with?"

"Nah, it was probably there at one point. That coat's been tossed in and out of airplanes, in and out of vehicles. The repellent could've fallen out anywhere. For all we know, some bear at the Kvichak River is sniffing at it right now."

"That'd be ironic." She draped the jacket back over the seat, and walked forward to the cockpit. After surveying the closeness of the seats, she motioned to Steve. "After you, kind sir. I'll get in once you've managed to wiggle your butt into your seat."

A minute later they were ensconced in the cockpit, Taylor in the copilot's seat, Steve in the captain's. She surveyed the panel in front of her wistfully. How long before she sat there for real, as part of the actual flight crew departing for a medevac? Whatever the time span before her upgrade, she couldn't wait.

Stifling her longing, she got back to business. She scanned the panel in front of her. Most of the flight instruments were familiar to her—she had seen similar gauges in all of the planes she had flown—but the instruments peculiar to a jet were new to her.

That was part of her attraction to the Learjet: it was a highly complex aircraft that demanded a lot from a pilot in the way of brains as well as pure physical skill. If she wanted to prove to the world that she was a competent pilot, securing a slot as a Lear crew member would do it. Her reconnaissance of the cockpit felt like the first step to that, as if she were an explorer charting potentially dangerous territory. If she couldn't digest the intricacies of the jet, she'd flunk the first test.

Even so, her initial foray into learning the new aircraft thrilled her. Everything about the Lear seemed to have an effect on her.

Once Taylor had adjusted her perch, Steve flipped on the master electrical switch. The annunciator lights came up a millisecond later. A curious sensation passed through her the instant the beams of red, orange, yellow, and white flooded the darkened cockpit, and the hair on her nape stood on end. She'd never been in there at night before, and it made her shiver.

"You know, Steve," she confessed, "when you flipped the master on to power up the lights, I felt like it was hardwired directly to me." She glanced around the cockpit appreciatively.

"I know I've been in here with you before, but this time it feels different somehow."

It animated her, the thought that some day she could be in command of the sophisticated aircraft in which she now sat. Just studying the Learjet cockpit made her feel mesmerized.

"Steve?"

He dropped his hand from the master switch. "Hmmm?"

"Do you think you can lust after an inanimate object?"

"What do you mean?" he asked curiously.

"Well, if I could give a name to what I feel when I look at the Lear, I'd have to call it lust. It gives me a hard-on. Of course, I don't have the equipment for that, but you know what I mean."

Steve smiled as he shook his head in amazement. "I don't know, Taylor. Maybe you should see a therapist about that," he joked. "Is there something I don't know about you?" He cocked his head and peered at her, then broke the pose to laugh. "If you knew what I know about flying this bird, you'd look at it differently. It can bore the hell out of you. But enough of that . . . what do you want to know first?"

Arching one eyebrow, she held her hands up in a fill-me-with-knowledge gesture. "How do you get out of coffin corner?" she asked slyly.

"Coffin corner?" He gaped at her. "How do you know about that?"

"I hear things." She grinned, glad to have surprised him. She figured he assumed she didn't know anything about the Lear. But then she had to admit, "I don't know what it is, but I know you don't want to get in it. So tell me."

"All right. The technical answer is: you wind up in coffin corner when your limiting Mach factor runs up against your stall speed."

Now it was *her* turn to gape at him. "Huh? Plain English, please."

His wry expression had *gotcha* written all over it. "Okay. It's easier to explain using a few props. See this thing here?" He pointed to a black-and-white-striped needle on the airspeed indicator.

"The barber pole?"

"Yeah, the barber pole. It displays your limiting Mach factor. That's like a never-exceed speed in a plane that is unable to reach the speed of sound." He glanced at her to gauge her comprehension, then nodded and continued. "The barber pole changes position with your altitude, indicating a lower critical airspeed as altitude increases. Your stall speed is a constant"— he tapped on a red tick on the airspeed dial—"but the Mach factor changes as you climb. The barber pole is constantly lowering, and the stall speed stays fixed . . . and when the two connect, like around forty-three, forty-five thousand, you've entered coffin corner. You can't fly any slower to stay below the limiting Mach because you'll stall, and you can't fly any faster to prevent the stall because you'll exceed the limiting Mach. The proverbial rock and a hard place." He tipped his head back and barked an anxious laugh. "The only thing you can do to get out of it is descend. You better hope you can."

She could see that the thought of encountering that kind of no-win situation had him rattled. She attempted to reassure him by noting that he'd never find himself in a similar plight. "You'd have to be brain-dead to get yourself squeezed up against the edge of the envelope like that," she pointed out. "I don't think you'd ever do that."

"Well, let's hope." He grimaced, obviously running the scene he'd just described through his mind. "Anyway," he muttered, "let's talk about something else. How about the rest of the gauges up front?" He launched into a description of the rest of the panel, then started on the engine fire extinguishing system.

"Hey, want to know a tip on handling passengers that are getting too obnoxious?" Steve asked her at a breaking point. "This is a trade secret—only Lear pilots know it. Keep it in your hat."

"Hey, mum's the word. Tell me." Taylor welcomed that comment. She felt like one of the members of the Learjet clan, hearing privileged information. Almost like a secret handshake.

Of course, she was sure the tip Steve had ready for her was not *that* exclusive, but it served her fantasy to ignore the reality.

Steve smiled at the funny look on Taylor's face, then started to talk about ornery passengers. "Okay, say you've got some rock band that you're flying from gig to gig. They get pretty loose after a concert, and they're taking it out on the plane. If you want to turn their lights off, just do this."

He pointed at a silver lever, next to a sign stenciled on the metal of the panel that read: PRESSURIZATION. "Remember, I told you this controlled the cabin pressurization, right? Just like in the King Air. Well, usually it's set on automatic, and it takes care of itself. But if you want, you can set it on manual, and change the cabin pressure yourself. If the guys are cutting up too much in the back, just raise the cabin pressure to, say, twenty thousand feet. That decreases the oxygen content of the cabin air to what it would be that high, like on the top of a mountain. That puts them to sleep in about a minute. Works every time."

Steve chortled about that.

Taylor shook her head, squinting at him. "You think this is a Learjet secret?" She laughed. "That's one of the first things I learned when I got upgraded to King Air captain. I thought you were going to tell me something I could use someday. Sheesh."

"Hmmm." Steve fingered his blond moustache, then shrugged. "Yeah, I guess you would've heard about that by now. Anyway, I've told you everything I can about the stuff up front, so I guess we're done for now. Unless there's anything else?" Preparing to leave the cockpit, Steve reached to flip the master electrical switch to Off.

"Don't turn that off," Taylor said, gesturing at his hand. "I kinda like sitting in here with the lights on."

The feelings Taylor was drawing from her surroundings still charged through her system, and she wanted to enjoy them a bit longer. Even though she wasn't sure what prompted them, she knew she'd feel somewhat differently if it had been daytime and someone else was discussing the Lear with her.

But it wasn't daytime, and it wasn't anyone else talking to her.

Almost without thinking, she dropped her hand on Steve's thigh and began tracing geometrical figures on it. The denim swished softly as her fingers scratched on it.

With a raised eyebrow, he studied the hand on his thigh before looking up. "What does that mean? You frustrated because I turned you down the other night?"

She leered at him. "Hey, I'm a red-blooded woman. You can't keep ignoring me forever—"

"Yeah, I can. At least when we're in the middle of a public place." He snickered. "One of the ramp rats could walk up on us and we wouldn't even notice until it was too late."

"Do I look worried?" she asked, arching an eyebrow. Any fear of being caught in an intimate position with Steve was outweighed by other emotions—she couldn't describe the way she felt sitting in that Learjet.

What did the psychologists call that, transference? Assigning her strong attraction to the Learjet to the closest human that resembled it: Steve, a Learjet captain? Even if she couldn't have what she wanted—command of the sleek jet—she *could* have him.

The urges were powerful. Looking away from him, she glanced out the side window. Nobody was around anymore. The interior of the hangar filled her view—large metal tool-boxes bordered the walls, standing like high-tech building blocks. She sighed, then turned back to Steve. Her hand traveled farther up his thigh.

"You're braver than I thought, Taylor," he murmured in amazement. "Either that, or kinkier than I thought. What's gotten into you?" When she shrugged, he studied her for a second before he decided to call her bluff. Reaching over to her cheek, he ran his hand downwards to trace the contours of her neck and collarbone. His touch evoked a sharp intake of breath from her. Encircling his fingers with her own, she led them to her lips and slipped them into her mouth. Gently she sucked on them one by one.

"So, nobody's here," she murmured as she moved from one finger to the next. "You ever wanted to join the mile-high club?"

NINETEEN

Taylor slowly opened one eye, focused on the ceiling of Steve's condo, and shut the eye again. A second later, both of her eyes blinked open and she rolled over on her side with an annoyed look on her face. The medevac call that had summoned Steve to the hangar earlier that morning couldn't have been more frustrating.

The no-holds-barred sex from the previous night had left her eager for more. After a few hours of sleep she had initiated another round—still wired by the thoughts of Learjets flashing through her head—but as soon as she had Steve as interested as she was, he'd gotten beeped. Talk about coitus interruptus.

Rolling gingerly onto her back, she tried to ease into sleep again. An early rise wasn't needed that day. She had woken with an odd thought ricocheting around in her mind, and she wanted to capture it once more. That might require a return to snooze land.

As she snuggled under the covers, several images lingered still: the chime of the doorbell at Robert and Julie's Girdwood chalet, the tone of the other woman's voice inviting her inside, the sights around her. Another memory needled her from the deep recesses of her mind, too. She had noticed something as she had stood in the chalet's foyer, something vaguely important.

What had she noticed? Had she seen something, had she heard something? What was it?

The picture, submerged slightly below the conscious leve
her mind, refused to surface. Try as she might, she could
pull it to the top of the pond. Narrowing her eyes, she glar
at the clock radio near her head and promptly forgot her ment.
salvage expedition.

It was nine o'clock, and she had work to do.

Like call the LifeLine headquarters at the hospital, talk to
one of the nurses. She still had questions about Robert Berndt
and his accusation directed at Nate Mueller. Was he mentally
limber enough to make those kinds of judgments? He had been
spouting off means, motive, and opportunity like a homicide
detective, but where would his troubled mind have gotten complex ideas like that?

Should she believe Robert? She didn't want to—Nate was a
friend, after all—but if she'd been pursuing leads that held no
promise, she'd better figure it out right away. Maybe Carter
Masterson *had* surprised a burglar. Many items pointed to another reason for his death, but stranger things had happened.

Maybe one of the flight nurses who knew of Berndt's condition could apprise her of how it could have affected him.
Surely they would know something about head injuries, or at
least know to whom she could talk. It was worth looking into.

Tossing the covers aside, she sat slowly and swung her legs
carefully over the bed's edge. Surveying the bedroom as her
feet dropped to the floor, she stood. Steve's sleeping quarters
were so cozy that she hated to leave them. From the thick down
comforter puddled on the bed to the sheepskin rug tickling her
toes, the room spoke of a man who enjoyed the sensual nature
of his environment.

Trotting to the bathroom, she glanced toward a framed di-
ploma on the wall. Graduate, bachelor's degree in aeronautical
science, Embry-Riddle Aeronautical University, Daytona
Beach, Florida. That had always impressed her, that certificate.
She'd wanted to go to E-RAU, but didn't have the money for
the degree that would guarantee a job as a professional pilot.
No wonder Steve held a command seat in an aircraft like the
Learjet.

When she sat down to pee, she realized how sore she was.
That puzzled her. It hadn't been that long since their last
romp—had their intimate play just been a bit intense?

Oh, well, either way the pang from her crotch was like a

reminder of the evening's fun. Better than thinking about the interrupted morning attempt.

Five minutes later, after she collected her scattered clothing and dressed, she was in the kitchen investigating the cupboards. The rumbles from her stomach suggested that it was past her breakfast time, and she hoped Steve had something around she could snack on. She really didn't have the time for a full meal; she had plans for the day and her late start didn't help matters.

As one half of her brain scrutinized the refrigerator, the other half scheduled her day. She decided the first thing she needed to do was call Cook Inlet Medical Center and chat with one of the flight nurses.

She reached into the refrigerator and snagged a box of Cherry Pop-Tarts. Not much else complied with her new eating style; the only items in the icebox fit for a vegan were the condiments, a loaf of bread, and a large bottle of pickles. Oh, and some wilted lettuce that was stashed in a corner.

With a Pop-Tart in one hand, she looked around the apartment. She needed to make a call. Trotting toward the end table next to the couch, she grabbed the phone resting on top.

Clamping the Pop-Tart firmly between her teeth, she dialed the phone.

Two hours later, Taylor stood in front of the neuropsychologist who had treated Robert Berndt after his head injury. In a medical community as small as the one in Anchorage, it was easy for one of the LifeLine nurses to steer her in his direction.

"I'm glad you were able to see me on such short notice, Dr. Lelevier." Taylor extended a hand to shake. She stood next to a table she had commandeered in the middle of the hospital's lunch room. Behind her a queue of people, some in the white lab coats of technicians, loaded trays with food served up by uniformed cafeteria workers.

"Well, a man has to eat," Dr. Lelevier quipped. "As long as you don't mind if I talk with my mouth full, this'll work out just fine." He dropped a book on the tabletop to reserve it and gestured at the serving line. "Let's go get something to eat before we start to talk."

Following him toward the end of the queue, she grabbed a tray. She was pleased the doctor had been so easy to recognize in the crowd; his description of himself had been right on track.

As he had said on the phone, he was tall with blond hair cut short and a clean-shaven face.

What he hadn't mentioned was that he looked so young.

From what he'd told her, she believed he was a man in his forties or fifties. After all, he was the only board-certified neuropsychologist in Alaska. Certainly he'd spent a great deal of his past in school mastering the study of the brain-behavior relationship.

However, her first glimpse of him gave her the impression that he was a recent grad school enrollee, maybe in his early thirties. Undoubtedly his young features gave the relatives of his patients pause. They wouldn't want a neophyte supervising the care of a spouse or child, especially when a problem as serious as a head injury was involved. But the fact that he'd examined Robert Berndt spoke well of him. Surely Julie Malcolm had lined up her partner's care team, and as a nurse she would know to select the best.

After picking out some food, Dr. Lelevier placed his tray on their table and sat down. Taylor draped her leather flight jacket over her chair back and set her bowl of soup across from him.

"So, what can I do for you?" the doctor asked as he poked a fork in his broiled snapper. He looked up from his lunch as he steered a hunk of the fish into his mouth.

"Well, as I said on the phone, I have a term paper to do for my Psych 203 class at UAA, and my chosen topic is head injuries." She spooned up some of her spicy lentil soup and sipped it tentatively. She hoped her story sounded plausible. Age thirty-seven made her a bit old for a university sophomore, but she had read recently that the mean age of college students at the University of Alaska, Anchorage, these days was thirty-five, though that seemed hard to believe.

"I was told you were *the* expert on head injuries in the whole state," she continued, "and I wanted to get some information on them from you, stuff that I probably wouldn't see in a textbook." She quietly slurped up one more spoonful of soup. "Since the subject of head injuries is so broad, I wanted to select just one detail to concentrate on. I picked an obvious one: how a head injury affects a person's ability to think, to reason. That's what most people focus on when they think *head injury*, and that's what scares them the most. Losing their ability to think."

Lelevier paused to butter his roll. "Have you done some re-

ch on that subject at the university library? I don't want to
e you with things you've already read."

"Don't worry, I'll stop you if you repeat anything I've cov-
ed so far. I doubt you will, though. The information I get
om you will be less dry than what I got in the books, since
t's based on your interpretation of the texts."

"Okay, that's fine. As long as you don't let me get up on
my soapbox." Lelevier popped a chunk of dinner roll in his
mouth and chewed. "Let me see if I'm reading you right." He
swallowed and took a sip of water. "I think what you're calling
'thinking,' or 'reasoning,' is probably what the term 'abstract
attitude' refers to. That is a person's ability to see beyond the
concrete images in front of him to the meanings behind them.
The act of using abstract attitude is called abstract reasoning.
We do that every day without even acknowledging it." He
wiped his mouth with a napkin. "Was that what you were interested in?"

"Yes, exactly. Let me see if I can simplify what you said."
She dipped her spoon in her bowl of soup and stirred absently
as she thought. "Simple reasoning would be like holding a rock
in your hand and knowing it's a rock. It's gray, it's round, it's
hard . . . it's a rock. However, looking at that rock and knowing
what you can do with it, like use it as a tool or a weapon,
would be 'abstract reasoning,' right?"

"Yes, you've got the definition exactly. Then, to answer your
original question: abstract reasoning is profoundly affected by
a head injury. Almost nonexistent after a severe head injury,
as one would expect when the brain is badly damaged." Dr.
Lelevier took another stab at his snapper and followed it with
some more water.

"Does abstract reasoning ever return to a head injury victim?
Or is loss of it like a life sentence without parole, where you'll
never see the light of day again?"

"Interesting analogy," the doctor laughed. He arched his eyebrows and shook his head, as though he wasn't sure what kind
of person would phrase a comment like that. "Anyway, abstract
reasoning can return in some cases; it never returns in others.
If it does reappear, the amount of time that lapses before that
occurs can vary as well. Every head injury is unique. You can't
predict how one will progress. That's why the study of head
injuries is so fascinating for me. Anything and everything can
happen."

Taylor nodded her head and studied the soup bowl in f.
of her. Chances were good that Robert hadn't retained his a
ity to reason abstractly. If so, where had he gotten the ideas
expressed concerning a mastermind behind the robbery of Ca
ter Masterson? Surely generating a thought like that would re
quire some abstract reasoning.

Resting her spoon on her plate, she tilted her head and
frowned. "Why don't we put this entire textbook description of
abstract reasoning in a real-life situation? That will make it
easier to understand, when it's in a familiar context."

The doctor squinted at her, confused. "Surely your psychology instructor will be able to follow your paper. He's probably
read volumes about abstract reasoning. Why do you have to
elucidate for him?"

Taylor grinned sheepishly; at least, she hoped it was sheepish. She was having fun with the charade, but wasn't sure she
had her student disguise perfected.

"I want to use this paper for other classes if I can," she lied,
"and that means other instructors will have to read it. Instructors that may not be as well-versed in psychology." She
shrugged.

"Ahhh, I see now. A little double-duty for the paper." Lelevier smiled and nodded. "I did that in grad school. So what
kind of a real-life situation do you have in mind?"

"Okay, here it is." She glanced at the table, attempting to
hide her face. She wasn't a good liar, but she needed Lelevier
to believe she'd just concocted the following real-life situation.
"Say a head injury patient answered some fairly complex questions, yet you know he has lost his power to reason abstractly.
It doesn't make sense that he came up with the ideas he did.
How could he have made those deductions?"

Dr. Lelevier glanced at her and placed his fork at the edge
of his plate. "That's a rather specific situation. Do you have
someone in particular in mind?"

"Oh . . . oh, no. This is all hypothetical. I haven't even come
up with a story that goes with that situation, but it will revolve
around what I just said." She didn't know what had happened
during Lelevier's sessions with Robert, but she hoped she
wasn't duplicating something they'd actually talked about. If
the doctor connected the ex-pilot to what she said, he'd clam
up rather than break patient confidentiality. She forged on. "I
want my term paper readers to feel like they're in the midst of

a novel, rather than a piece of stuffy academic drivel. What works for Psych 203 wouldn't work for English 213."

"That's a good idea. I wish I'd done that on some of my papers in school. Maybe my professors would've given me better grades if my writing had been more fun to read." Lelevier picked up his fork and started arranging the remains of his snapper. He appeared oblivious to any link between Taylor's story and anything he had discussed with Berndt. "Let's see, to get back to your question . . . The easiest way for him to mimic abstract reasoning is to rely on past knowledge."

"What do you mean by that, past knowledge?"

"Well, a head injury doesn't destroy knowledge you've had for a long time, but it does erase things you learned recently. If he could connect a present-day scenario to something he'd learned in the past, he would sound like he was answering a question he'd never encountered before. Something he supposedly couldn't do."

"Where would he get this past knowledge?" As she spoke, she could feel something clicking in her head, but the cogs weren't meshing yet.

"Oh, anywhere. Maybe he recognized similarities between the present scene and something in a book. Perhaps he remembered something that was said to him."

When the doctor spoke those words, something in Taylor's mind fell into place with an almost audible click. Placing her index finger on the bridge of her nose, she attempted to arrange her thoughts in order to ask a question.

But even as she readied her question, Dr. Lelevier was scanning the cafeteria and noting the people bussing their trays over to the dirty dish cart. He glanced down at his watch and frowned. Looking up, he said, "I'm out of time here. I hope I've given you what you needed for your research. I'm interested in seeing the final product of your work . . . your approach to term papers is unusual. Maybe you could drop it by?" He picked up his tray and stood. "I never thought of constructing a term paper so it read like a novel. What kind of a novel do you have in mind, anyway? I'm a big mystery fan . . . maybe you can make it a mystery."

Taylor shoved her chair back and stood up, forgetting the question she wanted to ask. She reached out to shake the doctor's hand. "Mysteries, huh? Well this subject's definitely turning mysterious."

• • •

Upon exiting her Suzuki in front of her cabin, Taylor found her feet squishing in the slimy remains of last fall's dead leaves. She hadn't disposed of them before the snow fell, and they coated the gravel of the walkway like a garden slug's trail down a dandelion stalk. She thrust her key at the door's knob several times before it slipped into the lock, then shoved the heavy butcher's block slab open when it connected.

Once inside the A-frame, she tossed her coat on the love seat and marched toward a stack of receipts piled on the kitchen table.

"Where'd I put those," she muttered to herself. "It was written on those directions . . ." Several receipts and memos of various colors and sizes rustled as she thumbed through them. When she came to a scrap of typing paper, she extracted it from the assortment and stopped to peer at it.

Flipping the scrap over, she scanned the scribbles on it. "Okay, here we go. Seven eight three"—she reached over to dial the phone, then glanced at the scrap again—"nine nine one five. That sounds right."

She tapped her foot to the rhythm of the ringing phone. Several seconds passed. "Hello?" answered a lilting voice as the sound of a stereo muted in the background.

"Hello, Julie? This is Taylor." She drew a breath—story time again. "I was hoping to find you home; I need a favor. I'm preparing my garden for the spring planting and I need some tips. When I was talking to you and Robert I recognized a familiar smell, the same thing I smelled last year when I was getting the flower bed ready." She laughed, and hoped it didn't sound too artificial. "You know how the dandelions and the chickweed smell when you pull them, like salad greens. Makes me want to bring out the oil and vinegar. Anyway, is Robert a gardener? Can I ask a few questions?"

"Yeah, Taylor, he is a gardener. He's got plenty of time for that now, you know, and that's exactly what you smelled. Robert was working in the yard before you arrived yesterday."

Aaaah. "So, how much does Robert know about planting in Alaska? Boy, I sure could use some help with my vegetable garden. Everything except the potatoes died before I could harvest last year."

"Well, I know planting here in Alaska takes some planning. Robert did a lot of reading about it before he started his vegetable garden, then went to all of the greenhouses and talked to the experts. If he was here, I'm sure he'd've been glad to give you some hints about how you ruined your garden last year—"

"He's not home? Rats." Just as well . . . she wasn't sure what she'd have said to him anyway. Fabricating garden trouble might've been more than she could handle. She'd never planted anything but an innuendo. "I guess I'll just have to fumble along by myself. Maybe I'll call later if I get really worried."

"Do you want me to ask him to call? He's just out for a walk, he wanted a cinnamon bun from the Bake Shop. Why don't you give me your number?"

"No, that wouldn't work. I'll be out working on the garden, may have to run for supplies. I'll call later. Thanks for your help, though. Bye." She cradled the phone and blew out her breath.

Yeah, thanks for your help, she thought. She never connected Robert with the garden smells she'd noticed the other day; it didn't occur to her that he was someone who had a green thumb. That usually wasn't a *guy thing*.

She walked to the refrigerator and peered in. The pitcher of orange juice looked good, so she took a hefty swig. As she swirled the pitcher to mix the pulp before her next drink, a thought flashed into her mind like an LED display.

If Robert knew gardening— and the use of organic pesticides—could he have been responsible for spiking Steve's sandwich with nicotine? And if he had, why?

Contemplating the possibilities made Taylor's face blanch. Endless minutes passed as she stood in front of the open refrigerator, her white-knuckled fist wrapped around the pitcher of orange juice.

TWENTY

Whenever Taylor had things bothering her, she gravitated toward airplanes. The atmosphere of the airport and its environs seemed to soothe her rattled thoughts, enabling her to concentrate. So, a few minutes after ending her conversation with Julie Malcolm, she climbed into her Suzuki and set out for the LifeLine hangar.

Twenty minutes later—after a drive down from the Hillside, seemingly done on autopilot—she swung into the parking lot sandwiched between Old International Airport Road and the north side of Runway 24R. Few cars remained in front of the offices that bordered LifeLine, but Nate Mueller's beater Honda slumped by the front entrance.

Inching into the slot between his car and the concrete blocks of the building, she killed the engine and clambered from the driver's seat. She'd hoped everyone had headed home for the day, leaving the office and hangar empty, but no such luck. Oh well—at least she only had Nate to contend with. He was okay, wouldn't pester her.

At least, not too much.

She walked into the LifeLine office and was greeted by the sight of Nate shuffling through a stack of paper on his desk. She glanced at her watch: 4:50 P.M. Almost time for him to go.

Upon hearing the front door swish open and close, he looked up from his handful of various and sundry items. "Hi there, Taylor," he greeted her. "What are you doing here? You're not on duty for an hour or so." He looked pointedly at his own wristwatch. Then he glanced over his shoulder toward the locker room and turned back to face her. He lowered his voice. "You got any news to report?" he asked. "How'd your talk with Robert go? I forgot to ask you that when I talked to you last night."

She blanched at his question. She didn't want to talk to him about *that*. He'd be astonished to hear what Robert Berndt had accused him of, and if it was true, it might be dangerous to let him know she had knowledge of those suspicions. Should she be worried?

But then she shook her head subtly and made a decision. She didn't think Robert's accusations held a lot of weight—considering his mental handicap and her faith in Nate—and she wasn't going to let their existence color her conversation. She doubted there was any risk in telling Nate of her earlier talk, but if some risk appeared she'd deal with it at that time.

She unzipped her jacket as she walked across the room. "I heard some interesting things in Girdwood, Nate," she told him, unwittingly lowering her voice, too. "Some things you may not want to know. About your involvement in Carter's murder." She sketched out her talk with Robert Berndt, and watched her friend's face for traces of trouble. If his mien hardened, she'd be alerted to a problem.

But nothing untoward appeared. Nate's face paled as she divulged Robert's suspicion, but that seemed to be disbelief, not wariness. That relieved her.

"Is Robert nuts?" Nate squawked after she had finished. "How could he think I'd do anything like that? I don't need money badly enough to plan the robbery of one of my coworkers, especially if it led to his death. How could he believe that?"

She nodded slowly, digesting Nate's reaction. Either he was a consummate actor, or his indignation rang true. Her fear of him—slight, but not nonexistent—hadn't been warranted.

"Exactly," she echoed. "How *could* he think that? I was under the impression that he was unable to do complex thinking like that." She perched on the edge of Nate's desk and leveled her gaze on him. "I was wondering about that, so I checked into it. Got some curious information from two different sources. First I talked to Robert's doctor, the neuropsychologist—" Using her hands to punctuate her words, she condensed her lunchtime conversation for him.

"What Lelevier said didn't mean much to me," she concluded, "until I called Girdwood and spoke to Julie Malcolm. She told me that Robert has gotten into gardening since his departure from flying." She was monitoring the expression on Nate's face as she spoke, but she saw nothing.

"So?" He stroked his chin in a thoughtful manner. "Why does that matter?"

She wrinkled her nose. She had forgotten to tell him that nicotine was also used as a pesticide and was available to gardeners. No wonder he didn't see the relevance. Promptly, she filled him in.

"Aaahh." He nodded at her as it dawned on him. "Then if Robert knows gardening, he could have gotten the nicotine and laced your sandwich the other day. Is that what you're thinking?" When she raised her eyebrows to signal her confirmation, he aimed a questioning look at her. "But why would he do that? And more important, *how* did he do that?"

"Well, when I examined what Julie had said under the context of what Lelevier had told me, I started to see some connections." She pushed herself farther away from the desk's edge, so both of her legs dangled over the carpet. "If he was a gardener, and read books about it, he has the past knowledge the doctor said he'd need for abstract reasoning. I'm sure one of the gardening books mentioned how deadly nicotine could be, and he might have picked up on that." She hesitated and arched her eyebrows. "But do you remember what I said the other day? 'You'll find Carter's killer if you find the poison?' That's not making any sense now. Robert *could* have spiked the sandwich—that wasn't a very elaborate murder scheme— but does he still have the kind of brain power to concoct a complex murder scheme like the one for Carter? I mean, it was sophisticated enough to slow down the cops for a while." She wiggled her feet, staring at her toes. "I just can't see that, Nate."

"Yeah, neither can I." Nate glanced down at his wristwatch and frowned. "Hey, it's past five. I gotta get going." He pushed his chair back and stood.

Taylor peered at him with her best schoolmarm expression. "Got a hot date, Lothario?"

He grinned, seeming to be pleased by such a risqué nickname. He certainly didn't have a reputation as a womanizer; she hadn't even seen him with a member of the opposite sex, ever. "I *do* have a hot date," he exclaimed, astonished. "I can't believe it. Cute little number from the Alaska Airlines ticket counter." Wiggling his eyebrows á lá Groucho Marx, he snagged his coat from the rack and vanished out the door.

She watched him go with a contemplative expression on her face. He was awfully quick to leave. Granted, he said he had a date—an odd factor in itself—but he made little mention of his innocence when she'd relayed Robert Berndt's accusation to him. She would have thought a man with clean hands would be more avid in his own defense. Instead, he had focused on the possibility of the other man's involvement in the nicotine fracas. Either he thought his ex-coworker's suspicions were laughable, or . . .

She shuddered. *Nah. That couldn't be.*

Stifling those thoughts, she jumped from the edge of Nate's desk. She peered out the window and scanned the empty parking lot—nobody out there, nobody but her in the office. Finally alone, she was able to do what she had wanted to do all along: climb into an airplane and clear her mind. There was nowhere better to do that than a cockpit.

Marching through the locker room, she shoved the hangar door opened and stepped into the cavernous structure. Her footsteps echoed across the nearly unoccupied enclosure. Only one of the King Airs sat in its slot—the other King Air and the Lear were gone. She figured the twin of the aircraft remaining had been dispatched earlier on a medevac, as the Lear had been.

Heading for the lone aircraft, she nodded. Looked like the other flight crews had been working hard that day— here it was, nearly time for the evening shift to begin, and the day shift hadn't ended for them.

Climbing the airstair to the King Air's cockpit, she slipped into the left-hand pilot's seat. *Aaah.* Now she was comfortable, ready to do some thinking. She still hadn't come to a decision about the Robert Berndt situation. It looked like he could have poisoned the sandwich with nicotine—but could he have schemed to murder Carter Masterson? Was he a more likely suspect than Ed Guralnik or John Wisdorf? Both of *them* were smart enough to figure out the nicotine strategy, and both of them had motives for murder, too.

Puzzling over that, she leaned back in the pilot's seat and meshed her fingers behind her head. Thinking mode. She had a lot of that to do.

Then she started and sat forward. *Wasn't it about time to go on duty?* She didn't want to pull the same stunt she had the previous day, forgetting that she was on call at six o'clock P.M. not A.M. Sliding her jacket cuff up, she checked her Seiko. It read 6:03.

Shoving a hand inside her flight jacket for her pager, she flicked it to the ON position. Less than a millisecond later, its irritating *wheep-wheep . . . wheep-wheep . . . wheep-wheep* blasted across the confines of the cockpit.

"Damn!" she yelped in an octave two times higher than the one in which she usually talked. "I wasn't expecting that!" She gulped, forcing her heart back down into her chest were it belonged. Glaring, she unclipped her pager from the waistband of her Levi's and peered at its display.

"Taylor Morgan, Seth Roberson, call for dispatch to Chenega," it read. *Hmmm. Duty called.* Extracting herself from the captain's seat of the King Air, she trotted down the airstair and marched toward the phone in the office.

A minute later, she had the hospital's nighttime LifeLine dispatcher on the line. "Evening, Nora, this is Taylor. Were you really trying to scare the hell out of me with that page, or was that nothing but coincidence? I had *just* turned it on. I mean, I still had my hand on the switch when it beeped me. God! I just about swallowed my heart!"

A chuckle prefaced Nora's reply. Taylor could envision the sight of the plump woman giggling, her round cheeks and rounder body jiggling in unison. "Sorry, Taylor. I didn't think about that when I dialed you." She laughed again. "Anyway, we got a call from Chenega just a second ago. Guy cut his hand off chopping wood; he's losing blood. A lot of blood. The health aide has the wound wrapped, but you gotta get him out of there quick. I beeped Seth to meet you at the hangar—"

"I'm already at the hangar, Nora," Taylor interrupted. "I'll be waiting for him when he rolls in. Who else is going with us?"

"I think Patty Yanosheck and Joyce Parret are on duty tonight." Taylor heard a rustling as Nora perused her paperwork. "Yeah, it's Patty and Joyce. They're on the way. Any problems with the weather?"

"I don't think so, but I'll be checking on it as soon as I hang up on you. Okay?"

"Okay. Have a good flight."

TWENTY-ONE

An hour and a half later, the King Air was cruising over the Sargent Ice Field. To the right sat the Ellsworth and Excelsior Glaciers, glistening in the evening sun with bites of pink and orange crowning their craggy surfaces. To the left the blue-white fingers of Nellie Juan and Chenega Glaciers splayed across the southwest reaches of the Kenai Mountains. From an altitude of six thousand feet, the entire gray-blue expanse of Prince William Sound graced the view. Numerous glaciers dotted the northern and western shores of the five-hundred-square-mile sound, the immense Columbia Glacier foremost in view as it inched down from the hills to the water's edge.

Spring had made more of a dent in the snow fields of the sound than it had made near the Anchorage Bowl. The vivid dark green of spruce trees peppered the foothills centered on the many islands, large and small, that checkered the white-capped water in front of the King Air. The aircraft dipped its nose as it started its descent to one of the landfalls.

"We're heading down, ladies," Taylor Morgan called out into the cabin where the flight nurses sat. Swiveling in her pilot's seat, she peered at them anxiously. "It's going to get rough here pretty soon. Stow anything that needs it. Cinch down your belts." She turned back to her copilot, Seth Roberson, who was guiding the King Air toward their destination: the village of Chenega on Evans Island. "You've been in here when it was blowing, right?" she asked him.

The young man pushed his glasses back up on his nose and nodded. "Flew in with about a twenty-knot wind blowing. It'll be worse tonight, though, won't it?"

"Yeah. That's what the weather forecast for the west side of the sound said, and when I called Chenega for weather at the village they said it was woofing pretty good already. But if you've been in there in the wind before, you can handle the landing."

"Little on-the-job training, huh? How'd I get so lucky?"

Taylor cracked a smile. "Comes with the territory. How do you think you'll learn enough to get upgraded to captain if you don't get to try the tough stuff?"

Arching his eyebrows, he shrugged. End of conversation.

As she pondered the vicious winds that awaited their arrival at Chenega, she remembered the violent beginnings of the village itself. Old Chenega—the word "Chenega" meant "along the side"—had sat on the south shore of the island of the same name, and evidence showed that humans had lived in the settlement for hundreds of years. But the massive earthquake that struck Alaska on Good Friday, 1964—reading 9.3 on the Richter scale—had devastated the town. A thirty-five-foot-high tsunami swept over the small village, and a group of elders died when the church they were hiding in was washed out to sea. In total, twenty-three of the sixty-eight villagers were killed by the awesome force of nature.

Unable to face the anguishing memories of the tragic end to Old Chenega, residents built a new Chenega fifteen miles to the south on Evans Island. More than twenty contemporary homes were erected, along with a school, an office building, a community hall, a store, and a Russian Orthodox church. The one-hundred-plus residents now even enjoyed indoor plumbing—a rarity in the Alaskan bush communities.

Even as Taylor smiled, thinking about the successful rebuilding of Chenega, the first of the anticipated gusts slammed into the King Air, rattling her teeth. "Damn," she cursed. "Here we go." She turned toward the cabin to check on the nurses.

"You guys all strapped down?" she asked, scanning the twin blond heads sitting behind her. "This is just the start of an E-ticket ride at Disneyland."

Thirtyish Patty Yanosheck and fortyish Joyce Parret nodded. They'd ridden through similar turbulent skies, and knew what to expect. Both of the nurses sported bright golden hair, though the shoulder-length cut of the younger woman was more platinum. The French braid that held the older woman's tresses away from her angular face gleamed more dully in the cabin's dim light.

"We can handle this," Joyce reassured Taylor. "I'm more worried about the patient during the flight home to Anchorage. This wind won't help anything if he's in bad shape."

"Well, first we've got to get down to him," Taylor complained. "That won't be fun." Just as she spoke a second hard gust slapped the King Air, followed by another and another. In a matter of seconds they were deep in an ocean of air, and the surf was up. The heavy chop battered the plane like an enormous woodpecker, hammering at its fuselage.

Glancing at her copilot, she noticed a slight green tinge to his cheeks. "You okay?" she asked. "You're not going to lose it, are you?" Though many people believe that pilots never get airsick, she knew that wasn't entirely true. She'd known aviators that flew with one hand on the control yoke and the other on a sick sack. That was rare, but not unheard of. Even *she'd* been nauseous at times.

"I'll be okay if I concentrate on my flying," Seth advised his captain, wiping the sweat off his forehead.

"All right, then. We'll be down in a few minutes." The terrain around the aircraft was already segueing from mostly gray and white to mostly green, and the taller peaks for the Kenai Mountains were retreating behind the King Air's tail. As they approached the waters of the sound, the whitecaps broke furiously against the boulders scattered on the pebble-strewn beaches.

Evans Island appeared in the aircraft's Plexiglas windshield, and Taylor could see the three-thousand-foot gravel airstrip that ran northward from the end of Crab Bay into a valley surrounded by thousand-foot hills. She remembered from previous experience that those low promontories channeled the wind down the runway like a funnel, churning and warping the gusts into currents like white-water rapids.

Drawing her attention from the nasty conditions outside, she reached to tune the radio to 122.9, the local traffic advisory channel. "Chenega traffic," she transmitted, "Lifeguard three-lima-lima is four south for landing to the north."

After a minute of listening for any radio response from other aircraft in the area, and after a scan of the terrain around them, she nodded to Seth. "It's all yours. Set it down before you blow your guts."

Grimacing at her graphic comment, he turned ninety degrees to line up with the airstrip's final approach. Reducing power to the aircraft's twin PT6–50 engines, he nodded at Taylor. "Arm the autofeather, give me flaps forty, and drop the gear," he said. She reached to lower the landing gear and the flaps. The whine of the electric motors that extended the King Air's extremities combined with the whine of the wind to sound like instruments tuning up in the orchestra pit.

The gusts persisted, bursting over the hills, smacking the aircraft like an irritable child slugging a Bozo-the-Clown punching bag. Taylor tensed, ready to step in if Seth had any difficulty coaxing the King Air onto the ground. The twin-engine turboprop continued to jump and dance down final, making her stomach churn and twitch with every wallop from the wind.

The concentration was evident on her copilot's face as he fought the heavy machine—she had no doubt that he had completely forgotten about his earlier queasiness. At least *that* was something good about the difficult weather.

The landing threshold of Chenega's strip—not much more than reflective panels pounded into the dirt—loomed ahead of the aircraft, only fifty feet below them. Seth's grip on the copilot's control yoke tightened, and Taylor's own hand hovered by her own control yoke in case she needed to grab it. She knew she should trust him to get the plane down, but she had a hard time doing that. Regardless of who actually held the flight controls, she was ultimately responsible for the safety of the aircraft. She couldn't forget that.

Dipping and swerving, the plane continued to react to the buffeting of the gusts as it neared the ground. If anything, their proximity to the runway increased the violence of the wind. It seemed Mother Nature had decided to test the occupants of the King Air in several ways, and she wanted to know what they were made of. Cranking up the volume of the churning air, she applied the thumbscrews.

Then, suddenly, the bottom of everything seemed to drop out from under the King Air. Twin shrieks of fright burst into the cockpit from the cabin, matched by a throaty cry of, "Oh, shit!" from Seth Roberson. Taylor felt her stomach lurch up her esophagus, and she barely contained the bile that threatened to erupt. Like a giant fist had flattened it, the aircraft slammed onto the gravel surface of the Chenega airstrip with a heavy *whump!* The speed of the headwind it had landed in made it decelerate like it had just tripped over a giant rubber band stretched across the ground.

"Damn!" Taylor croaked. "What the hell was that?"

"Hey, that wasn't me! I didn't do that!" Seth insisted, his eyes wide in terror. He appeared to believe that Taylor was going to blame him for the extremely hard landing, like he had miscalculated his flare point and stalled the plane ten feet into the air. "It must'a been a downdraft. Probably came right off that hill over there." He pointed at a mound with vertical cliffs that hung down to the water's edge. The tops of the spruce trees that blanketed the hill were waving erratically under the blasts of wind.

"Don't worry about it, Seth," Taylor assured him. "I know you didn't blow the landing. I could feel what the airplane was doing."

"The gusts are really bad, but I didn't expect that downdraft," he apologized, sounding as though he felt she still thought he could have prevented slamming down on the strip.

"Like I said, Seth, don't worry about it. The same thing could've happened to me. Anyway, you're going to have to stay in here and keep an eye on things while I go out and help Joyce and Patty. The wind's just too strong to leave the plane sitting alone." She could feel the King Air tremble when the wind hit it like massive bellows. Even the heavy twin-engine turboprop could be rocked by the strong gusts. Directing her gaze slightly farther down the airstrip, she waved to her left. "Okay. Pull up into the loading area. We've got somebody that needs to get out of here."

TWENTY-TWO

When Seth taxied the plane into the gravel square, Taylor could see a group of eight people marching down the path from the village. They huddled over a stretcher, the four men grasping the handles tightly, fighting the air blasts that threatened to turn the entire litter over. "Damn," she swore as she recognized their trouble. "Those people can barely stand in this wind. It's going to be a bear getting the airstair door open."

"Oh, we can handle it," protested Seth, "the two of us together—"

"It's not going to be 'the two of us.' Remember, you're going to stay up front." Wrangling herself out of her seat, she trotted to the rear of the plane and beckoned for the nurses to follow. "Go ahead and keep number two running," she yelled back to her copilot. "If the wind shifts, you may have to move to keep the nose into it."

Even with all three of the women working, lowering the airstair door took a great deal of effort. Not only did they have to strain to push it out against the wind, they also had to prevent the same wind from tearing it from its mooring as it descended. Once it was down, though, Taylor, Joyce, and Patty stumbled down the steps, battling the gusts as they went.

The three of them met the human convoy fifty feet down the path and escorted them to the plane. As they matched their pace to that of the villagers, Patty and Joyce made a visual inspection of their patient, waiting to check his vital signs until they were back inside the King Air and out of the near-gale-force bluster.

One anguished-looking Native woman clung to the uninjured arm of the man being carried, and three other women trailed close behind her. Who were they? Taylor wondered. His wife and her friends, afraid that he would die from his wounds before he got medical help?

Not if *she* had anything to say about it.

But one sight of the hurt man, and a look at the wrapped stump of a right arm, made Taylor shiver. Even with her hair blowing across her face, obscuring her eyesight, she could tell he was in trouble. His dark Alaskan Native complexion had lost any semblance of its original deep olive tint and was as white as a that of a Caucasian. Sweat plastered his coarse black hair to his brow, only occasionally lifting away from his skin when a particularly strong blast of air pounded him.

"His heart rate is pretty rapid!" shouted Joyce to Patty, raising her voice to be heard over the scream of the wind. She had her index and middle fingers pressed against her patient's carotid artery, feeling for a pulse. Until they had him inside the plane, where their equipment was stowed, she couldn't do any better. "Not much of a pulse, either. We got to get him out of here, right away!" She raised her eyebrows at Taylor, her body language signaling the severity of the situation.

Taylor knew what the problem was in an instant. Other than the obvious one— the loss of his hand—the man was showing the classic signs of shock: pale, sweaty skin; elevated heart rate; low blood pressure. Any worsening of his symptoms could mean loss of consciousness, even death. He had to get to a hospital.

Dashing ahead of the stretcher, Taylor ran up the steps of the airstair in preparation to grab the litter's front handles as the carriers lifted it into the King Air. While the men switched positions to protect the stretcher from the wind as they elevated it, another furious gust hammered them and they nearly dropped the man on the ground.

"Hang on, guys!" Taylor urged them. "We're almost in!" Reaching for the end of the wooden handles, she grunted as she and the others eased the stretcher into the cabin. The whole time, they struggled to prevent it from getting blown against the sides of the door or snagging on the airstair support cables. Any bystander, unaware of the emergency nature of situation, would have laughed at the Keystone Kops routine everyone performed as they fought the gusts.

But finally, the stretcher was in. Taylor and the nurses strapped it onto the aluminum bench built into the cabin's wall, readying it for the flight back to medical help.

Still breathing hard, Taylor left the nurses to their work—Joyce taking vitals, Patty starting an IV line to administer fluids—and ran back to the rear of the King Air. Adrenaline surged through her bloodstream as she directed the village men outside in raising the airstair. But just before they closed it, a woman trotted over with a Tupperware container in her hands.

Rapping on the metal door, she yelled over the shriek of the wind blasting into the cabin. "Here!" She lifted the plastic box through the crack into Taylor's hand. "Don't forget this!" Without any further word, she ran back to her companions, who slouched nearby with the wind at their backs.

Setting the container on the cabin floor without looking at it, Taylor signaled the men to shove the door closed, then latched its handle. The whine of the gusts abated immediately, and she relaxed. She could feel her heartbeat pounding in her ears, and she leaned over to catch her breath.

The Tupperware box on the floor caught her eye. Curious, she reached for it and peered inside. "Yikes!" she squawked. Inside, lying on a pile of ice cubes, rested the injured man's severed hand. She shuddered at the rude shock.

Extremities—without bodies attached to them—were frequent passengers on the medevac planes, but normally they were wrapped in sterile gauze. Apparently in the excitement the village's health aide had remembered to pack the hand in ice but had forgotten to cover it in bandages.

Taylor grimaced and held out the Tupperware to Patty. "Here. Here's the guy's hand. Will they be able to reattach it, the condition it's in?"

Peering at the plastic box, Patty shook her head. "I don't know. They usually can't reattach hands, and since this one is going to be in bad shape, it'll be even more unlikely." She reached out for the translucent container. "But we gotta take it along anyway. Thanks."

Joyce interrupted the conversation concerning the hand to point at her patient. "Come on, Taylor. Let's get out of here. This guy isn't doing any better. He's pretty shocky. We may need to intubate him, and that'd be rough to do when we're caught in the turbulence. If there's better air at altitude, let's head for it."

"Yeah, right." Taylor took one brief look at the Native man on the bench, then headed back to the cockpit. "Come on, Seth," she called as she stepped through the bulkhead's door. "Time for us to get out of here." Sliding into her pilot's seat, she glanced outside to make sure none of the villagers were near the propeller, then engaged the number one engine.

Forty-five minutes later, the ambulance carrying the injured man was disappearing around the LifeLine hangar corner, lights flashing and siren whooping. Cook Inlet Medical Center, and a surgeon that might be able to reattach the severed hand, was only minutes away.

Breathing deeply to calm herself, Taylor watched the ambulance depart. The adrenaline buzz that had accompanied her back from Chenega had finally begun to ease once the Native man had been unloaded from the King Air and transferred to the other vehicle.

Sighing, she shook her head. The flight crew and the nurses had done everything they could to ensure a good outcome; now it was all up to the patient himself. If he had a strong constitution and a will to live, he'd be fine. Well, maybe not fine— how would he deal with his day-to-day activities with only one hand?—but it could have been worse.

During their climb out from Chenega, still caught in the wild turbulence, the man had lost consciousness and quit breathing. That meant intubation—the insertion of a tube down the trachea—to allow for artificial breathing. Both Joyce and Patty had their hands full with that process: tilting a patient's head back and threading the rubber line through his windpipe was no easy task during the best of times. With the aircraft lurching up and down and from side to side, it had been nearly impossible. As the time his body went without oxygen lengthened, the amount of irreparable damage done to the brain increased, and they were sweating it.

But Lady Luck had been riding shotgun on board the King Air that evening. Only less than a minute of fumbling with the intubation apparatus had passed before the plane broke into calmer air. When Taylor leveled off, the nurses had the tube in place in seconds. Even though the man hadn't gained consciousness, at least he was receiving oxygen. Then it was just a matter of getting him to the Anchorage hospital.

As Taylor stood next to the King Air, watching the emergency vehicle race off, she shuddered. Disaster had loomed too close for comfort that time. She pondered whether the injured man would ever realize how fortunate he'd been. Or if he would do nothing but curse the loss of his hand and the stupidity that had caused it.

Beetling her eyebrows, she acknowledged that she might look at the accident only in the negative, as well. If she had chopped her own hand off, could she bring herself to smile about what other things *hadn't* happened? She doubted it. The inability to open a jar—or do countless other tasks—would haunt her every day. She certainly couldn't command an airplane without a hand—how could she bear to live in a world where an aircraft cockpit was out of her reach?

Literally?

Caught in her depressing thoughts, she jumped when Seth Roberson touched her shoulder. "I'm heading inside to do paperwork," he told her. "You coming?"

Drawing a deep draught of the nighttime air, she shook her head. "Naw, not yet. My flight case is still in the King Air and I got to go get it. Just leave the flight log on Nate's desk, I'll sign it when I come in. You can split." Waving at her copilot, she turned toward the aircraft.

Once inside, she hiked up to the cockpit where her flight case sat tucked behind the captain's seat. She reached to grab it, then paused, changing her mind. The excitement of the Chenega flight had served to make her forget why she'd come to the hangar that night in the first place. She still had a mystery to unravel. It was coming to a head, and she knew clues would start to fall into place if she was smart enough to put them together. She better get back to it.

Sliding into her pilot's seat, she made herself comfortable and began counting the clues on her fingers. She realized that was kind of a sappy move, but she had no paper to write on and she needed to make a list.

She held out her index finger—clue number one. Several days ago, she and Steve had only one suspect for Carter Masterson's murder—Ed Guralnik. Ed's behavior when he'd joined her for lunch seemed to confirm his guilt, and she was sure she had confronted a likely murder suspect.

Out came her middle finger—clue number two. A day later,

John Wisdorf was added to the list. His resentment of being
passed over as a Lear pilot—and his possible involvement in
the death of another captain—made him a second suspect,
seemingly as viable.

But only one of them was the actual murderer. *Who?*

Squinting out the window, she tapped the two fingers on her
teeth, then withdrew her hand from her mouth to add another
item to the first two.

Her ring finger joined the gathering—clue number three.
Someone had spiked Steve's lunch with nicotine, an incident
she felt was related to the main crime, Carter's murder. But,
once that had happened, hints to the guilt or innocence of Ed
and John became muddled.

Where Ed had a good reason to kill Carter, he was not as
obvious a suspect in the connected poisoning; where John's
reason to kill Carter seemed more circumstantial, his background pointed at him for the poisoning. Surely, a former nurse
would know how deadly nicotine was.

Then she unfolded her pinkie—clue number four. That one
really had her stumped. She'd discovered a third suspect in the
sandwich tampering, Robert Berndt. For some reason, her intuition had her leaning toward Robert as the force behind the
nicotine *application*, but she couldn't link him to Carter's
death. Certainly, his head injury had left him without the necessary intellectual skills, the abstract reasoning skills, needed
to commit a successful murder.

Those two crimes, the murder and the poisoning, *had* to be
connected. She was sure of that.

Taylor stared out her window into the deepening darkness
around her and snorted. She couldn't figure the puzzle out. All
those clues, but nothing snapped together into a recognizable
form.

How stupid can you get? she chided herself.

As she tried to sort everything, she saw a ramper drive a tug
across the asphalt toward the King Air, preparing to hangar the
plane. It was Wendell, a teenage high school dropout who
worked the night shift. Obviously, he didn't see her sitting in
the cockpit, since once he reached the plane he just clambered
lazily from his seat and idly hooked the tow bar to the aircraft's
nosewheel. As far as he could tell, nobody was watching him;
he could be as lackadaisical as he wanted.

As the tug dragged the King Air toward the hangar, she

leaned forward. Time to climb out of the cockpit. With her knees creaking, she stood and cracked her neck.

Oooh, she thought. How'd she get so stiff?

Shrugging, she reached behind her seat for her flight case and dragged it into the cabin. As her eyes surveyed the vacant darkness, she spotted a paperback book lying on one of the seats. She recognized the title: *A Cold Day for Murder* by Dana Stabenow. A murder mystery set in Álaska. Undoubtedly one of the nurses had been reading it on the way from Anchorage to Chenega.

She snatched it up. She'd leave it in the office, where its rightful owner could claim it. Put it in the lost and found, wherever that was. She'd have to ask Nate for its location tomorrow.

Suddenly, she stared at the book and her gaze widened. Her cheeks drew back from her cheekbones. Of course; how could she have missed that? Her grip on the volume's spine tightened and a surge of adrenaline shot through her body.

Of course.

TWENTY-THREE

A wash of charcoal had bled into the granite gray of the evening sky by the time Taylor had left the King Air and headed back into the LifeLine office. The tone of the sky matched the darkness of her own thoughts as she'd traipsed across the hangar's concrete floor.

Once settled behind Nate Mueller's desk, she examined and signed the flight paperwork left for her by her copilot, a standard procedure she could do easily while her mind dealt with other matters. An occasional pair of car headlights flashed past on Old International Airport Road as she looked up from her work and scanned the dim parking lot. Her Suzuki was the only vehicle occupying the lot. That, too, matched the emptiness of her mood.

With the paperwork concluded, she leaned back in Nate's chair. Drumming her fingers on the armrest, she contemplated the evening's significant event—her startling discovery of the clue that enabled her to link Berndt to Carter Masterson's murder. Finally, she had a suspect she could be sure of. Whereas the quasi-evidence she had on Ed Guralnik and John Wisdorf had flaws, she could easily connect Robert to the murder.

But what could she do about it?

As with the other suspects, she didn't really have any hard evidence. She hadn't seen him shoot Carter, hadn't overheard him bragging about the crime, hadn't found a smoking gun. Was her suspicion credible enough?

Pushing her chair back from the desk, she stood. She wanted to think about the situation some more; she *needed* to think about it some more. She'd better head back into the hangar, to her cocoon, where her mind worked so much better.

Upon nudging the heavy door open, she flicked a switch on and bathed the hangar with light. She glanced around. The entire complement of LifeLine aircraft sat at the ready in their slots—by the time she had returned from Chenega with N433LL, the other King Air and the Lear had returned, too.

She'd brightened when she'd entered the hangar earlier and recognized the sleek form of the jet—that meant Steve had completed his flight. She could probably catch him at home, and talk to him about what she'd discovered about Berndt. Get a second opinion, as it were, concerning what to do about it.

But then she'd hesitated. He still didn't know anything about her continuing search for their coworker's killer. She'd better keep him out of it; do all of the figuring on her own.

Heading back into the hangar from the office, that's what she resolved to do: figure it out on her own. She couldn't count on Steve for help, but at least she could get some assistance from his jet. Considering the way the sleek aircraft made her feel, perhaps it could make her think better, too.

Taylor made herself comfortable in the Lear's copilot seat, appreciating the ambiance of the cockpit. She flipped on the interior panel lights—she certainly remembered the feeling their glow gave her and she wanted to experience it again. Even the smell inside the Lear tantalized her, acting like a high-tech pheromone.

As she decided what to do about Robert, she reached for the systems manual that was poking out from a wall pocket. Treating the manual like a pacifier, she leafed through it absently as she thought. Her gaze was unfocused, and none of the pictures or diagrams really registered while she thumbed the pages.

The sound of a door swinging open in the far corner of the hangar broke into her reverie. She started, and lowered the manual into her lap. Who would be here at this time of night? Had a medevac been dispatched? She glanced at her pager—*she* hadn't been beeped; must be somebody else. She leaned forward to peer out the cockpit window, but the Learjet faced away from the noise. With her view blocked, she strained to hear something.

The echo of conversing voices grew stronger as two sets of footsteps approached. She recognized the loudest voice: it was Wendell, the teenaged ramp attendant who had hangared her King Air earlier. The young man was talking to someone about the Lear. She perked up.

"You know," said Wendell, "it's really swell seeing you again. Bet you're glad to get back into the Lear, huh? I heard you got hurt, but I didn't know when you were going to come over to the hangar. Welcome back."

"Well, I'm glad to be back, too, Wendell. Things were kinda tough, but I'm okay now." Taylor's eyes widened in surprise when she recognized the familiar mumble of Robert Berndt. What the hell was he doing there?

Her silent question was answered instantly as Robert continued to talk, and what he said made her quail. "I'll be taking the Lear out for a bit," he announced. "I need to get back into the swing of things. It's all fueled, right?"

"Sure," Wendell replied. "I topped it off myself earlier. But where's your copilot?"

"Don't need one for this flight. It's Part 91," Robert answered. "Go ahead and drag it out with the tug. I'll put this in the back."

Back inside the Learjet, a quiet groan crawled up Taylor's throat. She paled and sucked in her breath. Didn't Wendell realize that calling the flight Part 91 was a bullshit answer? You never flew the Lear single pilot. Ever.

Then she acknowledged that the ramper wouldn't know much about things like that. After all, he wasn't a pilot.

Peeking around the cockpit door, she saw Robert Berndt walk past Wendell and cross the hangar. Thoughts ricocheted about her head as she tried to analyze the situation.

The comments made to Wendell made it sound like Robert planned to take the Lear on a flight, but that didn't make any sense. Didn't he realize there was a valid reason for his removal from the pilot roster? He couldn't fly anymore!

However, that minor detail was not germane at the moment, because it appeared he *was* going to fly the jet. His belief that his injury hadn't made permanent damages—provoked by his anosognosia—must be responsible for his brash act. Perplexed, she continued to watch him approach. As his steps neared, her anxiety grew.

"Shit," she cursed under her breath. "I'm a sitting duck. As soon as he climbs in here, he'll see me."

And what would he do then?

She had no way to gauge his reaction to finding her. Obviously, he planned to fly the Lear, but to where? And how frantic would he get if she prevented him from doing so? Would she pose a threat just because of her presence in the jet?

Or, would she pose a more serious threat because he had seen through her previous questioning of him? Would he realize she had figured out his involvement in Carter's death? Would that make him a danger to her?

She shivered. Robert had proven he was capable of murder.

And he was walking her way.

"Oh, God," Taylor whimpered.

Though she felt the pounding of her heart would alert anyone to her presence in the Learjet, she still tried to conceal herself. She slumped down in the seat, hoping Robert would not see her before she had a chance to dash off. Maybe he would go straight to the rear of the aircraft when he entered and she'd have time to dart out of the cockpit.

Unfortunately, she had no more time to speculate on slipping out of the Learjet. The clunk of footsteps on the concrete hangar floor approached. While she flattened herself on her seat, she heard him reach the jet and start up the airstair. The corrugated vinyl covering the steps crinkled as he climbed them.

Fleeing before he spotted her was now a moot point.

Seconds later his oddly distorted voice rasped in the cockpit. "Who's in here?"

As a surge of adrenaline blasted through her system, Taylor pulled herself up from where she huddled. She was thinking maybe she could play it stupid.

But she had no chance to try any escape plan. When Robert Berndt realized who sat in the copilot's seat, he growled and hefted his flight case and swung it in a giant arc toward her head.

She thrust her hands up to deflect the blow, but her defense did nothing but redirect its strength. A metal-trimmed corner of the rigid leather case struck her cheek, glancing off the cheekbone and smashing the side of her nose. A spurt of crimson spattered on her upheld fingers and a sickening *crack!* echoed across the confines of the cockpit. An immense pain radiated from the bridge of her nose, sweeping crosswise on her face like a tactile explosion.

She saw the blinking annunciator lights on the instrument panel fade, then shrink and black out.

TWENTY-FOUR

As blackness segued into gray, Taylor struggled back into the real world from a hazy dream. In the dream, she had been striving unsuccessfully to push a severed hand away from her face as it pounded repeatedly on her nose. But the hand was surprisingly strong for a disembodied extremity, and for some reason her arms couldn't move to protect herself. When the hand turned into a fist and connected a roundhouse punch to her cheek, the pain woke her.

For an instant she didn't know where she was and what had happened to her, but as soon as she opened her eyes it became clear. She was lying flat on her back, staring at the Learjet cabin's ceiling. The hard, cool surface pressed against her spine and buttocks was the wall-mounted patient bench. Her hands had been bound—she could feel some kind of soft restraint twisted around her crossed wrists. Her legs couldn't function, either. Though she couldn't see them, she knew they were tied, too. When she tried to sit, web straps—the patient seat belts, she imagined—prevented her from moving. Giving up, she dropped onto her back against the aluminum beneath her.

Unsure of her predicament, she tuned in to the noises around her. The soft "whoosh" she heard was the sound of the Learjet engines, churning softly as they impelled the aircraft through the air.

Fuzzily, she acknowledged what was going on. They were going somewhere. Where, she did not know, but it was curious.

How had Robert gotten the Learjet in the air? He was no longer competent to fly the machine. She shivered when she contemplated what had been going on as she lay unconscious in the cabin. He had remembered enough about the jet to get it airborne, but that was the easy part. Performing a safe landing would definitely tax his weakened mental faculties.

Not thinking straight, she continued to examine that minor aspect of the current situation until the major aspect smacked her up aside the head—regardless of how he got the Lear airborne, he had taken her along, trussed like a Thanksgiving turkey.

She blanched when she realized what that meant. He was on to her. He knew that *she* knew about him and the murder, and he planned to do something about it. Obviously, they were enroute to a place where he felt comfortable disposing of her.

Frantically, she tugged at her restraints. She had to get free; she couldn't let him get any further toward her eventual end. Tugging and flopping, she strained to free herself. The frenzied thudding of her body against the bench ricocheted across the cabin, bringing a reaction from the cockpit.

"Oh, I see you're awake," boomed Robert Berndt's baritone as he peered at her from the front of the Learjet.

Taylor jerked and craned her head over her shoulder to see him. "What the hell are you doing?" she croaked. "Why am I tied up?"

Smiling, he widened his gaze. "Isn't it obvious?" He wriggled awkwardly out of the Lear's left-hand seat and edged into the cabin. In a few long-legged strides he stood at her head.

As soon as he appeared next to her, she jumped. "Jesus!" she squawked. "Get back up front! You can't come back here, there's nobody flying!"

"Hey, the autopilot is on. I don't need to be up there. No big deal."

Terrified, she gaped at him. "Are you kidding? You can't leave the cockpit unattended. What if something happened? What if there's traffic? What if Center calls?" Any number of disasters could occur—didn't he know that? Was he crazy? He'd obviously forgotten some of the basic premises about how to fly the Lear.

That scared her more than the idea that he may mean her harm.

What else had he lost? What had happened between the time

*when he'd put her lights out and when she'd regained con-
sciousness?* She didn't even want to think about it.

"Don't worry," he reassured her. "We're up around flight
level three-five-zero. There's nobody up here this far north.
Plus, I've got the radio on speaker. If anyone calls, I'll hear it.
Anyway, you're not really in any position to do anything about
it." He cackled, sending a shiver down her spine.

"But why am I tied up?" she asked. Then she pleaded, "I
haven't done anything to you." Would he fall for that? How
much did he know about what she'd conjectured?

"Well, that's true, you haven't done anything to me. Yet. But
you will if I give you the chance." He stared at her pointedly,
like a parent getting ready to scold a misbehaving youngster.
"As soon as you left the other day, I knew what you were
doing. I can't believe you thought I'd fall for your cock-and-
bull story. Asking me for ideas about solving Carter Masterson's murder. Come on, you weren't trying to help the police
in their investigation, you were checking *me* out. Trying to get
me to say something incriminating."

She gawked at him incredulously, trying to look innocent.
In a way, though, she was innocent. He was right—her story
had been bullshit—but she had not been after him when she
had visited Girdwood. John Wisdorf and Ed Guralnik had been
her real prey. His guilty conscience must have made him think
otherwise, though, and where she'd had a smidgen of doubt
about his guilt earlier, he'd unwittingly convinced her of it
completely by what he'd just said.

Arms akimbo, he peered at her. "What was it that tipped you
off? The nicotine flavoring I added to Steve Derossett's sandwich?" When he got no response from her but a blank stare—
damn, she'd been right about that, too—he nodded. "Yeah, I
thought that was too much. In retrospect, that is. I guess I'm
lucky the poison didn't kill Steve, like it was supposed to. Two
Lear captains dead within a week would have been a stretch.
Even those stupid police detectives would have started wondering, then." He gazed moodily out one of the cabin windows.
"Well, you can't blame me for trying. I was just so pissed when
Nate refused to rehire me, even though there was an opening.
What the hell did I shoot Carter for, anyway?" He glared at
her like he blamed her for it, and she shrank from his look.
"Do you think I was just stealing from him, like I tried to make
it look? Wrong. I just had to make room for myself on the pilot

roster, where I belong. There's nothing wrong with me—anybody with any sense can see that. My injury didn't turn me into a bumbling idiot. Shit, I can do—"

Taylor decided to break into his bitter rambling and find out what *she* needed to know. "Where are we going?"

He squinted at her, a bit perturbed by her interruption. "Oh, just a short stop in Nome to refuel, then a jump across the Bering Strait to Russia—"

"Russia? Are you nuts?" She choked on his words. "You don't have permission to fly into Russian airspace." The best ending to an unauthorized venture into foreign territory would be a military escort to the nearest airport; the worst ending would be getting shot down. He should know that. It became apparent that he wasn't thinking logically if he thought he could just waltz into Russia, and she sure didn't want to be on the Lear when the first Russian Mig fighter appeared.

Fearing for her life—for the second time—she attempted to dissuade him from his plan. "Robert, why would you want to go to Russia? There's nothing for—"

He held up his hands to stop her. "Hey, think about it. I can't get my old job back here in the U.S., no matter what I do. But if I land in Magadan or Providenya, in *my own Learjet*, offering my services for hire, they'll jump on it, no questions asked. Things are so screwed up there, and so corrupted, they'd never bother checking on where the Lear came from. Or where I came from." He grinned, obviously proud of himself for devising what he believed was a no-fail plan. "Hey, I read the paper and watch the news. I know what's going on over there. One look at this Learjet and I'll have them eating out of my hand." He crowed in delight.

"But what about their fighters?" she questioned. "If they see us crossing the international date line without clearance, they're guaranteed to fire on us. Not even this Lear can outrun a Mig."

He cocked his head and looked at her smugly. "Oh, I don't think I'll have to worry. I'll be talking to them long before that." He turned to return to the cockpit. "Anyway," he called over his shoulder, "you don't have to think about any of that. When we stop in Nome for fuel, you won't be going any farther."

Her heart spasmed in her chest. What did he have in mind? Obviously he wanted to kill her, but when and how? Would he wait until they had landed, or would he kill her before they reached Nome? There'd be no difficulty in tossing her lifeless body out of the Lear at the end of the runway after they'd touched down. *Egad.*

In a panic she jerked at her bonds again, her body bucking and straining against the seat belts. She felt some give as the knots in her restraints tightened, but she could not break free. Her breath rasped; she grunted and groaned in her frantic effort to escape.

"Hey, don't bother trying to get away," Robert advised from his pilot's seat. "That'd be a waste of time. Just relax and enjoy the ride. I wouldn't want your last minutes to be a drag."

TWENTY-FIVE

"Enjoy your last minutes." Robert's final comment rang in Taylor's ears like a death knell. The irony was not lost on her. She'd finally found herself flying in her dream ship, and it had metamorphosed into a one-way cruise to oblivion. Talk about a macabre twist to the Cinderella story—her elegant carriage hadn't turned into a pumpkin, but a hearse.

Breathing hard, she attempted to compose herself. Focusing only on the problem meant a sure death; she had to allow her mind a chance to examine the situation for a solution. She had to get free. Terrified thrashing would serve no purpose. She needed to be logical, use her brain where her brawn had proven useless.

Obviously, Robert Berndt wanted to murder her, but when? He had her strapped down on the patient's bench—what was he waiting for?

Maybe he was working up to it, she thought. He had shot Carter Masterson with a rifle—a somewhat impersonal way to kill—but using a gun on her while inside the Lear would be suicide for him. Her death would require something much more hands-on, like strangulation or slashing. Could he bring himself to do that, face his victim as her life seeped from her body? You couldn't get any more intimate than that.

But whatever he had in mind, she had to thwart his plans. She had no ideas about how she could do that—she certainly couldn't go *mano a mano* with an adult male and hope to subdue him—but the first step was clear: get out of her restraints. Maybe something would come to her as she struggled with that.

It had to.

Craning her head, she squinted down toward her hands. Whatever held her chest down was preventing her from arching her back so she could look at them directly, but she had to catch a glimpse. Whatever Robert had used to bind them was tough. Light, but tough. As strong as she was—comparatively speaking—she hadn't had any luck in tearing it.

By tilting her head and stretching, she could finally see her hands, tied crosswise together at her waist. Her ankles were bound with the same material as her wrists: sterile gauze—an item always on hand on medevac planes—had been cut from one of the supply rolls and wrapped several times around her extremities and knotted. And as she'd suspected, the bench's seat belts were snugged down over her body, one at chest height and one near her knees.

Hmmm. She could just untie her feet and unlatch the seat belts, but first she'd need her hands free. That was going to take some thought, figuring how to tear the bandages. They were made to withstand a lot of force—she'd need something sharp to cut them.

Narrowing her gaze, she thought about what to use. Her teeth? No, couldn't get her hands to her mouth with the seat belt cinching them down. A sharp edge of the bench? No, for the same reason: she couldn't move her arms across her body, just slightly up and down and side to side.

Then she grinned, delighted. Good thing Robert didn't think to search her before he'd tied her up. If he had, he'd have found the small knife in her right jeans' pocket. Wiggling her hands to her pocket, she poked her fingers into its opening to grab it.

And froze.

"Damn," she whispered. Wrong jeans. She cursed her lax housekeeping tendencies. The pair of pants with the knife—her Levi's 501s—were sitting at home, in the wicker basket that held her dirty clothes. If she had done her laundry in a timely fashion, she would have emptied the pockets and discovered the small blade in time to transfer it to her clean jeans.

But nooo.

Grimacing, she wracked her brain for another object she could use to cut the gauze restraints. She fumbled near her waist, trying to feel something pointed or sharp. There was nothing there.

But when her fingers traced the fly of her jeans, she brightened. *Yes! That'd work!* Her relaxed housekeeping attitude was serving her well this time: the clean jeans that she'd grabbed the other day were *not* 501s. If she'd had her choice, she would have waited for her 501s to complete the wash-and-dry cycle, but instead she'd picked a different pair. A pair with a *zipper*, not a button fly.

Eagerly, she spread the fabric lip of the jeans' fly and exposed the zipper inside. The zipper tab itself had a number of sharp edges on it, and she maneuvered her hands to drag the gauze across its angular metal points.

The threads of the cloth snagged on the points. Tugging hard against their hold, she heard a tiny *rip!* as the metal cut a few strands of the cotton.

She took a deep breath, unaware that she'd been holding it for the past minute or so. *Whew!* It would take some time—at three to four threads per pull—but if she continued to drag the gauze across the zipper tab, eventually the bandages would part and her hands would be free.

Setting to her task, she vigorously rubbed her cloth restraints over the zipper tab. *Ckkk ckkk-ckkk.* The minute scratching noises sounded like the strains of a victory parade's band. She had won! She would get free!

As she ground the gauze across the zipper, back and forth, back and forth, she caught a whiff of a unique odor. She paused in her hurried work, and sniffed again. It was an unusual odor, but it had a touch of familiarity to it. The identity of the odor was right below the surface of her consciousness, but she was unable to break it free.

While reflecting upon the scent, she quickly glanced forward over her shoulder to see if Robert had noticed her busy hands. Fortunately, all indications told her he hadn't. As far as she could tell, he was fantasizing about his successful escape from murder charges.

But she was going to change *that*.

Satisfied that Robert was occupied with something else, she turned back to her work. Still, the smell lingered and she paused again. It had an unusual tang to it, some kind of spicy accent. It hinted of a hot Mexican dish, maybe something with jalapeños in it.

Then an additional dose of the spicy musk prodded her memory and it all came back to her. She recalled what the smell was and where it had first stung her nose.

It was bear repellent. A friend of her brother had purchased a spray can of the stuff when planning a float trip down a river known to have an active bear population. Playfully, he'd squirted a little in her direction—a suitable bit of fun with his friend's kid sister.

"Yikes!" she'd squeaked. "What is that junk? It makes my nose feel like someone just reamed it out with steel wool. Yuck!"

That memory swept across Taylor's mind as she lay in the Lear's cabin. She *knew* it was bear repellent insulting her nostrils. It probably came from the can that dropped out of the jacket of the man that had been mauled near King Salmon.

And that can was somewhere nearby.

Her mind snapped to attention as she recalled how just a trace of the bear repellent had nearly blown her nose off. What would a full dose of it do to a person?

Leaping on that idea, she concocted a plan in a few seconds. She had to find that repellent.

But first she had to cut through the gauze restraints. Bending to her task, she bore down on it. She was nearly done, and in a few seconds the final *rippp!* told her she was free.

With her hands finally mobile, she quickly and quietly unlatched the seat belts and untied her feet. The next job was getting hold of that repellent. Easing herself down from the aluminum bench, she stood on trembling legs. Glancing over her shoulder, she saw Robert was still occupied with his own thoughts, so she tiptoed to the rear of the plane. That's where the repellent had to be.

As she neared the back of the cabin she knew she was getting close. Her nose burned, her eyes teared. She felt like she was slicing onions.

Dragging her hand across her face did nothing to stem the tide of tears pouring from her eyes, nor did it stop the mucus dripping from her nostrils. She found herself in an annoying rhythm: she'd swipe at her nose, peer around the area for the can, swipe at her nose again. Finally, she located what she searched for.

Tucked in the farthest corner of the Lear's cabin, she saw a cylindrical blue-and-white aluminum can with the words Nox-um-out Bear Repellent printed on the side.

Grabbing it, she stuffed it up the arm of her long-sleeved T-shirt and wheeled around to check on Robert. He didn't appear to have noticed anything, and hadn't been watching her too closely. He probably figured his job of tying her down was foolproof; undoubtedly, he believed she was completely cowed by the thought of her imminent death, and wouldn't try anything.

But as she crouched near the rear of the aircraft, she heard him cough and calmly turn around in his seat to inspect his prisoner's bonds. Obviously he still expected to see her immobilized on the bench. But his inspection told him she had broken free. He gaped at her for a second before he scrambled out of the cockpit, furious. He was going to make her pay for her impudence.

"Damn you!" he shrieked. "What are you doing? How'd you get loose?" He tore his eyes away from her and scanned the cabin near him for a weapon to punish her. "Aaargh!" he bellowed, snatching the fire ax from its cradle next to the extinguisher. "That was a bad choice!" He grasped the ax between his hands and stalked toward her.

TWENTY-SIX

Taylor rotated from her position near the rear of the cabin and faced him. "Oh, yeah? Try this on for size!" she yelled. Robert saw trouble in her eyes and hesitated for a millisecond, then rushed toward her again with the ax held high above his head. Guttural croaks emerged from his throat. She forced herself to wait until he was within six feet of her, then yanked the spray can out of her sleeve. "Hah!" she cried and pressed its nozzle to deliver the final blow.

Robert screeched to a halt, anticipating harm to himself . . .

But nothing happened. . . .

Jabbing at the button, she jerked and shook the can but no noxious, pepper-laden fumes spurted from its nozzle. "Shit!" she cried, astounded. "What happened?"

Robert had held his position for a moment, but as soon as he realized her weapon had failed, he leaped at her with a bellow.

She gaped at the man bearing down on her with an ax above his head, then without even considering what she was doing, she met him head-on and rammed his solar plexus.

"Whoof!" he grunted as he bent over, trapping her under his torso as he recoiled from her strike. He retched, clutching at one of the nearby seats to steady himself, and the ax clattered to the floor.

Hearing the ax fall, she tried to wrench it away from him. There was her chance! But he had the presence of mind to grab her before she could struggle free, and he wrapped her into a lethal bear hug. With her snared between his arms, he struck at her again and again with his fists.

"You've done it now!" he screamed as he punched her. "This is gonna be it!" His mostly ineffective blows rained down on her shoulders and back, but when one connected with the side of a breast, she screamed in pain.

He reached for the spray can in an attempt to disarm her, but she moved her arm back to keep it away from him. She wouldn't let him have her only defense. Yelping, they thrashed about in the aisle, bouncing back and forth between the seats and the patient bench.

Then Robert wrapped a long leg behind her and lunged forward, tripping her and falling directly on top of her. She shrieked as she fell backwards, and at the last second she flung the spray away from her attacker. He *wasn't* going to get her only weapon.

The can whacked sharply against the metal leg of the seat behind her and a *kawhoom!* filled the air as its side split. The contents of the can spewed out through the ruptured aluminum. Everything for several feet, including Taylor's hair and Robert's eyes and face, was covered with an acrid coating of the cayenne pepper mixture.

Even though Robert had instinctively shielded his face from the explosion, his arm movement was too slow. The fiery and volatile repellent coated his eyes and the sensitive inner layers of his nose.

He shrieked in agony as the compound varnished his mucous membranes. The lungful of air he sucked in sent even more of the mixture coursing through his nasal cavities, and he raked his fingers over his face as his anguished cries filled the cabin.

While he writhed on the narrow aisle, Taylor strained to separate herself from the human pileup. Wiping at her own tearing eyes, she pushed away from him and stood on unsteady legs. Agog at his tortured throes, she stepped over him and shook her head. What had that repellent done to him? It was meant to be used on a large animal—what would it do to a human? Had she blinded him?

But she didn't have time to worry about his pain. She'd immobilized him, but not for long. She still needed to enact the rest of her plan. Mopping her face with her sleeve, she walked away from him and began to wriggle into the cockpit of the Learjet.

Once in the captain's seat, she glanced out the side window. The entire northwestern sector of the state was clear. Not a cloud to be seen, even from thirty-five thousand feet. The western reaches of the Alaska Range were disappearing behind the Learjet, their massive peaks glowing in the pink light of a setting sun. The farther north she traveled, the longer the daylight hours lasted—it was like she was chasing the sun, dogging its heels as it slipped below the horizon. The Kuskokwim Mountains and the thousand-mile-long Yukon River spread across the skyline ahead of her. Spring hadn't come to the northern tiers of the state, and most of the view was the white-and-blue of snow and ice.

Breaking away from her momentary lapse into sightseeing, she shook the cobwebs out of her mind. She had important things to do; she couldn't allow distraction. Taking a deep breath—the air still tinged with the acrid scent of the cayenne pepper spray coating her hair—she scanned the panel in front of her. Where did that switch go? she wondered as she surveyed the instruments. Finally, she nodded and placed a finger on the top half of a red button marked UP located in the lower right quadrant of the panel. Holding the button down, she watched it do its magic: the air began to filter out of the cabin.

Then she started and stared at the pressure gauge. "Good lord," she murmured. She had been venting the oxygen out of the cabin without taking care of air for herself. Quickly, she grabbed for the oxygen mask next to her head.

Once she'd donned her mask, she turned a dial marked PASS MASK from NORMAL to OFF. By doing so, the discharge of the passenger oxygen masks in the cabin became a function only she could control. They wouldn't automatically drop down as the cabin air got purged, and Robert would be unable to grab one of them.

As the needle on the cabin altitude gauge crept upwards, she bit her lip in anxiety. "Come on, baby, come on!" she muttered to the system, as though her words could effect its actions. "Come on, you're not going fast enough! Come on!" Her heart pounded an up-tempo march in her chest in response to her desperation, and the pulsing of the thick carotid artery in her neck matched it, throb by throb.

The cabin altitude needle continued to inch up and Taylor's

ears began to pop as the air pressure changed. "That's it, keep going! Come on, go faster, go faster!" she yelled at the gauge, rapping on the glass. "He's gonna notice what's going on and try to get up!"

When she looked back into the cabin, she noted that Robert had changed position from where he had fallen, but his hands were still furiously wiping his face.

"What the fuck did you do to me!" Robert screamed from the cabin's floor. "I can't see! I'm blind!" His eyelids were clamped shut and he lay in a fetal position.

Then he removed his hands from his face and began to feel about. As he figured out where he was, he moved into a kneeling crouch. "I know you're up there, bitch! I can't see you, but I'm going to get you anyway! You're going to pay for what you've done to me!" He reached out and grasped one of the stretcher legs and pulled himself up onto his feet. Fumbling in the unsighted dark, he attempted to feel his way forward to the cockpit.

"No, don't do it!" Taylor cried through her mask as Robert walked and paused . . . walked and paused . . . on his way toward her. "Leave me alone!" she yelled. "Stay back there!"

His forward progress continued for a few more tentative steps, then his knees lost their stability. They turned into putty and buckled underneath him, dropping him to the floor. She stared at him, then glanced at the cabin altitude gauge. It read 21,500 feet. At that height, the cabin's oxygen level was low enough to make him lose consciousness. She scanned the other pressurization instruments, then whipped around to her view of the cabin. She was in time to see him collapse onto his belly.

A sense of relief washed over her when he was silenced. Looking at his inert form, she cried out in triumph to the empty cabin. "He's down! My God, I did it! I've got control of the jet!" She turned toward the front of the cockpit and flipped a lever to prevent the cabin from being repressurized, refilling with air. "This'll keep you down for a while."

TWENTY-SEVEN

Taylor sucked on her oxygen mask, a myriad of thoughts whirling about in her head. She'd solved the primary problem—how to get free from and subdue Robert Berndt—but solving the primary problem brought more trouble to the forefront. Like how the hell did she get down? The Learjet was almost completely foreign to her, and its temperamental nature made it probably the worst jet in the world from which to learn.

She needed help. Reaching out for her transponder, she set its four digits to 7700, the emergency signal. The minute that emergency signal appeared on radar screens at the Air Route Traffic Control Center all kinds of bells and whistles would sound. She smiled grimly at the idea of what her distress call would set in motion. It seemed rather ironic, getting her fifteen minutes of fame because she'd stumbled into a life-threatening situation.

After checking her COMM-1 radio for its selected frequency—133.3, the appropriate setting for Center in that part of the state—she flipped the OXY-MIC switch to ON and prepared to speak to someone who might prove to be her guardian angel. Clearing her throat—the cayenne pepper spray had rendered it clogged and hoarse—she transmitted. "Anchorage Center, Lear six-zero-four-lima-lima, on one thirty three point three, squawking seventy-seven hundred, is declaring an emergency." She nearly choked on the words—she'd never, *ever*, been in a situation like the one she found herself in right then.

"Four-lima-lima, Anchorage Center. Radar contact. State emergency," responded a methodical, soothing male voice. The controller on the other end of the radio line didn't appear flustered by the word *emergency*. Either he was unflappable or he was trained to reply in a neutral tone regardless of what he heard.

She suspected the latter.

She sighed when she got an answer to her call. Finally, a voice from a human who had no wish to do her harm. She felt herself start trembling in relief, and she hoped that didn't show in her own voice. If he could be cool, she could as well. She wasn't going to give in to her anxiety; she didn't have time for that.

"Anchorage Center, I'm not sure what to call this emergency," she confessed. "A kidnapping? An assault? At any rate, the critical problem is that I don't know how to land this aircraft. I'm going to need some help."

The untroubled tone in the air traffic controller's voice vanished immediately. So much for training. "You don't know how to fly an airplane? And you're in a Lear?" His disbelief was almost palpable.

That didn't reassure Taylor.

Even so, she answered him in a deliberate voice with a tone that did not reflect the atmosphere existing in her mind. By all rights, she was terrified, but she wouldn't allow herself to show it. That wasn't her style.

"Negative, Center," she answered. "I do know how to fly, just not a Lear. I'm a King Air captain," she added. "I'm not a complete neophyte. But I will need some help in getting down."

That was a dramatic understatement.

"Four-lima lima, Anchorage copies." The controller was back to his calm, professional tone. "You're filed for Nome. Is that still your intended destination?"

"Well, I'd like to get vectors back to Anchorage. Lot more runway for landing there. I'm not sure where I am now, but if you can get me reoriented I can follow the jetways back." Then she glanced at her gauges to confirm that she had enough fuel for that return trip. When she saw what it read, the blood drained from her cheeks. She was aghast. Very little remained.

Damn! Robert Berndt had miscalculated the Lear's range, or hadn't bothered checking the aircraft's fuel level at all. What had he been thinking? No wonder LifeLine management had taken him off the pilot roster. The low fuel level meant the jet could get to Nome, but just barely.

Trying to disguise the tremor in her voice, Taylor amended her request for a steer back to Anchorage. "Cancel that, Center. I'm going to have to continue to Nome. And I'll only get one shot at a landing when I get there. I'm pretty low on fuel."

Another understatement.

"Roger, four-lima-lima. Cleared to the Nome Airport via direct. Maintain flight level three-five-zero. Winds are light and variable at Nome. Plan on an approach to runway zero-two. That's a straight shot from your location and will keep you away from an approach over town. I'll notify Nome Radio to keep any other traffic out of your way. Are you familiar with the Nome Airport?"

"Affirmative," clipped Taylor. "Been in there numerous times." She could hear the strain in her voice, accompanied by the heartbeat thumping in her chest. She wiped one clammy hand on the leg of her jeans.

"Okay. Then you know runway zero-two is nearly at sea level, 5,576 feet long. It has VASI lights, which will be on. Should I tell Nome Radio to notify the airport fire truck to stand by at the runway's end?"

"Yeah, that might be a good idea," Taylor concurred. "You also better have a search and rescue team ready, in case I don't make it and have to dump it into Norton Sound. It's gonna be close."

The thought of crash-landing in the frigid water of the ocean set her to shivering. Even if she pancaked the Learjet onto the water's surface—without serious injury to herself—its thirty-seven degree temperature would suck the life out of her in a matter of minutes. Maybe it would be better to plunge nose first into the sea and kill herself instantly, rather than get caught inside a sinking aircraft, left to endure the terrifying death of suffocation.

The controller's soothing voice eased her away from her fatalistic thoughts. "Four-lima-lima, Anchorage Center. Don't give up. Someone's looking for a Lear pilot to talk you down when you get to Nome."

She grimaced. "No need. I've got a name for you." It was time to call in the big guns. As much as she hated asking for aid, with anything, she realized that her independent nature could get her killed in the next few minutes if she listened to it. She had to use her head; this day was not the day to insist upon doing things by herself. Clearing her raspy throat, she informed the controller, "I'll give you the number of the man that usually flies this actual aircraft. His name is Steve Derossett, and he's at—" She rattled off his number, hoping that he was home. Boy, did she need his help *this* time.

"Roger, four-lima-lima. I'll get him on the line right away."

Taylor didn't even bother to reply to his confirmation, to acknowledge it. The common courtesy of radio communication was not on her mind—she was much too busy looking at the fuel quantity gauge. The needle seemed to be ticking downwards visibly and she tried to concentrate on the imminent landing, not on her lack of fuel.

As she pondered that, another concern entered her mind. While the jet descended, the amount of oxygen in the atmosphere would rise, along with the oxygen in the cabin. Her gaze narrowed as she contemplated what would happen when they reached an altitude where Robert would wake.

"Oh, shit!" she exclaimed when it dawned on her what that would mean. What could she do about that? She couldn't keep squirting him with bear spray every time he moved.

And he probably would regain his senses at the same time the approach and landing at Nome challenged her. Not a good situation.

She glanced into the cabin anxiously, looking for the crash ax Robert had wielded against her. If she could find it, she could whack him in the head and knock him unconscious. If she hit him hard enough, he'd remain out for a *long* time, long enough to get the Lear on the ground without his interference. She reached down to unclip her seat belt.

Then she hesitated. From what she'd learned from the flight nurses, she knew that the trauma of a first head injury made getting a second head injury life-threatening. The brain just couldn't recover from further damage. If she smacked him on the temple—hard enough to put him out for a number of minutes—she'd likely kill him. He'd survived his first injury, but a second would be lethal.

Could she live with being a murderer, herself? Granted, he planned to kill her, but could she lower herself to his level?

She shook her head. No, she couldn't. She'd have to think of something else to subdue him.

The sting of her wrists reminded her of how he'd tied her up, and she decided she'd try the same with him. But this time, she'd make sure he couldn't tear free of his bonds like she had. For all she knew, he *did* have a knife in his pocket even though she didn't.

She prepared once more to leave the cockpit, then remembered she better tell ARTCC before she left. "Anchorage Center, four-lima-lima," she transmitted, unsure what the controller would do when she told him she had to leave the cockpit unattended for a moment. *Yikes.*

"Four-lima-lima, Anchorage Center, go ahead."

Taking a deep breath, she told him she'd be off frequency for a bit, then abruptly pulled the oxygen mask from her face. Certainly, she had cut out his reply, but she didn't want to hear it anyway. She had other pressing matters. Propelled by the intensity of the adrenal hormones flooding her body, she jumped from the cockpit.

The vapors in the cabin stung her eyes and nostrils as she moved down the aisle toward Robert. What's good for the goose is good for the gander, she thought. She hoped that the old cliché still held true. Grabbing up one of the rolls of sterile gauze, she lifted his limp arms and tied his wrists together and cinched them to the nearby bench's leg. That'd hold him.

As she worked, she started to feel some discomfort from her lungs. Their burn reminded her that she needed some air, and she'd forgotten that she'd purged most of it from the aircraft. At a cabin altitude of 21,500 feet, the oxygen level was insufficient to keep her going for much more than a minute or two. Making a final knot of the gauze, she stood and swung around on leaden legs to wobble toward the cockpit and her oxygen mask. After gulping just one quick breath from it, she headed back to her handiwork.

Robert's ankles came next. In a matter of seconds she had him trussed up like a Christmas goose. She quickly surveyed his restraints, and once she'd decided he would not present any trouble, she turned away from him. At the last second she paused, then returned, snatching a roll of surgical adhesive tape from the supply cabinet. She didn't want him pulling the same trick she had when she'd ripped free from *her* restraints. She'd augment the gauze with a band of tape, preventing him from tearing anything.

As she applied the tape, her vision started to blur again.

Stripping the last piece of adhesive from the roll, she could feel her muscles weaken. She knew she had to get back to the cockpit and her oxygen mask, but she hadn't completed her task yet. Quickly finishing the final steps, she stumbled to the front of the jet and grasped for the mask dangling from the wall. When she pulled the mask over her mouth she sighed in relief. The cool flow of air into her lungs felt like the nectar of the gods pouring down her throat—the oxygen tasted that sweet. Gasping, she collapsed on the pilot's seat and sucked away.

Suddenly, she remembered whom she'd left hanging on the other end of the radio. She needed to know if they'd found Steve. "Anchorage Center, four-lima-lima is back on frequency," she reported. "Do you have my flight instructor on the line yet?" Had he been home? That night was not the night for him to be at the movies, sulking because she was out doing something without him.

But she doubted he would have enjoyed sharing what she was doing right then.

"Negative, four-lima-lima," Center reported. "We haven't found him yet. But we're still trying. Someone else is looking for another Lear pilot as well, and we'll get somebody here as soon as we can. It's time for you to descend now, however."

Taylor settled down into the pilot's seat and snugged down her seat belt and shoulder harness. She hoped she wouldn't need them. But if nobody appeared to talk her through the landing, the chances seemed good that she would. She steeled her resolve—it was not time to give up, regardless of what faced her. "Okay, Center. Four-lima-lima is ready."

"Roger. Four-lima-lima, descend and maintain four thousand feet. Nome altimeter is two-niner-niner-zero. Report Nome Airport in sight on this frequency."

"Four-lima-lima copies. Wish me luck." Taylor prayed that her unprofessional comment wouldn't be the last one ever heard from her.

So many unknown factors would accompany the imminent landing at Nome. Could she handle the Learjet, given her lack of knowledge of the aircraft and its temperamental nature? Apprehension gnawed at her resolve. Had she come so far, had she overcome so many challenges, only to meet her end during the last minutes of the battle?

TWENTY-EIGHT

With a quick flick, Taylor disabled the autopilot. Pushing the steering yoke forward, she lowered the aircraft's nose to initiate the descent into Nome. A moment later her radio crackled again. "Lear four-lima-lima, Anchorage Center," broadcasted ARTCC.

"Anchorage Center, four-lima-lima, go ahead." A concerned look passed over her face—was this further trouble? She didn't know if she could handle any more. Her self-preservation instincts were wearing thin. Overstressed, she felt herself on the ragged edge of breaking, ready to lose it. At any moment, she might turn into a blubbering idiot.

But then she firmed her jaw. No. That was what happened to other women with other lives. Not her. She wouldn't fall apart—she'd face her uncertain future head-on. Her pride wouldn't let her to do anything else. If her current predicament led to her death, she wanted others to remember her as a pilot who fought against overwhelming odds, only to be overcome by them in the end.

Not as a woman who froze when met by a life-threatening problem, never attempting to solve it.

"Four-lima-lima," replied the ARTCC controller, "I finally contacted Steve Derossett. He's on his way but doesn't know how soon. You doing okay still?"

"Affirm, Center." She glared at the radio as though it had betrayed her. *Help was on its way, but who knew when?* A sudden sweat broke out across her body—she could feel it soaking the armpits of her T-shirt.

"Okay, Miss Independence," she scolded herself. "You're on your own. You better hope your balls aren't bigger than your brains." During her entire life she'd wanted to do everything her way, without directions or guidance. Determined to figure things out without help, she had found herself in jams numerous times. Usually she wriggled out of the situation using her head. But this time it would be different—if she screwed up now, she'd pay dearly for her mistake. Probably with her life.

Grinding her teeth, she squinted at the panel, not really focusing on anything. Finally, she shook her head. She was jumping to conclusions—who said she couldn't handle this alone?

Then, without warning, the blare of an alarm exploded into the still air of the cockpit.

A sound like a car's burglar alarm began yelping, ricocheting off her eardrums. The effect of the shrill, strident *Whoop! Whoop! Whoop!* of a warning horn caught her unaware and jolted her senses as though someone had jabbed her with a cattle prod.

Was that the cacophony that would attend the end of her life? And what did it mean?

Desperately, she flicked her eyes from gauge to gauge on the panel in front of her. Warning horns always meant something was wrong: the pilot had switched something to the wrong setting, something was too fast, something was too slow. But what? A myriad of instruments could display improper readings.

It was difficult to think clearly with the alarm bellowing, but she tried to concentrate. The bleating of the horn became stronger and faster as the Lear continued to accelerate. That was a clue.

Her eyes closed tightly as she tried to think. Was the jet flying too fast? Did she just have to get it slowed? Was it that easy? She remembered questioning Steve about that exact factor when she asked him about coffin corner. He'd said that you could get into trouble if you exceeded certain speeds, just like in the planes she flew. The speeds had different names, but those different names meant basically the same thing.

Praying she'd interpreted the alarm correctly, she made a move toward the flight controls. She had to slow down, and that meant a power reduction, so she throttled back. That should do it, she figured.

The oxygen mask stifled the sound of Taylor's anxious gasping as she glanced at the instrument panel in front of her to monitor her velocity. But the tension across her shoulders tightened as the airspeed continued to increase. What was going on? she wondered. She had decreased her power—why wasn't the Learjet slowing? It showed no signs of behaving as she had expected it to, and that frightened her.

It appeared that all of her hours spent in Cessnas and Beechcrafts did her no good in the Learjet, which was a completely different animal from the propeller-driven planes. She felt so impotent, so ignorant. Here she'd believed herself an accomplished pilot, able to handle nearly any problem in the sky, but she'd found herself flying an aircraft that followed none of the rules she'd previously learned.

And it had the power to kill her, easily, if she misjudged it.

As the panic built in her, something clicked in her head. It tickled the inner recesses of her brain, forcing its way to the surface. Hadn't Steve commented on something in the past, telling her that descending in the Lear was somehow different from descending in a prop plane? What had he said?

She struggled to recall, then the memory she sought finally emerged. Her eyes darted frantically across the instrument panel in response to what it told her. "Speed brakes," she whispered to herself. "You can't just use power to change your speed on descent, you have to use your speed brakes. Your spoilers. Where'd the control for those go?"

She scanned the panel. There were so many gauges, and so few that she recognized. She felt like an imbecile. Not just for her lack of knowledge about the Learjet, but for getting herself in that situation to begin with. Why hadn't she left the search for Carter Masterson's killer to the police? And at the least, why hadn't she discovered the murderer well before she found herself trapped in an aircraft with him? She would pay for her impetuosity and stupidity with her life.

Finally, she spotted a silver lever marked SPOILERS. "Okay, here it is," she murmured. With her shaking right hand, she toggled the switch to the EXT position. She felt a slight tremor as the speed brakes extended and she glanced out the cockpit window to confirm their deployment. She found she was unable to see the spoilers from the cockpit, but she wouldn't go back into the cabin to check them, she'd have to trust they were out.

Glancing at the airspeed indicator, she noted its decrease. Apparently, the speed brakes had extended. Their drag was slowing her down; no need to touch the throttles. The wail of the warning horn was abating. What she had done had worked.

Finding the solution to the current problem comforted her, but she knew she couldn't relax. The Lear was obeying her at that time, but things were sure to get tricky again.

Like when she landed at Nome.

As she stared at the runway in the near distance, two extremes tore at her. She felt daunted by what would undoubtedly become an increasingly more difficult situation, but she also felt empowered by successfully meeting the challenge of one riddle. More complex enigmas were likely to appear, but she felt much more brave now that she'd shown the smarts to haul herself out of her scrape.

Again.

"I *am* going to get this ship on the ground in one piece," she whispered to herself. "I'm a good pilot. I can do it." She prayed that her confidence was born from true prowess and not from an inflated ego.

TWENTY-NINE

Inside the Lear cockpit, the needle of the altimeter was ticking down as the jet slid toward the ground more than one mile below it. At a descent rate of four thousand feet per minute, the Learjet had less than sixty seconds before Taylor needed to level off her approach. She knew it was time to start the next step in the landing. "Anchorage Center, four-lima-lima has Nome Airport in sight," she transmitted.

"Four-lima-lima, Anchorage Center. You're cleared for a visual approach to the Nome Airport. Remain on this frequency— Mr. Derossett just ran in, and he wants to talk to you."

She nearly choked when she heard those words. *Steve had finally made it to ARTCC!* She wasn't on her own anymore! She wanted to blurt out everything to him—that Robert Berndt was the murderer, that he'd kidnapped her, that she'd subdued him and took over command of the Lear, that it terrified her— but she stilled her tongue. She didn't have time to say any of that, and surely the tall, blond man had deduced most of the story already. And if he hadn't, he'd learn it soon enough.

It would have to wait until she was on the ground.

Preparing to speak to Steve, she made a perfunctory scan of the instrument panel. He'd want to know exactly what was going on with the jet—her speed, altitude, distance from the airport—but her brief glance across the fuel quantity gauge made her suddenly stop and focus intently on it. The picture of it mortified her. Her first words to him cracked in panic.

"Steve," she cried. "First problem! My fuel is *really* low! I knew the fuel was low, but I can barely see anything registered on the gauge!"

Her breathing quickened once more, and her pulse began to race when another dose of adrenaline flooded through her system. Sweat trickled down her back like she had just finished a five-mile run in record time, and the same profuse sweat had her bangs plastered on her forehead. Dark rings circled the fabric of her shirt.

"Okay, okay, hang on, Taylor," Steve soothed her. Like the air traffic controller, he was able to speak calmly when faced with an emergency. She hoped his composure came from his faith in her ability to handle the situation, not because he suspected things had gone too far to correct. "Don't panic. How far out are you? What's your altitude?"

"I'm three minutes out, descending through six thousand feet. Can I make it? How well does the Lear glide, power off?"

"Well, it's not much of a glider, but I don't want you to worry about that. From six thousand feet you could just sail in. You've done dead-stick landings—this'll just be another one of those."

"Are you kidding? I've never done any of those that weren't staged. This is gonna be for real. . . ."

"Take it easy, you'll squeak in. It's probably not as bad as you think."

"Bullshit, Steve!" she swore, losing her cool. "I know how to read a damn fuel gauge! It's fucking empty!" The anxiety of the situation showed itself in her words, and she could hear tension in the snap of her voice. The edge to her tone embarrassed her—no matter what had warranted it, she hated showing any sign of fear like that.

"Don't think about the fuel," Steve coaxed Taylor. "Just think about the landing. If the fuel is that low you're gonna have to nail it, first time. No go-arounds, hit it first try. Concentrate on that. I know you can handle it, just go do it and prove me right."

Taylor could tell Steve was a believer in the power of attitude—if he made her realize she had the ability to do what was needed, he knew she would. But if she started to think of failure, she *would* fail.

"Maintain a steady approach," he warned her, "no wild maneuvers. Make sure you've got everything lined up way before you make it to the airport. When you're low on fuel, a steep turn can slosh it around in the tank. You don't want it to splash to the wrong side of the tank and cause a flameout."

Shuddering in response to the thought of an engine quitting on her—a flameout—Taylor turned back to the matter at hand. "Okay, okay," she assured him, regaining her control. "I'll make it in real steady. Now what else do I have to do? I'm getting pretty close."

"How close are you now? Within ten miles?"

"Probably," she affirmed. She glanced at her distance measuring equipment and stated it for sure. "Yeah, I'm ten DME out."

"Okay, then you need some flaps, right?" Steve suggested. "Remember that flaps can't put up with much stress, so slow down a bit."

"Got it. Reducing power," she indicated. "Flaps coming down." An electrical motor ground as the flaps dropped.

A black arrow crawled down a white arc on the flap position gauge. "Flaps eight are extended and confirmed by the panel," she announced, watching the arrow. "I'm going to twenty now." She reached lower the flap switch further.

"Okay, now—"

As she readied for more directions, the instrument panel lit up like the traffic signals at a congested intersection. "Shit!" Taylor cried. "My panel looks like a Christmas tree, Steve! What happened?"

"What lights are on?" Steve asked coolly.

Ignoring him, she anxiously repeated, "I've done something wrong, Steve. What did I do? The panel's showing me something's not right! I don't know what I did!" All of the blood drained from her face as her eyes darted randomly across the gauges. She had kept her panic bottled up inside her for most of the flight, but her hold on it was slipping.

And she hated herself for showing it.

"Calm down, Taylor, calm down!" Steve ordered her, losing some of *his* coolness. "I can't tell you what you did until you tell me what's lit. Look at the panel."

She blew out a breath and relaxed her tensed shoulders. She couldn't let herself lose it. "Okay, I got something, I got it," she reported. "There's two of them on both sides of the upper annunciator panel." The phrase MSTR WARN was stenciled on the two lights that were blinking furiously, flashing that unknown message at her. "They must be the master warning lights. What the hell does 'master warning' mean? What's wrong?"

Before Steve could answer, Taylor spotted another red light that was glaring at her from the upper edge of the instrument panel. "Wait, wait, I got another one lit up, Steve. It says SPOILER."

"Damn," Steve cursed. "You must have put your speed brakes up during descent. Where'd you learn that?" Then he realized she had no time for questions like that. "Never mind. Just get them down, that'll put out the light. You can't have both flaps and spoilers extended at the same time, so put the spoilers down."

She toggled the SPOILER lever and heard the mechanical grind of their motors. As they flopped down onto the top surface of the wing, she heard the *ta-thump! ta-thump! ta-thump!* of her heart begin to slow. She shuddered as she examined what had just happened. "If you hadn't been here talking me through this," she said to Steve, "what would I have torn up by having the flaps down with the speed brakes out?"

"You would have figured it out pretty quick, that wouldn't have been a problem. You just would've scared yourself senseless."

"Hey, I'm doing a pretty good job of that right now, Steve. What if something else goes wrong and we can't catch it soon enough?"

"Just don't think about it," Steve said soberly. "Pay attention to what you have to do."

"Okay." She wiped a hand over her sweaty forehead. "I'm getting nearer to the airport and my flaps are down to twenty degrees. Is that right? Is that enough?" She was starting to become wary of doing anything with the aircraft—the surprise of unexpected aural and visual warnings had her jumpy, gunshy.

"Anyway," she continued, "I'm getting slowed down for the landing, Steve. Slipping past one forty-five . . . almost one forty. Time for gear?"

"Yeah, now you're getting it. I'll make a Lear pilot of you yet."

"If I don't kill myself first," she muttered to herself. Then she reached out for the tiny wheel-shaped lever used to lower the landing gear and pushed it down. The whirring of an electric motor was barely distinguishable above the pounding of her heart, but she could hear the *Clunk, Clunk . . . Clunk!* which indicated to her that the gear had come down.

Then a combination of hoarse coughing and angry cries diverted Taylor's attention from the gear extension. "What the hell have you done to me?" Robert Berndt screamed from the floor of the cabin. "You tied me down, I can't get away!" The descent of the jet had allowed enough oxygen to enter the Lear to begin reviving him, and he wasn't happy.

Goggle-eyed, Taylor ventured a glance around the door into the cockpit. Robert lay on the floor next to the stretcher, wriggling his hands furiously in an attempt to break his bonds. She felt sure of the integrity of her restraint handiwork, but still cringed when she saw him wrench at them.

"Don't do it, Berndt!" she yelled at him. "We're coming in for a landing any minute and I have to have my mind on what's going on with the jet. Don't try to get away and come up front! Stay there!"

"What?" Robert cried. "You're trying to land the Lear?" He continued jerking at the bandages wound around his wrists, more frantically. "Come back and untie me, or you'll kill us! I have to be there up front! You won't be able to do it!"

The words from Robert Berndt were exactly what she *didn't* want to hear. He believed she couldn't land the Lear—was he right, and were she and Steve wrong? Had her confidence in her abilities been nothing but wish fulfillment?

Locked to the Learjet's flight controls, she tried to remain cool as things came apart around her. The runway was five miles away and the landing was imminent.

THIRTY

Trying to ignore Robert's intermittent screams from the cabin, Taylor punched the push-to-talk switch on the control yoke. She needed to let Steve, and the ARTCC controller, know where she was and what she was doing. Without radar coverage that far north, they were in the dark. The flight service station at Nome *could* see her, but she wasn't talking to him—ARTCC had to relay everything to Nome FSS. Her moist fingers nearly slipped off the switch's knurled knob as she toggled it, and her eyes stung as beads of sweat trickled into them. The beat of her heart pounded into her ears, reverberating like the thumping of a war drum.

"Steve," Taylor transmitted, "I'm on a straight-in, five mile final." Tension tinged her voice as she spoke.

"Okay, Taylor. Flight service just reported that you came into sight a minute ago. The fire trucks"—she thought she heard him choke a bit on those words—"are standing by, and he's listening for any traffic on the other frequency. There doesn't seem to be anyone around, so you've got the field to yourself. How's the fuel situation?"

A quick glance at the fuel quantity gauge reassured Taylor that she would make it to landfall. "The level is really low, but like you said, I'm close enough to the runway to glide to it if I have to. I hope they keep everybody out of my way, this isn't gonna be anything I can try again. No go-arounds."

She wiped a hand across her wet cheek where the oxygen

mask was plastered on her skin. Even though she didn'.
it anymore, she hadn't had time to take it off. "Looks like
time for me," she cracked in a tone of false bravado. "H
go. Wish me luck."

"You're not going to need luck," Steve said emphatica
"You know you can do it and so do I."

Let's hope those are not going to be famous last words, Tay
lor thought, and grimaced.

Even before she was able to catch her breath, the first test
of her ability to get the jet down on the ground appeared.
"Steve, things look wrong," she said. "I'm too high, my descent
isn't right. I'm not in position, it doesn't feel right."

She glanced down at her altimeter and back up to the scene
in front of her. "It's looking like I'm liable to overshoot the
runway. How much room does the Lear need for landing?" she
asked. "I'm gonna have to touch down right on the numbers,
aren't I?"

"Yes, right on them. You gotta nail this landing. That runway
at Nome is adequate for somebody who knows what they're
doing, but—"

His unspoken inference was not lost on Taylor. She was
terrified that her lack of knowledge was going to handicap her
fatally.

"Just don't land long, Taylor," Steve warned. "You're not
going to have a lot of room to play with. Nome isn't Anchorage
International, remember."

The pounding of Taylor's heart acted like a physical excla-
mation point at the end of *that* statement.

"And don't forget your fuel level," he admonished her. "No
wild maneuvers, keep it lined up. Just because you're not where
you want to be doesn't mean you can rocket around."

"Yeah, right, I remember." Taylor reached for the flap lever,
ready to initiate the full flap configuration. "I'm gonna put out
full flaps. I'm still too high and I gotta do something about
that."

"No, Taylor," Steve advised her, his voice cracking. "Not
full flaps, that's too drastic for you! You don't know the airplane, you don't know how it handles in that configuration. It'll
lose too much speed too fast with full flaps and that's hard to
handle."

"Hey, I gotta get this jet down before I run out of room! I
have to use full flaps!"

Three seconds passed before he conceded. "Okay, you're the one sitting at the controls, Taylor, you're gonna have to call the shots. Put 'em down to full but add power to make up for the drag of the flaps. Go to about seventy percent right now, or you're going to stall."

With her heart pounding staccato in her chest, she lowered the flaps and eased the power levers forward. "I don't like this, Steve," she moaned. "I'm descending faster, but the jet doesn't feel right."

"Be careful," Steve cautioned Taylor. "The Lear gets pretty testy with full flaps. Watch your airspeed close, don't let it pull you below the power curve—that'll end up in a crash for sure."

"I'm still too high!" Taylor shrilled when she drew her gaze up form the airspeed indicator and looked out at the runway again. "What else can I do?" Her eyes scanned the instrument panel apprehensively, but it didn't tell her anything.

"Well, there's one more thing you can do, but it's not an approved maneuver and I don't know how well you could handle it—"

"Steve!" she yelled in desperation. "Tell me, I gotta try it! If I run off the end of the runway I'll kill myself! Tell me!"

"Okay." Another second-long pause indicated Steve's hesitancy. "The spoilers. Extend the spoilers."

"Spoilers? That'll bring up all of the warning lights again! You told me no spoilers when the flaps are down."

"Yeah, I know. It's not supposed to be done," Steve acknowledged, "but if you're that high you have to do it. Just ignore the lights, you can get away with it."

Taylor winced, unhappy about doing something unauthorized by the people who know the Learjet the best—its manufacturer. "Okay, I'll do it. I have no choice." She reluctantly reached out for the spoiler lever. "Here they come, I'm activating their extension." She toggled the speed brake lever and the spoilers began moving slowly into position on the wing.

"Taylor, wait! Wait!" Steve screamed. "I didn't tell you what to expect! You don't know what's gonna happen when you do that—"

Interrupting his message, a violent buffeting began to pound the ship like a giant thrashing the jet furiously with an enormous mallet. Once the spoilers had reached full extension the pounding increased, nearly doubling in its ferocity, and the pummeling was accompanied by a frenzied rattling of the flaps.

It sounded like a demon's frantic drumming on a set of steel cymbals. The spasmodic agitation of the jet nearly prevented Taylor from maintaining her hold on the flight controls.

"S-St-Steve!" she wailed, her voice becoming a quavering stutter as the buffeting knocked her from side to side. "Th-this ship-p is going to come ap-p-art! W-what can I d-d-do?"

"Get it down on the ground as soon as you can! Do it fast!"

"I'm t-t-trying, I'm try-ingggg!" The near end of the runway loomed ahead and the VASI lights at its border told her she was still too high. "I'm way a-b-bove the flight p-path but I'm d-d-descending too fast and I'm t-too sl-sloww! When does this ship st-stall?"

"What's your airspeed now?"

"A-b-bout one-ten! Is that too sl-slow?" Taylor screamed over the tumultuous racket filling the air. "When am-m I g-gonna get a warning horn-n?!"

"The Lear has a dirty stall speed around one hundred! Keep it above one hundred until you're within fifty feet of the runway!"

"I'm c-coming up on the threshold r-right now, at fifty feet! I d-don't think I can do it, St-Steve!" Taylor cried. "I'm afraid I'm g-gonna fly int-to the ground-d, I don't know the r-right landing alti-tude for this ship! It-t doesn't feel right t-to me!"

The lights surrounding the approach end of the runway gleamed in the twilight right in front of Taylor.

"I'm p-putting it down-n, Steve!" she yelled. "I'm r-running out of room-m, I gotta do something! Shit-t, here comes the run-n-way! Steeeve—"

The yellow centerline on the runway loomed ahead, dwarfing everything in her field of vision. Sucking in her breath, she pulled back on the control yoke, waiting for the familiar feel of an aircraft touching down easily beneath her.

"Taylor, be careful!" Steve howled. "It's gonna hit hard! It's not gonna flare at the bottom of—"

Steve's warning was overridden by the sound of the jet slamming down onto the runway. With a squeal and *whomp!* the tires of the main gear impacted with the asphalt, screaming as the brakes bit into the metal hubs surrounding the wheels.

A *pow!* ricocheted into the air as the tire on the left side of the aircraft exploded, disintegrating. Pieces of shredded rubber flew off both of the tires as the nearly locked wheels skidded

he asphalt. Streamers of dark gray smoke blossomed
d the gear.

e shriek of the screeching tires didn't even register to Tay-
ner heart hammered so frantically. Her eardrums received
rapid beat of her pulse: the *wham! wham! wham!* sounded
e kettledrums being pounded on by a timpanist performing
riotous orchestral finale.

"Taylor, Taylor! What's happening! Talk to me!" Steve
screamed into his microphone.

"It won't straighten out! It's skidding!" were the final words
in her last transmission.

THIRTY-ONE

At seven-thirty A.M., the rays of the morning's sunlight dappled the low vegetation covering the rolling hills surrounding Nome. During the spring and summer, the sunrise came early in the northern reaches of Alaska and the long shadows of the dawn had evaporated even before much activity developed around the town.

Only pilots moved around on the airfield, readying their mounts for eight o'clock departures to settlements with odd names: Golovin, Shaktoolik, Shishmaref, Elim. The clatter of fuel trucks echoed across the quiet airport as they rumbled from plane to plane.

Half a mile to the north of the terminal and the commercial ramp sat a silver-and-burgundy Learjet, squatting on the bumpy ground to the side of Runway 02. Its bedraggled appearance resembled that of a boxer recovering from defeat in a prize fight. As though it had received a left hook to the face, its nose gear was torn away, leaving the front of the fuselage resting directly on the turf below.

Chips of paint from the aircraft's belly had flaked off near deep wrinkles in the fuselage. Nicks and scratches covered its body, and a grimy coat of muddy dirt had dried on its skin, making it look like a hog emerging from its wallow. The metal surfaces of the flaps showed vague dents on them that resembled cellulite on a fat woman's hips.

The main gear under the wings were still intact, though one

of the tires was blown out and most of the other had peeled off its metal hub. The wheels had created deep ruts when they plowed through several of the low hummocks that covered the ground surrounding the runway.

Upturned clods of soil and shredded vegetation clearly marked the jet's exit from the runway, and it had come to rest at the base of a shallow hill. At the edge of the runway, several of the standards that carried the runway lights were bent over, their globes shattered.

Taylor Morgan stood near the nose cone of the Learjet, looking at the whole scene without any focus in her swollen, black-and-blue eyes. Several bruises and abrasions held prominent positions on her face, and a cervical collar surrounded her neck. Mottled skin around her broken nose added nasty splotches of green and yellow to the colorful display. Dirt, mud, and blood caked the fabric of her long-sleeved T-shirt.

She just stood there, staring.

Occasionally she ran her hand over the painted metal exterior of the jet as though she was reassuring an injured pet. She didn't appear to be doing much but mindlessly surveying the damaged aircraft.

The time she had spent in the small Nome health center had given her an opportunity to reflect on what she had just gone through. Rather than focusing on how she had handled a potentially fatal event, she had centered on more philosophical reflections.

Had Robert Berndt's murder of Carter Masterson been a crime of passion? Was it the only way he thought he could get back to the life and aircraft he dearly loved? Had he decided to risk killing himself while fleeing to Russia rather than rot in a prison cell, unable to fly again?

Trapped in her thoughts, Taylor did not hear the footsteps approaching until a hand ran under her hair and stroked the top of her neck.

"Yikes!" She winced as the touch prompted her to swing around.

"Oh, damn. I'm sorry. I didn't mean to startle you." Steve Derossett lightly rearranged the position of the cervical collar, a look of apology on his face. "How bad's your neck?"

"Well, it's not my neck that hurts when I turn, it's my side. My ribs are black and blue from when the Lear made that sudden stop on landing, and I connected with the shoulder harness. It kept me from hitting the yoke, but left behind some pretty wicked marks. I look like I need a collar for my whole damn body."

He fingered the contraption around her neck. "You're going to have to find a bow tie to pin on the front of that thing," he grinned. "For formal occasions only, of course."

She pointed a finger at him. "Hey, no jokes. It hurts when I laugh." Then she smiled: it was the best she could do to reciprocate for his attempt to make her feel better. "So, is the King Air ready to go yet?"

"Yeah, it's being fueled right now. I hope the trip back to Anchorage will be more peaceful than the dash up here last night. I'm still recovering from the anxiety attack I was having then."

Her smile segued into a grin when she saw the look on his face. "Were you worried about me?" Even though she'd figured he'd be concerned, it pleased her to hear the words.

"Well of course I was worried," he stressed. "Last I heard from you was that panicked radio transmission you gave as you slid off the runway. When I blasted out of Anchorage in the King Air all I had was word from Nome flight service that the jet hadn't burned. That didn't tell me much. I kept calling the entire flight, but nobody knew anything." He gently dusted some of the dirt off her T-shirt. "I didn't know anything for sure until I had tracked you down at the health center."

"That sure was nice, seeing you walk through the door about one this morning," she agreed soberly. Then a teasing mien brushed across her face, prefacing her next comment. "I didn't know *how* I was going to get home, Steve. Not enough money in my wallet to buy a ticket. And the Lear wasn't going anywhere, so I couldn't take it." One of her eyebrows arched slyly.

A moment later her smile dissolved as she remembered the thoughts that had occupied her before he arrived. "So, what's the deal with Robert?" she asked. "Did I say enough for the cops to arrest him?"

"Hey, just your kidnapping and taking the jet was enough for them to hold him." He glared at the Learjet pointedly, then shook his head. "Detective Franklin and another officer are coming up to escort him back to Anchorage—they'll probably charge him with the murder soon. I'm sure Franklin will have questions for you, too."

Her pained expression made him add, "Not right now, though.

After you've gotten back to Anchorage. Once you get settled down and taped back together."

She averted her eyes. "Good, I didn't want to wait around here for Franklin to arrive. I want to go home."

"I don't blame you for that, you've had your share of excitement for today. And yesterday." He laughed, then took a more solemn tone. "I wanted to ask you how you figured it out. Carter's murder, I mean. It never occurred to me to ask you that at the clinic. Last time I talked to you, the puzzle hadn't started to mesh, either for you or for me. What'd you see?"

She puffed up as much as her ribs would allow. Even *she* was surprised by how it had come to her. She deserved to do a little bragging, and some boasting would do wonders for her bruised ego. "Remember that medevac to Chenega I went on?" she asked. His blank look made her realize he *hadn't* known of it, so she added, "Well, I *did* go on a medevac to Chenega. When I got home, I noticed a paperback lying on one of the seats. I guess one of the nurses was reading it. Anyway, that gave me the clue that tied things together."

"A paperback? What could you get from that? Did it remind you of something?"

"Well, in a way it did." A ground squirrel peeked out of its nearby burrow, momentarily catching her attention. When it disappeared back underground, Taylor looked up at Steve. "Yesterday I found out that Robert could've been the one who poisoned your sandwich, but I didn't know why he would. I couldn't connect him to Carter's murder, and that's what I thought the nicotine poisoning was related to. I didn't think he had the brain power left after his injury to plot a successful killing. Then I saw that book." She arched an eyebrow. "What if I told you that that book was a murder mystery? Does that ring any bells?"

She grinned broadly when she saw his features draw back and his gaze widen perceptibly.

"Well, yeah," he said. "Me and Nate gave him a bunch of books like that when he was convalescing, and he loved them. He's been a murder mystery fan for years." Steve stared at the ground as he mulled that thought over, then glanced up. "Yeah, I got it now. He probably took the plan for Carter's murder straight out of a book he'd read. Same thing for hanging the blame for the murder on Nate."

Taylor nodded vigorously, then changed her mind about doing that when the motion jarred her ribs.

He peered at her for a second, then spoke again. "But what I still don't—"

The nearby growl of a single-engine Cessna rolling for take-off overrode his words and he clamped his mouth shut. The plane lifted off gracefully and arced to the south, the rotating beacon on its tail flashing as it roared overhead.

"What I was saying before I was rudely interrupted"—he grinned at the disappearing Cessna—"was why would he kill Carter in the first place? Carter hadn't done anything to him, as far as I know."

Taylor nodded more slowly, drawing things out. "I think it had to do with his inability to acknowledge what his head injury had done to him. You told me that he didn't believe there was any reason for LifeLine to take him off the pilot roster. Obviously he thought he could still fly, otherwise he wouldn't have taken the Learjet like he did." She ran her hand up and down the cervical collar absently. "Remember when he came into the office all ready to go back to work? He said he'd heard about Carter's death and knew LifeLine would have an opening for a Lear captain. That was kind of coincidental, wasn't it?"

"Yeah, I guess so. Robert just happens to read about it, so he decides to drop by." He stuffed his hands in his pockets and studied the ground. "He's exactly what they were looking for, exactly when they were looking for it."

"Yup. He killed Carter to open up the pilot roster. He was sure LifeLine would just throw him back in the Learjet without even thinking about a relationship between Carter's death and his appearance."

"Okay, that explains why he'd kill Carter. But why did he go after me?"

"You don't think Robert had a reason to kill you?" Her eyebrows rose. "Come on, don't you remember what I'd said about the nicotine on your sandwich? That it might've been an attempt to get *you* off the Lear captain list?" She glared at him for doubting her. "That's exactly what it was. Berndt said that when his first attempt at clearing a space for himself didn't work, he tried again. That's when he doctored your sandwich. Not only did he hate you for having one of the jobs he thought rightfully belonged to him, he was going to have to try again in creating another vacancy. Getting rid of you killed two birds with one stone. As it were." She smiled at her pun.

"But that doesn't make any sense, Taylor. LifeLine had refused to rehire him several times. Why would he still try to get me off the list? Kill me to make room for himself?"

"Hey, we're talking about a man who can't even acknowledge the effect of his head injury. He thought he was okay, that LifeLine was being illogical by not rehiring him. Obviously, he couldn't see that killing other pilots to create an opening for a Lear captain was the illogical move. For that matter, it wasn't working, either. You're still here." She chortled. "And so am I."

"Don't laugh, Taylor. That nicotine-laced sandwich could've killed you."

"Yeah, well. It didn't." She wrapped an arm around his waist and cocked her head as she peered up at him. He pulled her a bit closer, evoking another wince from her.

"Sorry," he muttered, and eased his grasp. "Anyway, you did a great job with the jet, considering what you were up against."

"Oh, come on." Taylor tried to tilt her head up to frown at him but the cervical collar prevented that. Then she stepped away and her gaze traveled over the crumpled heap that used to be a Learjet. "You know, I still feel like a complete imbecile for what I did to the jet last night. I figured I could've done a little better – "

"On the contrary," Steve interrupted. "I can't believe you were able to get it on the ground without completely destroying it, everything considered. It doesn't look all that bad, anyway." His gaze traveled the length of the aircraft slowly. "I'd have to say it was a pretty hard landing, but all of the damage is fixable. Just some wrinkles on the skin and an amputated nose gear. It could have been worse, a lot worse."

"Well, it shouldn't have happened," she grumbled. "I can't believe I was conceited enough to think I could handle the jet if I got control of it. There must've been a better way to prevent Robert from killing me."

"Yeah, but you certainly came up with a unique way to get Robert's attention," Steve chuckled dryly. Then curiosity lit up his eyes. "I just can't figure out how the hell you remembered what I told you about the pressurization system. I couldn't believe it when you told me what you did. How did you relate a joke about unruly passengers to controlling Robert? That one has to go into the textbooks on Lear trivia."

She only scratched her neck under the collar, and shrugged. "That was the easy part, putting him under by venting the oxygen from the cabin. Getting around him to reach the pressure controls in the first place was the hard part. That bear repellent worked pretty good for that," she cracked. Then her eyes glazed over as she recalled the abortive attempt to blast him with the pepper spray. When it hadn't gone off as anticipated, she'd nearly had a seizure. "Speaking of bear repellent, how's Robert doing? Were they able to get that stuff off his face?"

"Yeah, they got him cleaned up," Steve reassured Taylor. "He's doing a lot better than you are. Remember, he was completely strapped down for that bumpy ride off the side of the runway and you weren't able to put many marks on him when you two were wailing on each other." He looked to his left, toward the small terminal that served Nome Airport, then back at her. "I bet a videotape of that would be pretty hilarious, you know? Robert and you trying to knock each other out in the middle of that cramped cabin."

Taylor shivered as *that* image flashed through her mind. She wasn't going to forget that for a long time.

Steve noticed her expression and gingerly rubbed her neck. "Hey, forget it. That's yesterday's news. Anyway, Robert just has a little rash on his face from the repellent, but that's the least of his worries."

With a hand wrapped around her elbow, Steve guided Taylor back toward the terminal, one hundred yards away. LifeLine's King Air was parked next to the building; smaller planes waiting for passengers surrounded it.

"That ramper from Nome Air was nearly done fueling the plane when I left," he said, "so we better get going." He nodded toward the King Air and gestured.

As they walked along the side of the runway, he glanced down at the anxious, hangdog expression on her face. "So, you want to be my copilot on the way home? We've never flown together, it might be fun. You look like you could use some fun."

"Does this fall under the heading of 'getting back up on the horse that threw you'?" she grumbled.

"I guess so, but you know this horse a lot better than the one that tossed you. I figured you'd like a taste of something you're used to."

"Okay, I guess I can humor you. But I'm not flying right

seat; *you're* flying right seat. I haven't been demoted to copilot from captain yet." She rubbed her cervical collar again. "Anyway, I haven't slept for about thirty-six hours and I might fall asleep halfway home. You can be captain then if you want."

"Hey, that won't be any different than last night. You being asleep at the wheel, I mean." He smirked playfully.

She glared at him. "Smart ass. In that case, I'll stay up the whole time." Then she rubbed her chin thoughtfully. "That may be a good idea, anyway. I have to forget the way the Lear felt, get my King Air touch back. I'm still on duty for tonight, aren't I?"